# VANESSA JAMES

## the devil's advocate

D0815951

## *Harlequin Books*

TORONTO • NEW YORK • LONDON
AMSTERDAM • PARIS • SYDNEY • HAMBURG
STOCKHOLM • ATHENS • TOKYO • MILAN

Harlequin Presents first edition June 1985
ISBN 0-373-10793-5

Original hardcover edition published in 1983
by Mills & Boon Limited

# CHAPTER ONE

How absurd, Luisa thought. If someone were to open the door and look into the room now, a stranger for instance, it would appear totally calm, at peace. *I* would appear totally calm.

She set down her sewing and looked round at the room, trying to see it with an outsider's eyes. A fire burned in the grate; two lamps, with red shades, threw warm pools of light on the blue and russet rugs her father had once brought back from Tashkent. A clock ticked; in front of the fire Tamara, the Siamese, stretched and flexed her claws as she dreamed. Heavy old velvet curtains shut out the night, and Luisa herself, curled catlike on the bumpy old chesterfield, stitched the final square inch of her embroidery. She peered at the petit-point, at the webs of tiny stitches, the design of summer flowers, cabbage roses and peonies. It was almost finished.

With a sigh she thrust the needle back into the work and pushed it aside. Her eyes strayed again back to the clock, as they had a hundred times already that evening. Past midnight, almost one. She stood for a moment, listening intently for the sound of a car engine, for tyres on the wet road outside, but there was nothing. She was not calm, she thought irritably, far from it. The calmness was an illusion, a fake. Not even the embroidery, so time-consuming, so intricate, had been able to soothe her tonight. Where *was* Claudia?

Impatiently she paced back and forth, and then, on impulse, crossed quickly to the door, across the landing, and into Claudia's little attic bedroom. It was in chaos as usual, the tiny mantelpiece piled with invitations, coffee cups, ashtrays; clothes dropped on chairs, tossed on the floor, a table littered with expensive make-up, dirty cotton wool, necklaces, rings and bracelets. Luisa hesitated; she hated Claudia's room, hated its disorder.

She paused and then opened the door of the huge old wardrobe. Why she did it, she didn't know. After all, the coat would still be there, the dresses would still be there, however much she might wish they weren't, that she had never come in here, looking for the new box of embroidery silks which were stored there—and found them.

Of course they were still there; she stared at them, her face quiet, perturbed. She ran her hand gently over the smooth brown fur of the jacket, and she felt again the panic grip her stomach. *Where* had they come from? Even she, uninterested in clothes, could tell they must have been terribly expensive; one of the dresses was a St Laurent, pure silk.

The fur, from Harrods, was new. There was no way, she thought, that Claudia could afford such clothes. Her secretary's salary at Morrell & Kennedy was even lower than Luisa's at the gallery; Harry might have bought them for her, but somehow Luisa doubted it. Perhaps someone had lent them to her, she told herself quickly, for the hundredth time. Perhaps there was a perfectly good explanation ... She'd tried to ask Claudia, earlier that evening, but she was going out, stalking around the flat in Janet Reger underwear, in a terrible temper with her hair, late for Harry as usual. 'I'm in a hurry, Luisa!' she had cried crossly, and slammed the door in her sister's face.

Luisa quickly shut the door and went back into the sitting room. She crossed to the windows, drew back the heavy curtains, and looked out over the square. The snow, falling late, for it was February, had almost melted earlier in the day; now the slush had frozen over; the trees, the pavements glistened white in the moonlight. Her own reflection, pale, ringed with an aureole of silvery fair hair, gazed back at her from the glass, till her breath misted it over and the ghostly face vanished. On an impulse, she pushed up the window and leaned out, breathing the cold air deeply, gratefully. Tiny icicles hung from the frame; she broke one off and held it in her hand, shivering at the sudden cold, a little dagger of ice that very slowly melted against the warmth of her skin.

Then suddenly she heard them; there was the roar of an engine, a screech of brakes, a burst of rock music from the car's stereo, as Harry braked sharply in front of the house. Quickly Luisa drew back, unwilling to appear over-anxious, to be spying, and shut the window, drew back the curtains.

Hurriedly, hearing the door downstairs slam, Claudia's feet on the stairs, she sat down on the sofa and picked up her embroidery. She must seem calm, she thought quickly. She mustn't lose her temper. But she must make Claudia explain; she still felt responsible for her. When would she not? she thought dully, as the front door slammed. She lowered her eyes again to her sewing.

'Oh, you're still up. I thought you'd have been in bed hours ago.'

Claudia paused, framed in the doorway, a cross and sulky expression on her face.

Composedly Luisa looked up at her. How beautiful she looked, she thought, and how aware of it. Claudia's thick dark hair, inherited from their mother, was tousled; her lipstick very slightly smeared. As Luisa watched her, she made a half-hearted attempt to smooth her hair, and then with a shrug, tossed off the thin silk stole that she had wrapped round her tanned shoulders. She shivered and went across to the fire, kneeling down in front of it by the cat, keeping her back to her sister.

'Were you warm enough in that?' Luisa gestured to the thin blue and gold stole.

'Oh, don't be boring, Lou.' Claudia sighed. 'Honestly, you sound like Aunt Con sometimes! Of course I was warm enough; cars do have heaters, you know.'

Luisa kept her voice steady. 'It's a cold night, I'd have thought you might wear the fur coat.'

Claudia swung round accusingly. Across the room, in the firelight, her blue eyes flashed.

'You've been in my room!'

'To find the embroidery silks. Yes.'

Claudia hesitated. Her face took on the expression Luisa knew of old, the nursery face, sulky, defiant. She took her time answering, settling herself crosslegged on the rug, staring across the room at her sister. She was calculating what lie she could tell to extricate herself, Luisa thought sadly, and from long practice, she kept silent.

Eventually Claudia shrugged.

'I see,' she said rebelliously. 'It's inquisition time, is it? That's why you waited up.'

Luisa sighed. 'Hardly an inquisition,' she said gently. 'But I did wait up. If I didn't, I'd never catch you, would I, Claudia? You'd always be rushing off somewhere. There'd never be any time for explanations.'

'What makes you think I have to give you any explanation?' Claudia snapped. 'A year from now I shall tell you to go to hell! I can't wait!'

Luisa smiled at her sadly. 'That's a year from now,' she said patiently. 'As it is, I'm still legally responsible. You're only twenty, Claudia, can't you see . . .'

'And you're twenty-five. So what? You're not my mother!'

Luisa felt a shaft of pain at her words and looked away. Claudia hardly remembered their mother, but she did, she thought sadly. Her mother certainly would never have done what she was doing now—she'd have let Claudia go her own way, just as she had always done. And perhaps she would have been right. It would be easier.

'Claudia, please,' she said softly. 'I didn't choose this situation, you know. But as it is . . .'

'Oh, don't pretend! You revel in it!' Claudia glared at her. 'You always have done, as long as I can remember. And since it's you that has the money—you that holds the purse-strings, there's not much I can do about it, is there?'

'That's not true!' Luisa stared at her sister indignantly. She had a temper too, she thought defensively. But Claudia was so impulsive, so impossible, that she always had to repress it—it wasn't fair. She forced it down, kept her voice even. 'Claudia, the money has nothing to do with it, and you know it. I didn't want it, I never did. And if it's any consolation, most of it's gone already.'

'On my school fees? I don't believe it!'

'That and other things.' Luisa looked away, and her sister's eyes narrowed suspiciously.

'Well, I can't think on what,' she said rudely. 'You never spend any. You never go out, never see anyone, never buy anything. All you do is work, come home, and work some more. Well, just don't expect me to live like that. You might as well be a bloody nun!'

'Claudia.' Luisa leaned towards her. She knew this technique of old; anything to change the subject, to draw off the attack. 'It's late. We've been over all this hundreds of times. I don't want to cross-question you, and I don't want to interfere. Believe me, I wish I'd never gone into your room. But I did, and . . .' She broke off, her eyes pleading. 'Claudia, you'll have to tell me. Where did all those clothes come from?'

'I bought them, of course. What else?' Claudia could not meet her gaze, Luisa saw. She looked away, turning her beautiful face to the fire. Luisa sighed, and Claudia tensed impatiently.

'I suppose you thought Harry bought them for me? You would think that! Just because I don't share all your puritan hang-ups it doesn't mean I'm a kept woman, you know. Not yet, anyway!'

'I didn't think that.'

Luisa hesitated. It would be so much easier to stop, she thought, to close her eyes to it all, to give in. But she knew she must not.

'Claudia, look,' she said gently, 'they're terribly expensive—even I can see that. I . . . I wondered if you'd borrowed them?'

She looked at her sister hopefully, and Claudia swung round with a look of scorn.

'Borrow them? Wear someone else's cast-offs? No, thank you! You think I'm going to go out with Harry—to the sort of places he takes me—in a lot of hand-downs?' She laughed. 'Hardly my style!'

There was a silence, and Claudia looked away, stroking the cat, her face suddenly thoughtful, her head bowed. Her thick dark hair fell forward across her face, so its expression was suddenly hidden. Luisa felt a dart of pity and sympathy for her; Claudia, who had grown up hardly knowing their mother, the two of them parked with an endless succession of nannies and aunts, as their father continued his endless peregrinations around the world. It wasn't surprising, she told herself, that Claudia should have grown up as she did, headstrong, wilful, never satisfied until she had exactly what she wanted, and then instantly bored with it.

'Clou, please, come on, don't let's quarrel . . .' She reached across to her sister impulsively, using the old nickname of their childhood. Claudia brushed her hand away impatiently, and then, with a sudden movement, turned and clasped it. Their eyes met, and Luisa saw her sister's mouth tremble, the huge dark blue eyes well with tears. She drew a deep breath; so she had been right.

'There's something wrong, isn't there, darling?' she said gently. 'Come on, you'd better tell me.'

'Oh, Lou!' With a tearful moan, Claudia drew her down on to the rug beside her. 'I'm in a mess!'

Luisa smiled wryly. She knew her sister's swift changes of moods; with her, defiance was always a prelude to confession. She put her arm round her comfortingly, thinking how often the two of them had played out this kind of scene before.

'It can't be so awful,' she said softly. 'Tell me. You know I'll help.'

'You can't!' Claudia gave a sob. 'Not this time. No one can . . .'

'Of course they can. I can . . .' Luisa forced her voice to remain calm, and soothing, but she felt inside the quickenings of alarm. Claudia was trembling.

'These clothes . . .' She hesitated. 'Lou, the money to get them. I . . . I stole it!'

Luisa stared at her in disbelief, feeling herself go rigid with shock and fear.

'You *stole* it?' She looked into her sister's troubled face, and Claudia blushed scarlet. 'Clou, you can't have done. You can't mean it!'

'I did!' Claudia tilted her chin. 'I was desperate for some money, can't you understand? It was after I met Harry. He was taking me to all those places—dancing, parties—and I . . . I wanted to look pretty for him. I wanted to wear the kinds of clothes all the other girls were wearing, and . . .'

'But, Claudia, you have lots of clothes already . . .' Luisa interrupted in bewilderment.

'No, I don't!' Claudia shook her off. 'Awful old things everyone's seen already! I wanted new things, I . . . I wanted to impress Harry, I suppose, and that awful old battleaxe of a mother of his, who looks down her nose at me every time I go there. I love Harry, Lou, I want to marry him, damn it!'

Luisa sighed. She had been hearing that refrain for the past three months, ever since Claudia and Harry had first met. Privately she thought Harry kind and good, but unlikely ever to cross his family to the extent of marrying Claudia. She looked away.

'The money,' she prompted gently. 'Claudia, never mind why. Where did you get it?'

'From the firm.' Claudia stared at her defiantly.

Luisa felt her blood run cold; she stared at her sister in disbelief.

'From Morrell & Kennedy? Claudia, you can't have . . .'

Her sister gave a sob. 'I did! It was such a temptation, you

see; it was so simple, that's what's so awful . . .' She drew in
her breath shakily, and turned away once more so the fall of
hair hid her face. 'I know you just think of them as family
solicitors. But they don't just handle small inheritances, like
yours. They act for all sorts of rich people.' She hesitated.
'There's this client of theirs, some stupid ancient spinster,
living up in Yorkshire, they've handled all her affairs since
the year dot. Well, she's mad on animals, potty about them.'
Claudia gave a harsh laugh. 'I even typed her will; the whole
damn lot's going to some stupid cat sanctuary!' She broke
off.

'So?'

Claudia shrugged. 'So, I thought, what a waste. And
then—well, every so often the firm sends off cheques for
her—it's interest on her shareholdings, and it goes to
different animal charities, umpteen of them. We have her
cheques, old Mr Morrell just used to fill in the charity's
name, counter-sign them, and then send her a monthly
inventory of where the money went. I typed the inventories;
I sent off the cheques . . . Well,' she paused, 'about three
months ago, when old Mr Morrell was taken ill, he left a
whole bundle of the cheques on his desk . . . I only took a
few of them, Lou, just on impulse to begin with, I don't
know why. Then I . . . I made them out in the firm's name,
and took them round to the bank and cashed them. Not all at
once, of course, they might have been suspicious. A few
weeks apart. No one blinked an eyelid, I cash cheques for
old Mr Morrell all the time. It was so *easy*, don't you see,
Lou?'

She stared at her sister pleadingly.

'But they had to be counter-sighed . . . there was the
inventory . . .' Luisa stared at her sister in mounting horror.

'Oh, that was nothing!' Claudia sounded almost boastful.
'I could copy old Morrell's signature with my eyes closed. I
typed the inventory—I just altered the figures . . .'

'You . . . you *forged* his signature?'

'Well, I had to, didn't I? They wouldn't cash them with
my name on, would they?' Claudia snapped.

Luisa felt suddenly sick.

'How much . . .' she hesitated. 'How much were they for,
Claudia?'

'Not much.' Claudia looked away, avoiding Luisa's eyes.
'Well, not to begin with, anyway.'

'How much?'

'Nearly two thousand pounds.' Claudia's voice sank to a whisper.

'*What?*' Luisa stared at her, rigid with shock. She felt her mind spin, and immediately begin the terrible endless calculations. How much of her own money was left . . .? If she sold the last set of savings certificates . . .

'Oh, Lou, I'm so sorry. I don't know what came over me . . .' Impulsively, Claudia turned and buried her face in her sister's lap. Absently, Luisa stroked her hair, held her close, until her sobs subsided.

'Claudia, listen.' She kept her voice quiet and soothing, knowing that the worst thing she could do would be to upset Claudia any further. She sighed. 'There's no point now in talking about that. I can't think how you could have done such a thing, but since you have, we'll just have to sort it out, shan't we? Now, listen to me. I have some money left . . .'

'How much?' Instantly Claudia sat up, her eyes alert.

'Enough, I think,' Luisa said slowly. 'So, tomorrow, we'll go in together, we'll explain what's happened, you'll apologise, and we'll pay the money back. I'm sure old Mr Morrell . . .'

'It's not as simple as that!' Claudia gave a wail of despair. The tears spilled over, and she clung to Luisa's hands.

Luisa looked at her in bewilderment.

'Clou,' she said gently, 'it'll be O.K., you'll see. You'll have to resign, but you never liked the job anyway. And Mr Morrell was so fond of . . . of our mother. For her sake, I'm sure he wouldn't . . .'

'Oh, Luisa! You don't *listen*! I told you a month ago. You can't even see old Morrell. He's ill, he hasn't even *been* in the office since the heart attack . . .'

Luisa paused. Suddenly her memory tugged at her, and she felt herself go cold with fear.

'Then . . . who can I see?'

Claudia's eyes met hers.

'Julius Morrell.'

'*Julius?*'

'Yes. *Now* are you so complacent? How do you rate our chances now? You think Julius Morrell is going to let me off with a polite little apology and a convenient cheque?'

Luisa stared at her sister, hardly seeing her. Instead her

mind flashed back to a summer's day years before. The day of her mother's funeral: standing by the graveside, with the sun beating down on their bared heads, and meeting a cold hard stare from a pair of steel grey eyes. A look of distaste, without sympathy, totally cold. Oh yes, that was the last time she had seen him, but she remembered Julius Morrell.

She drew in her breath shakily. 'No,' she said at last. 'In that case I don't rate our chances too high.'

'Don't you *see*?' Claudia leaned towards her urgently. 'That's why I've been in such a state this past week. I'd have had to tell you—I just didn't know how.' She paused. 'You see, Julius has been brought in to overhaul the firm in his father's absence. As soon as I heard that, I knew it was only a matter of time anyway. Oh, Lou!' She gave a wail of despair. 'He'll find out. He's ordered a complete audit. And once he knows . . .' She broke off, and looked down.

'You think he'd prosecute?' Luisa said shakily.

'I *know* he'd prosecute! He'd probably take on the case himself!'

'Even if I explained . . . if we give back the money . . .'

'It won't make a shred of difference. You know how ruthless he is. And he hates us! He hated Mother—you've always said so! Don't you see—he'd be delighted!'

Luisa felt her mind go numb with despair; everything Claudia was saying was true, she thought desperately. He would do that, it would be a kind of revenge, belated but savage, none the less sweet for being delayed. Claudia tugged at her hand.

'Don't you understand, Lou?' she cried. 'If that happens, I'm finished. Harry will never marry me then. Can't you just imagine his mother? She'd be delighted, of course . . . Oh, Lou, I wish I were dead!'

Automatically Luisa put her arms around her, trying to comfort her, though she felt like ice.

'There must be something we can do . . .'

'There's only one thing.' Claudia's voice was muffled, her face buried in Luisa's arms. Luisa felt her stiffen, hesitate. 'We . . . I . . . could go to Kit.' She broke off and gave another sob. 'Oh, Lou, I can't bear it. There's more, I can't tell you . . .'

'*More?*' Luisa reached down and lifted Claudia up, so her sister had to face her. She looked at her sternly, feeling suddenly sick. 'It's nothing to do with Kit, I hope?'

Claudia gave a wail of despair. 'Oh, I know what you think about Kit,' she said. 'But he's not so bad! He's better than his horrible brother. At least he's not cold, he . . .'

Luisa looked away. Her head had begun to ache; little sharp darts of pain moved behind her eyelids. She closed her eyes. Julius, and Kit. Would the past never go away?

'Luisa, listen, I'll have to tell you . . .' Claudia knelt up, and met her sister's eyes pleadingly. 'I . . . I told Kit. I told him yesterday. Well, I was out of my mind with worry, and he guessed something was wrong . . . so I told him. He said he'd help, Lou, he promised he would . . .'

'Help?' Luisa stared at her blankly. 'You mean, talk to Julius?'

'Of course not! He wouldn't give a damn what Kit said. No . . .' Claudia hesitated. 'He said he . . . could cover up for me.'

'Cover up for you?' Luisa gazed at her sister, her face hardening.

'Yes, *listen*, don't look like that! He said . . . if I could find a way of repaying the money, he'd see the books were fixed before the audit—so nothing showed, so they'd never be able to see anything had happened. Oh, Lou, can't you see—it's our only chance?'

'More lies, you mean?' Luisa could not keep the disgust from her voice.

'What does that matter?' Claudia stared at her angrily. 'That stupid old woman would have her money back, wouldn't she? We'd all be back to square one, minus the scandal. And then Harry and I . . .' She broke off. 'There's only one problem,' she muttered. 'Kit made a condition.'

'A condition?' Luisa drew in her breath sharply.

Claudia lowered her eyes. 'He said . . . he said he'd do it for me . . . if I . . . if I went to bed with him.'

'*What?*' Luisa felt the blood rush to her face; she stared at Claudia in horror. Defiantly Claudia looked up.

'Well,' she cried accusingly, 'is that so awful? He's always fancied me. He knows I'm not like you . . . I mean, it's scarcely a secret round the office that I'm . . . well, *modern*. He knows I sleep with Harry. Oh, for God's sake, Lou—I went on the pill when I was sixteen. Don't you see, it's a kind of a *joke*! Except he means it,' she finished dully.

'You think that's a joke?' Luisa's eyes blazed at her. 'It's the most disgusting thing I've ever heard!'

'Oh, don't be such a bloody prude!' Claudia glared at her, her face flushed, her eyes still shining with tears.

Something inside Luisa snapped. 'A prude? Is that what you call it?'

Claudia blushed; her mouth turned down sulkily. 'It would get me out of trouble,' she said hesitantly.

'If you had any moral sense whatsoever, you'd never have got into it in the first place.'

'Oh, shut up!' Claudia sprang angrily to her feet. 'I hate you sometimes, Luisa. Always preaching, always holier than thou. It's all very well for you to talk. You've never been in love in your life—you've never let a man so much as touch you as far as I can make out. So how can you possibly understand? I was desperate, can't you see? Desperate. And Julius is away. He's gone to Italy on that Red Brigade kidnapping case; he's coming back next week. By that time the audit will be done, and then I'm finished. Kit was my last chance, can't you see that?'

Luisa stared at her sister in silence.

'Julius is in Italy?' she said at last.

'Yes! But Kit's there as usual. He knows the place backwards, he's been there long enough. He has the key to the safe where the books are stored—he can fix it, Luisa, don't you see? No one else can.'

Luisa drew in her breath slowly, fighting the pain that shot behind her eyes. Her palms felt damp, and she rubbed them impatiently against her dress.

'Could I see Kit?' she said finally.

'Oh, Lou, *would* you!' Claudia sank to her knees again and took her hand. 'It would be all right then, I'm sure. If you offered to pay the money back. If Kit realises you know about it—I'm sure he'd back down about his ... little bargain. You could explain about Harry ... *Please*, Lou. I think it might work. Kit's so keen on you—he's always asking about you, and he doesn't like Julius much either. What good would it do Kit to tell his brother? Nothing! *Please*, Lou ...'

Luisa looked at Claudia's flushed tearful face, and a wave of love and protectiveness moved her heart. She didn't want to see either of them, she thought; just the idea of meeting them, now, made her throat dry; but if it had to be, better Kit than Julius.

'If I do this...' she spoke hesitantly. 'If I see him,

Claudia, will you promise me, absolutely, that you'll never do anything like that again?'

Impulsively Claudia flung her arms around her.

'Of course I will!' she cried. 'Oh, Luisa, bless you! I *knew* you would help me . . .'

Luisa looked away. 'Because of Harry,' she said gently. 'Because you love him . . .'

Claudia smiled happily, ignoring the tone of her sister's voice.

'You darling!' she cried. 'Oh, Lou, what should I do without you?'

'I can't imagine,' Luisa said drily. She stood up, slightly unsteadily. 'Could I see Kit tomorrow?'

'The sooner the better!' Claudia paused. 'How quickly can you get the money?'

'Quickly enough. Kit could arrange it, I expect. He handles the investments.' Luisa rubbed her hand against her forehead, trying to ease the pain, feeling suddenly exhausted. So many memories all jumbled and indistinct, were crowding in on her.

'It's strange,' she said. 'We saw them quite a lot once, when we were little. Especially Kit. Julius was older, always away at school. You wouldn't remember, of course.' She paused. 'We went to Scotland once, for the whole summer, just the four of us, with Aunt Con. Do you remember?'

'Vaguely. You and Julius were always going off together. It was pretty boring. I remember the house, though. It was on the edge of a loch, wasn't it?'

'Yes. Yes, it was.' Luisa shivered; the fire had burned very low. Absently she bent and poked at the coals, watching small darts of flame, blue and gold, flicker up, then die away again.

She sighed. 'It's so long ago. I'm not sure I'd recognise . . . Kit now.'

Claudia laughed. 'And whose fault is that? He was always trying to arrange a meeting, ever since I went to work there. It was you who wouldn't. You're stupid about all that.'

'Yes, maybe I am.' Luisa straightened up. 'Well, I'll see him tomorrow, shan't I?'

'Go in the morning,' Claudia said quickly. 'He's always there then. He uses his father's old office—the one at the head of the first stairs.' She paused. 'You will tread carefully, won't you, Lou—don't antagonise him.'

Luisa nodded. 'Maybe you'd better stay home tomorrow,' she said. 'Just till I've sorted everything out.'

'Fine by me. I can think of much better things to do anyway.' Claudia hesitated in the doorway, as Luisa turned away from her and crouched down before the dying fire, cradling the cat in her arms.

'Lou . . .' She hesitated. 'Do you think it'll really be all right? Will you be able to handle it?'

'Oh yes,' said Luisa, her voice level. 'I'll be able to handle it. I may only be a woman, but I'm more than a match for Kit Morrell.'

'And Julius?' Claudia called mockingly as she shut the door.

Luisa shivered, and did not answer. No, she thought silently, not for Julius. But that was all right; it was only Kit she had to deal with, not his celebrated barrister brother.

Unsought the memory of those cold grey eyes came back, and she shuddered involuntarily. It was the first time in her life she had seen hatred in another human being's face, she thought suddenly. She had been sixteen years old. Even then, she realised, even then it had carried such force that she had recognised it.

Oh no, she never wanted to encounter Julius Morrell again, and the one good thing in this whole horrible mess was that she still didn't need to.

# CHAPTER TWO

THE bus crawled. Anxiously Luisa looked at her watch, then leaned to the window, craning her neck to see down to the street below. They were still only in Piccadilly. The side streets, she saw, had been cordoned off; police cars were parked, blocking them off, their blue lights flashing. There had been another bomb scare that morning, in a Middle Eastern consulate, she had heard it on the radio. The centre of London seemed to have come to a complete halt. She hesitated; perhaps it would be quicker to walk?

But she decided against it. Deliberately she sat back in her seat, trying to calm herself. Claudia had said Kit would be there all morning. There was still plenty of time. She'd checked her last inventory from Morrell & Kennedy the previous night. If she sold the last bonds, there would be enough: just. She could give it to Kit in cash if need be, within a couple of days.

She drew in a deep breath, fighting her rising nervousness. There was so little left now. And she'd had another letter from her father that morning, from Rome this time, with all the usual pleas, the usual excuses. She would have to send him something too, and then ... She sighed. How much better it would have been, she thought sadly, if Aunt Con had never left it to her in the first place. Aunt Con had never liked Claudia. 'You might as well know, Luisa,' she'd said, in that clipped brisk voice of hers, 'that when I die, it's all coming to you. Not that there's much, but it's something.' She had laughed. 'If you've as much sense as I think you have, and you never marry, you'll find it useful some day.'

Luisa smiled sadly to herself at the memory. It was so typical of Aunt Con, who'd detested men all her life. Of course her prophecy had turned out to be only too true; she would never marry, she thought. And she wouldn't have Aunt Con's nest-egg either. But that didn't matter. It had come in useful. It had bought her father air tickets and whisky and the nearest thing he knew to peace of mind; it had bought Claudia an education. And now ... What did it buy now? she thought bitterly. An ugly obscene cover-up, that was what it bought.

As the bus suddenly jolted forward again, she felt a terrible trapped panic start to rise up in her chest. She must, somehow, handle it, because if it all got to Julius . . .

Suddenly, out of nowhere, came a scene from her childhood. Kit, flushed, persuasive, trying to talk his way out of trouble. She couldn't remember what it was, the memory was elliptic, shifting . . . But she saw Kit clearly, swinging round to where she watched, mute, in a corner, while Julius strode up and down the room, his face white with anger. Julius hated lies, even then, she thought miserably. Oh, if Julius found out, it was all over.

Her hands shook as carefully she pushed back the heavy mahogany doors she remembered so well from her childhood. In the hall she paused. It was just as she had pictured it, unchanged in the ten years she had carefully avoided coming here. The photographs of the firm's founders on the walls: Mr Kennedy, long dead, without issue. Old Mr Morrell, pictured when he was in his thirties perhaps, outside the Law Courts . . . She paused. The reception desk was where it had always been, off a small room to the left. If she was quick, and quiet . . .

She tiptoed across the hall, making for the stairs. Yes, she was in luck. The girl at the desk was absorbed in some magazine; she didn't even look up. Luisa hurried silently up the stairs. At the first landing she paused, making sure she was obeying Claudia's instructions, and her own memory. Yes, there was the small corridor away from the main offices. From above came the muffled sound of typewriters. It was the end door; all the other rooms on that little wing were for filing.

She drew in her breath, fighting down the panic. There was a carpet here, and her feet made no sound. Quickly she reached the door, and, giving herself no time to hesitate, her breath coming quickly and painfully, she tapped lightly, opened it, and went in.

There was a man behind the desk. As she opened the door he straightened up from some papers, obviously startled. He stood there, unmoving, just looking at her, as if frozen, and Luisa also stood still, her mouth suddenly dry, staring at him. He had gone white, seemed incapable of movement, as if he were seeing a ghost, and as they looked at each other

she saw the papers he held flutter from his hand to the floor.
Neither spoke, but the sudden movement of the papers
seemed to bring him back to life. His expression changed;
fleetingly his eyes travelled over her, from her feet, back to
her face. They rested there, too long. Then he smiled, a
smile she disliked instantly, for it managed to register both
admiration and insolence. He did not bend to pick up the
papers. Quietly Luisa pushed the door shut behind her.

The room felt oppressively hot and airless, and charged
with a peculiar tension. It was all Luisa could do to force
herself to stand her ground. Hesitantly she stared at the
man. He was dressed with an unexpected severity in a black
suit, with a white shirt and plain dark tie. She would have
expected something more flashy from Kit, she thought, a
little wildly, and he was much older than she had antici-
pated. Don't be stupid, she told herself, it's ten years since
you saw him, what do you expect? *Not this,* her mind said.

The man was startlingly handsome; there was now no
trace in his face of the weakness she remembered. The
planes of his face were harsh; deep lines were etched from
nose to humourless mouth; the dark auburn hair that fell
forward over his forehead did nothing to soften the drawn
brows, the cold distrust of his eyes. *You've changed,* she
wanted to say, but she could force no words out. Only a
second or two had passed, but they stretched, seemed
endless. It was he who spoke first.

'What a visitation,' he said. She saw his eyes fall to her
long slender legs, back over her body to her hair, her face.
Then he smiled, crookedly, insolently, and the curious spell
was broken. Luisa found she was suddenly furiously angry.
All the rage she had suppressed since speaking to Claudia
welled up inside her with a terrifying force. This cheap,
hateful man! How dared he smile at her like that, so
knowingly, after what he had said to her sister! The room
blurred for a second, re-focussed. She stepped forward.

'Mr Morrell?' she said coldly. 'You won't remember
me . . .'

'On the contrary. I remember you perfectly well.' His
voice, incisively cold, cut her off. 'It's Luisa, isn't it? Luisa
Valway.'

Surprise, and something in the way in which he said her
name, made Luisa hesitate. He sat down behind the desk,
and crossed his legs, leaning back composedly, watching her.

'Don't look so surprised.' He gestured to a chair in front of the desk. 'Do sit down. After all, you've a very memorable face. So have all your family, of course.'

Luisa felt the colour flame into her cheeks. She had not expected this, and he was so much more formidable than she had remembered. She cleared her throat.

'I won't sit down,' she said quietly. 'This won't take long. I think you must know why I'm here.'

'Must I?' He raised his eyebrows, and Luisa felt her temper rise again.

'I would have thought so,' she said scornfully. 'I've come about my sister.'

'Really?' he drawled. 'You mean you're still devoting your life to protecting her?'

He spoke quietly, and as he did so, his eyes met hers. His gaze, grey-eyed, cold, did not falter, and for a moment Luisa was reminded of his brother. She drew in her breath and steadied herself. It would do no good to get angry, she thought desperately, she mustn't antagonise him, somehow she had to be persuasive. She hesitated and then gave him the sweetest smile she could manage.

'Maybe I will sit down after all.'

'Do.'

He made no move, and so, nervously, she drew out the heavy chair. When she was seated, she clasped her hands together and leaned forward, fixing him with her eyes.

'Claudia's told me everything, you see,' she began. 'She told me last night.'

'Everything?' For a moment she saw his face change, saw something like anxiety come into his eyes and it gave her courage. She rushed on.

'Yes. She told me about the money and . . .' She broke off. 'Please, can't you understand?' She looked at him pleadingly. 'She should never have done what she did, but she does realise that now. It will never happen again. She's terribly ashamed, she's ill with worry about it. But we could repair the damage, I know we could!' She paused. 'I . . . I've checked all my investments. If they're sold, I can let you have all the money she took. As soon as you like. In cash if need be, so that it can be repaid immediately.' She broke off. His face had darkened, and the expression on it terrified her, but he said nothing.

'If only you would help us, the way you suggested!

Please!' She put her hands on the desk top, trying not to see
the expression on his face, trying not to let it deter her. 'You
see,' she went on falteringly, 'Claudia's in love—very much
in love, she wants to get married, in fact. But if all this
comes out, then it will all be finished. His family are very
well known, they'd never allow the marriage. It would break
her heart!'

'Would it really?' He gave her a cold smile.

'Don't you see?' She leaned forward, her eyes wide, her
cheeks flushed, determined not to let his tone intimidate her.
'If we can repay the money, no one has been harmed, have
they? Of course I understand that Claudia would have to
leave here, because—well, she's betrayed your father's trust,
and he helped her so kindly. But now——' She hesitated,
then ran on. 'Well, if your brother finds out what she's
done—and he will unless you do something—then it's
obvious what will happen, isn't it?'

'Is it?'

'But of course.' She stared at him. 'You told her
yourself—he'd prosecute. He'd be delighted. He hates us
both.'

'I see.' He stared at her for a long moment, then suddenly,
with a swift movement that startled her, he got up.

'I'm afraid I can't help you,' he said shortly.

Luisa stared at him in dismay.

'But you said to Claudia yesterday . . .'

'That has nothing to do with it.'

Suddenly Luisa felt her temper snap. She stood up too,
confronting him angrily across the desk.

'It has everything to do with it!' she cried hotly. 'How
dare you lead her on like that! Promising to help her, making
your sordid little bargain!'

'My what?' She saw him go white, and felt a wave of
triumph.

'Your bargain!' she cried without thinking. 'Your
blackmail, more like. You were always a liar—you haven't
changed much, Kit, have you, in ten years?'

'I don't know what you're talking about,' he began slowly,
but she cut him off.

'You know perfectly well. You mean you've forgotten the
convenient little cover-up you cooked up last night? You
have a very short memory!' She glared at him furiously, her
eyes blazing. 'The whole miserable affair is so disgusting it

makes me feel quite sick! But at least Claudia's sorry for what she's done, at least I'm trying to help her. All you're interested in is how you can blackmail her into going to bed with you. You're despicable!'

There was a long silence, during which his eyes never left her face. Then very slowly, as if reluctantly, he turned away and sat down behind the desk again. When he met her eyes once more he had recovered his composure, and he sat there for a moment, watching her with an insolent half smile on his face.

'So,' he said finally, 'I'm discovered. Caught out. By the pure sister.'

'How dare you! If you mean by that that Claudia's . . .'

'Oh, I know what Claudia is,' he cut her off. Then he shrugged.

Luisa felt a wave of despair flood over her. She had handled all this completely wrongly, she realised. She had abused him, lost her temper, and now totally alienated him. She lowered her gaze, and spoke quietly, trying to keep her voice level.

'I shouldn't have lost my temper,' she said coldly, 'it does no good. I'm here to tell you two things, and to ask one of you. Firstly, my sister has no intention of complying with your suggestion; secondly, the money can be repaid, as I said. Finally, I wish, for her sake, that you would help us, because I see no other way out.' She paused, and tilted her chin proudly. 'If I could, as you can imagine, I should take it.'

'You could go to Julius,' he said levelly, his face quite calm.

'You must be mad!' She stared at him in disbelief. 'He hates us, I told you. Because of our mother.'

'That was all a long time ago.'

'He won't have forgotten!' she flashed. 'He blames her for your parents' divorce . . . you must know that . . .'

'She *was* to blame.'

Luisa felt herself go white; it was true, of course, it was just a shock, hearing it said by someone else, by Kit, so flatly. She looked away.

'He might help.'

She swung round. 'Julius? He wouldn't help a dying man in the street!'

'Oh, really?' He stood up again, and gave her a cold smile.

'Then as you say, you've no option, have you, Luisa? You'll have to depend on me.'

She stared at him, confused by the silkiness of his tone, with its unmistakable underlying suggestion of threat. To her dismay, he crossed from behind the desk and came towards her.

She forced herself not to shrink back, to face him out.

'Will you help Claudia?'

He smiled. 'Oh yes.'

The relief was so sudden, so unexpected, that it almost overwhelmed her. She knew the joy she felt rushed to her face.

'Do you mean it?'

'Of course. With one little proviso.'

She froze, staring at him in dismay.

'No!' she cried. 'I've already told you, Claudia's in love, she'll never agree to . . .'

'I'm not talking about Claudia.'

He reached out and gripped her arm, urgently, just above the elbow, pulling her just a fraction towards him. He smiled down into her startled upturned face.

'I'm talking about you.'

'*What?*'

He gave a low laugh, an unpleasant, bitter laugh, and through her confusion she noticed for the first time the sensuality of his mouth, now so near her own.

'Well, after all,' he said insolently, 'when this bargain was suggested I hadn't seen *you*, had I? Not for . . . ten years. Now I do, and I wonder at my lack of perception in pursuing your sister. Why chase the easily obtainable?' His grip on her tightened painfully, and he lowered his face to hers. 'Here's metal more attractive, I'd say. Do you agree, Luisa?'

'Agree to what?' she stammered.

He smiled coldly. 'Oh, come now, do I have to spell it out? I will if you like. *You* come to bed with me, Luisa. Then I'll square things for your sister.'

Without thinking what she was doing, on a reflex of shock and something that felt like fear, she lifted her hand and struck him full across the face. The mark of her hand showed scarlet against his skin, and his hold on her slackened, though he did not recoil. She stepped back swiftly, her face white, her body shaking.

'You . . . you *bastard*!' she spat at him, the tears starting to her eyes. 'How could you . . . how could anyone . . .' Her throat felt constricted, the words would not come, and she turned to the door.

'I should think about it, if I were you. And all its implications.' His voice, cold, totally calm, stopped her in her tracks. She spun round.

'How dare you threaten me!' she cried. 'How dare you threaten my sister! I shall find some way out of this mess without your help—your foul suggestions. Wait and see!'

'Oh, I shall.' He gave her a cold mocking smile. 'But I think you'll come back to me in the end, Luisa, don't you?'

'I'd rather be dead!'

She stared at him, white-faced, for a second. Then, without pausing, she ran from the room, and slammed the door violently behind her.

When Luisa returned to the flat it was empty. Tamara came mewing to be fed, rubbing herself against her ankles, arching her back. Automatically, hardly knowing what she was doing, Luisa found a tin, opened it, fed her. Then she cleared the breakfast table, which Claudia had left just as it was. She looked into Claudia's room, thinking she might be in bed, but she was not. White sheets were tumbled on the floor; a thin ray of light lit up the heavy dust that covered the tables.

Dully, her limbs feeling leaden, Luisa went back into the sitting-room and sat down. She stared sightlessly at the cold ashes in the grate, holding herself tightly for warmth. She was surprised Claudia was not there, but even that emotion felt remote, blurred, compared to the icy numbness that gripped her heart.

She closed her eyes, but the images would not go away even then; they danced in her mind confusedly, with an ugly hallucinatory clarity, their sequence discordant, as random as a dream. He had pushed her—no, not that; he had gripped her arm, that was it, and pulled her towards him. The room had felt so hot, so airless, it had been impossible to breathe. She shook, and trying to calm herself, rolled up her sleeve. Yes, that was it. She bruised easily, and now the blue-black marks left by his fingers stood out clearly against her pale skin. Kit, she thought confusedly, and was suddenly possessed by a hatred for him so violent that it seemed outside herself, a malevolence, inhabiting the room.

She had no idea how long she sat there, locked in thoughts, in memories. But she was roused at last by the sound of feet on the stairs, the front door opening. She stood up shakily just as the door opened, and Claudia and Harry came into the room. Claudia was wearing the fur jacket, she saw at once, and her eyes met Luisa's immediately with a look of mute enquiry.

Luisa stared at her in dismay. Claudia looked terrible, she thought, moving quickly to her with a gesture of concern. Her face was chalk white; there were dark circles under her eyes; she was leaning on Harry's arm for support, and before Luisa could reach her, he helped her into a chair.

'What's happened?' she turned to Harry. 'Where have you been?'

He too looked troubled, she saw, his handsome boyish face clouded with worry. Could Claudia have told him?

'Luisa—I'm so glad you're back.' He stood looking down at Claudia worriedly. 'Claudia rang me this morning. She felt ghastly—I've just driven her round to the doctor's.'

'Clou . . .' Luisa knelt down quickly beside her sister, taking her hand; it felt hot and dry, feverish. 'Are you all right? What did he say?'

'It's nothing.' Claudia's voice was impatient. 'Probably 'flu or something. He's useless anyway, I can't think why I bothered. All he ever says is go to bed, get some rest and keep warm . . .'

Harry smiled. 'It wouldn't do any harm, darling,' he said gently. 'We have been burning the candle at both ends a bit lately . . .'

The intimacy of his tone, its quiet affection, evoked no response in Claudia. She looked away; Luisa blushed deeply.

'I'll light a fire,' she said briskly. 'You'd better stay at home today, Clou. I can stay too—I'll ring Luke at the gallery. I'm sure he won't mind . . .'

Quickly she busied herself, laying sticks and coal, clearing the ashes, trying not to hear the murmured conversation between Claudia and Harry. She fetched a rug, tucked it round her sister, and then stood looking down at her. Harry had perched himself on the arm of the chair, his arm round Claudia's shoulders, his face lowered near hers.

'Would you like some coffee, Harry?' she said stiffly.

He looked up, as if surprised, as if he had been oblivious

to her presence, and then stood up.

'I think I'd better go in to work, actually,' he said awkwardly. 'I'm late enough as it is . . .' He broke off and turned to Claudia. 'Will you be all right, darling? I'll come round as soon as I'm free this evening.'

'Oh *go*,' Claudia said irritably. 'The Stock Exchange will probably collapse altogether if you stay any longer . . .' She groaned. 'Oh, hell! And we were going to that party tonight . . .'

'We'll cut it. It'd probably have been god-awful anyway.' He bent down and kissed her cheek gently. 'You rest, darling. Luisa will look after you. I can get back here by seven at the latest. Tell you what—I'll bring a picnic, shall I? Some champagne . . . what would you like? Smoked salmon? Some pâté—I can drop by Fortnum's . . .'

Claudia turned her face away.

'You decide,' she said flatly. 'The very thought of food makes me feel ill.'

Luisa saw Harry's face fall, and she stepped forward quickly, shepherding him to the door, a little familiar ache of regret nagging at her heart. Claudia was so casual, she thought; if someone had ever spoken to her like that . . . She sighed and took Harry's arm.

'Why don't you ring later?' she said gently. 'She'll probably feel better then, and if not . . .' Her voice trailed away. It was unlikely Claudia would, she thought quickly, after what she had to tell her. But Harry had already recovered his spirits.

'Fine,' he said, smiling. 'I'll do that. I'll fix something special for us. All the things she likes. You too, Luisa, of course . . .'

Then he was gone, and Luisa went slowly back into the room. Claudia was still slumped in the chair, holding her slender hands out to the warmth of the fire. As soon as Luisa came in, their eyes met.

'Well?'

Luisa felt herself go cold.

'Claudia,' she said haltingly, 'it's no good, I'm afraid.'

'*What?*' Claudia's beautiful face flushed. 'What do you mean, it's no good—it must be! What happened? What went wrong? Couldn't you get the money . . .'

'No, I can get the money all right,' Luisa said quietly.

'Well, what's wrong, then?' Claudia's voice was shrill,

accusatory. 'It must be O.K., then. Didn't you see Kit?'

Luisa lowered her eyes, feeling the blood mount to her cheeks.

'Yes . . .' she said hesitantly, 'I . . . I saw him.'

'So?'

'He . . . he won't help us, Clou.'

Claudia fumbled angrily with the rug, trying to stand, then leaned forward, her eyes blazing dark in her white face.

'But he must help us! He said he would yesterday! He *promised* me, practically.' She broke off. 'Oh, God!' she cried bitterly. 'You messed it up, didn't you, Luisa? What the hell did you say to him? Oh, why did I tell you . . . why didn't I handle this in my own way . . .'

'It wouldn't have done any good,' Luisa said flatly. She knelt down by the chair and took her sister's hot dry hand in hers, but Claudia wrenched it away pettishly.

'Listen, Claudia, we have to think of something else. We *have* to. Kit can't help us, and I wouldn't take his help if he could do. He's . . . he's foul, Claudia . . . I . . .'

Claudia looked at her suspiciously. 'What do you mean, foul?' she said slowly. 'Kit's all right. If you've let all your old prejudices mess this up for me, Lou, I'll . . .'

'It's not that!' Luisa stared at her sister, her eyes wide. 'He . . . he stuck to his bargain . . .' she said finally.

'I see . . .' Claudia leaned back in the chair, her face set.

'No, darling Clou, you *don't* see.' Luisa reached for her impulsively. 'He . . . he changed his terms, there and then, for no good reason at all. He . . . he said he'd do it. But . . . but only if *I* went to bed with him . . .'

'*What?*' Claudia's eyes narrowed with disbelief. She stared at Luisa and then, to her amazement, threw back her head and laughed. 'Oh, my God,' she said weakly. 'How typical of Kit! What a joke. You, of all people!'

Luisa stared at her in disbelief.

'It was *horrible*, Clou,' she said fiercely. 'He . . . he had no shame whatsoever. He tried to get hold of me, and then . . .'

'And then you ran a mile, I suppose?' Claudia had stopped laughing, and was now looking at her appraisingly, Luisa saw, with a cold, thoughtful expression on her face. When Luisa didn't answer her, she looked away, reached impatiently for her bag, found some cigarettes and lit one. She drew on it deeply, coughed, then leaned back, her arm and hand extended, watching the thin grey smoke coil upwards in silence.

'Well, that's all right, then, isn't it, Lou?' she said finally.

'All right?' Luisa said in a quiet small voice; she felt the beginnings of fear grip her stomach.

'Of course. All right.' Claudia gave her a cold smile. 'I mean—you'll do it, won't you? Then I'll be in the clear.'

'Claudia!' Luisa stared at her in disbelief.

'Oh, hell, don't look like that!' Claudia flicked her ash in the grate. 'It's perfectly simple, isn't it? If that's what Kit wants—though I must say I think he's mad. But why not? What have you got to lose?'

Luisa's throat tightened, she felt tears start to her eyes; Claudia spoke flippantly, but she was clearly totally serious.

'Claudia . . .' Luisa's voice choked in her throat. 'You . . . you can't mean that . . .'

'Oh, but I do mean it.' Claudia stubbed the cigarette out impatiently, and turned to her, her face intent, tight.

'Well, surely you can see?' she said coldly. 'It's either that or I'm finished. It's not so much of a sacrifice, is it, for your own sister?'

'It certainly is!' Luisa stood up, colour rushing to her face, her hands shaking. 'I can't think how you can say such things, Claudia. To even consider . . . to ask me.' She broke off. 'He's the most hateful man!'

'No, he's not. He's extremely attractive.'

A memory of grey eyes, a mocking sensual mouth, came to Luisa; she reached automatically for her arm, for the bruises his fingers had left.

'No, he's not!' she cried hotly. 'And besides, that has nothing whatsoever to do with it. What he was suggesting was disgusting, obscene . . .'

'Was it?'

'Of course it was! It's just blackmail, pure and simple, of the most horrible kind . . .'

'Are you sure that's what's really worrying you?' Claudia leaned forward intently, her eyes burning, her mouth jagged with anger. 'Are you sure it's the blackmail you really care about, Luisa? Because I'd say it was something else.'

'Something else?' Her tone stopped Luisa dead, and Claudia gave a low bitter laugh.

'Oh, come on, Luisa, you can admit it to me! After all, I know you well enough, don't I? Look at you now!' Contemptuously, her eyes raked Luisa's pale oval face and

trembling body. 'You're scared, aren't you? And not because
of blackmail, because of sex. You're terrified of men, Lou,
you always have been. As long as I can remember you've
been like that—like ice. No man can get near you—you
never give one the chance, do you? Why even when we were
kids ... oh hell, what's the point?' She broke off angrily.
'It's impossible talking to you. I don't know what's the
matter with you—whether you've got some stupid hang-up
about your virginity, or whether you're just pure perverse—
God knows! You're twenty-five and you're on the shelf—
heavens, if Kit knew what he was in for he wouldn't bother.
No man would have much fun in bed with you!'

'Be quiet!' Luisa felt tears start to her eyes and covered
her ears with her hands. 'How can you say such things,
Claudia? It's not true! Just because I don't share your free
and easy morals it doesn't mean I'm ...'

'I know what you are, Luisa.' Claudia pushed the rug
aside angrily, and stood up. 'You're a stupid, frigid prude.
You can call it morality if you like. I call it being scared. I
know what you think of me, you've preached often enough.
But at least if I like someone I admit it—to myself *and* them.
All right, I go to bed with them. So what? I give them
something, they give me something. It's not necessarily ugly
or cheap or wrong, it's sometimes painful and sometimes
pleasant, but at least it's *free*. I don't hoard *my* purity like a
fortune in the bank!' She stopped suddenly, her breath
coming fast, as if aware she had said too much. The two of
them stood still staring at one another in silence. It was
Luisa who finally spoke.

'Is that what you really think of me?' she said finally, her
voice low, near to breaking.

'Oh, God knows!' Claudia turned away with a sigh of
exasperation, her temper finished. She sat down again
weakly, and when she turned to Luisa again, her face was
tired and haggard. She held out her hand.

'Lou,' she said, her voice more gentle, 'I'm sorry. You
know how I fly off the handle. But obviously I'm going to
see it differently from you.' She gave a low bitter laugh.
'After all, it's a simple choice, isn't it? Which matters
more—your precious purity, or your sister?'

'Claudia, no!' Impulsively Luisa crossed to her, taking her
hand and kneeling beside her. 'It can't be like that. It won't
be like that. There must be some other way.'

'To get you off the hook, you mean?' Claudia looked at her coldly, and Luisa let go her hand.

'Claudia,' she said slowly, 'I cannot, I *will* not do this. I know you can't understand, that for you it could just be something trivial, soon done, soon forgotten, but for me it wouldn't be like that, it would be *wrong*, going against everything I believe in ... I *can't*, Claudia. Not even for you.'

'I'd do it for you.'

Claudia spoke flatly, in a matter-of-fact tone of voice, and Luisa turned her face away miserably, because she knew it was true. Claudia stood up.

'Well, anyway, that's it,' she said dismissively. 'At least now I know where I stand. You keep your unsullied purity, your unstained reputation, and I ...' She shrugged. 'My own fault, of course. I have no right to blame anyone but myself, etc, etc. Except I damn well do, Luisa. I blame *you*.' She stopped at the door and turned back, her face wan, her eyes blazing with anger. 'And I shall go on blaming you. For the rest of my messed-up life!'

'Claudia ...' Luisa jumped up, but she was too late. The door of Claudia's bedroom slammed shut, and she heard the key turn in the lock.

She stood there for a few moments, unable to move, beyond tears now, her breath coming fast and painfully in her chest. Then she began to pace the room, back and forth, back and forth, like a trapped animal, trying to fight off the memories and emotions that Claudia had brought flooding back, trying to force herself to think clearly.

After a while she crossed out into the little hallway, hesitating outside her sister's door. From inside she could hear the sound of muffled crying, and she felt a stab of pain and love shoot through her heart. It was like that year, that terrible year, after their mother died. Claudia could hardly remember that now, but she could. The footsteps in the night on the bedroom floor.

'*I want Mummy, Lou, where is she?*'

'*Mummy's gone, darling. Can't you sleep? Come in with me, I'll hold you.*'

'*All night?*'

'*If you want.*'

'*You won't go away, Lou?*'

'*No, darling. Not ever. I promise.*'

Weakly Luisa rested her forehead against the cool walls, listening to the awful dry racking sobs that came from behind the closed door. Then, suddenly, she straightened, and went quickly back into the sitting-room. She picked up the telephone, hesitated, and then dialled a number. There was just one last chance, she told herself feverishly, the only one she had.

The number seemed to ring interminably; then it answered and she spoke.

'Hallo? I'd like to speak to Julius Morrell's secretary please. It's Luisa Valway.'

# CHAPTER THREE

'OH, for God's sake, Luisa, have a drink or something.'

'Luke, I can't. I've got to be there in a minute . . .'

'Rubbish, my dear, a little Dutch courage never did anyone any harm.' Ignoring her protestations, he poured two large brandies into some old chipped glasses. He gestured to the clock. 'It's less than ten minutes from here. Now calm down. Sip it slowly.'

They were in Luke's tiny flat above the gallery, hemmed in by Luke's paintings, by a lifetime's magpie collecting. Luke was wearing what he always wore in the evenings: a green velvet smoking jacket that had seen better days, and an incongruous vivid scarlet scarf about his neck. They gave an air of youth and gaiety to his features, belied by the deep lines of his face, the iron grey of his hair which—ever since he had been at Oxford in the twenties—he had worn obstinately and unalterably long. He leaned on the mantelpiece, his elbow finding a tiny resting place between a clutter of snuff boxes, an ostrich egg, and a collection of Victorian silk fans; the ancient gas fire spluttered. He looked down at her kindly.

'Better?'

'A bit.' Luisa smiled up at him wanly; she was so fond of Luke. She had known him since she was a child, had worked for him for five years. In the past, she had spent such happy evenings, talking, looking at pictures. . . . She spread her hands in a gesture of despair.

'I'm so tense,' she said apologetically. 'I didn't expect to have to see Julius so soon, you see. I . . . I thought he was in Italy, but his secretary says he came back unexpectedly. This evening is the only time he could see me.'

'Come on, Luisa my dear. What difference does it make? Now or next week—you've got to get it over with.'

'But in his *house*. It would be so much easier in an office . . .'

'Luisa, you're making a mountain out of a molehill. You're resurrecting all sorts of old memories, adding two and two and making six . . . It'll be perfectly all right, you'll see . . .' He paused. 'I've met him, you know—Julius, that is. Once when he was a boy, with his father and your mother.' He hesitated fractionally. 'I sold him a painting once, a few years ago. And he acted for a friend of mine, who'd got into a spot of bother. He's a brilliant counsel . . .'

'Oh, I know *that*,' Luisa said bitterly. 'Renowned for his ability to get a conviction.'

'Not in this case. He was acting for the defence. My friend owes Julius Morrell quite a lot.'

There was a mild reproach in his voice, and Luisa acknowledged it.

'I'm sorry, Luke. I'm on edge.'

He smiled and sat down, lighting one of the long black Russian cigarettes he always smoked, inhaling deeply. There was silence for a while, and Luisa looked around the tiny tranquil room, trying to calm herself. There was one great painting among the many that clustered the walls, jostling for space on the old-fashioned shabby wallpaper; she never liked to look at it, but it drew the eyes effortlessly by its power. It was a nude, of her mother, painted when she was perhaps Luisa's age; her limbs were tawny, the strong curves of her breasts and thighs were exaggerated with primitive strokes. She was lying back on a bed, propped up, her neck arched, her black hair falling across brilliantly patterned cushions; asleep perhaps, in a kind of easy, animal-like abandon. The painter had been her mothers lover—or so Luke said. Through the shutters behind her, you could see the sea, the clear light of the Mediterranean. Luisa forced herself to look at it; it was so like Claudia.

Luke's eyes followed her gaze; he seemed almost to read her thoughts.

'You know, my dear,' he said abruptly, 'I find Claudia much to blame in all this. I'm not sure you wouldn't have done better to stay out of it altogether. She has to grow up some day, you know, fend for herself. And she'd acted very badly. Old Teddy Morrell was devoted to your mother—he took Claudia on there purely because of that. After all, her record wasn't too good, was it?'

'She'd been through a lot of jobs. But there were reasons for that, Luke.' Luisa sprang quickly to her sister's defence, and he suppressed a smile. 'No, it's true! She could never settle at work—hated office hours. She'd be late, get herself fired. But she has been trying, really, Luke. Since she went to Morrell & Kennedy she's been much better . . .'

'Until this,' he said gently.

'All this was a mistake! Claudia's not really dishonest. She's terribly sorry for what she's done. Oh, can't you see, Luke?' She leaned forward impulsively. 'I have to help her. No one else can.'

'Well, well. Don't get worked up again, my dear.' He smiled and gestured to the painting. 'She's just like your mother, of course. Gets more like her every day. Lucia was always impossible—wild, impetuous, a heartbreaker. Such a heartbreaker. Didn't know what she was doing half the time, and wouldn't have cared much if she did. But no one could ever get angry with her for long. She was so beautiful . . .' He sighed, and looked into the fire. 'I remember the first time I saw her: she came into the room and—well, it was as if time had stopped. You couldn't look at anything else; nothing. She was so alive, so vibrantly alive, and then . . .' He broke off sadly, and shrugged, as if he could shift the memories. 'Dangerous thing, beauty.' He looked at her keenly. 'But then you should know that, Luisa.'

'*I* should?' She looked at him in surprise.

'My dear! And I thought I'd been training you all these years.' He laughed. 'Stand up—go on. There's a glass there. Now, look in it, my dear, the way I've showed you, and tell me what you see.'

Hesitantly Luisa stood up, and looked in the huge dusty gilt-framed mirror that stood perched on top of the mantelpiece. Luke watched her intently, sipping his drink.

'Well? What do you see?'

Luisa lowered her eyes from her own image. 'Nothing. *A blank, my lord.*'

She quoted the line lightly, hoping to deflect him, but Luke made a gesture of impatience. He stood up, and turned her face back to the glass. His keen eyes, faded blue now, but still sharp, traced the lines of her face.

'Perhaps,' he said slowly. 'A little. Not quite awake, but certainly . . .'

'Tired, you mean?' she laughed nervously.

'No,' he said, his voice serious. 'You know what I mean, Luisa.' He paused, and then went on as if he were cataloguing a portrait, measuring the distances between her features with his long narrow hands. 'Features, delicately formed; brows, classically spaced; complexion, pale—too

pale! Eyes . . . strange eyes, a little distrustful perhaps, and a
disturbing colour, amber almost, old gold. Hair extraordinary—Rossetti would have loved your hair; like light.
Difficult to catch, that.' He smiled at her reflection in the
glass. 'Not a modern face, of course, but then neither is
Claudia's. There's a savagery of line in her face—Fauviste;
your face—difficult to say. Not this century, certainly.
Almost medieval. Something about the way your eyes are
set . . . I've got it! You've never been to Venice, of course,
but there's a painting there, a Madonna, by Bellini, it's in
the Accademia . . . Yes. That's it!' She saw a light of
triumph at having placed something come into his eyes. 'I
have a copy somewhere, but you should see the original one
day.'

Luisa looked back at her own face in the glass, curiously,
as if she were looking at another person. She sighed. She saw
nothing of that, she thought dully. She saw only a pale girl,
curiously bloodless; herself. She turned away.

'Hardly vibrantly alive,' she said, unable to keep a note of
bitterness out of her voice.

'Not yet.'

He patted her shoulder lightly, thoughtfully.

'I think you'd better go, don't you, my dear? You don't
want to be late for your appointment.'

The odd spell of the last few minutes had been broken;
quickly Luisa looked at her watch.

'Oh, I must go, you're right.' She turned to the door.
'And you won't tell anyone, Luke, you promise? Nobody
knows about all this, you see. I haven't even told Claudia
about tonight . . .'

He laughed, and planted a light kiss on her cheek.

'My dear, the secrets I could tell! I'm the soul of
discretion. If it's any comfort, I think you're doing the right
thing. Let me know tomorrow what's happened—all
right? And if you want a shoulder to cry on, you can always
come back here afterwards . . .'

Luisa let herself out, slipping quickly past the shrouded
paintings and statues in the gallery below, and out into the
cold night air. It was already dark, and the air was dank,
smelling of wet grass, damp privet, soot, against her skin. The
moon was rising, white as a bone, veiled with thin cloud, just
above the park on the hill. She quickened her steps on the
steep pavements, and at the corner hesitated. There were

only street lamps lighting the way ahead of her, and she looked back momentarily at the warm cluster of little shops by the gallery, the pub; on the night air, the chink of glasses, the music of the jukebox drifted. Resolutely she turned her back, peering at the tall white houses ahead of her. Opposite the park, his secretary had said, the fourth house after the turning. At the gate she paused. It was not too late, she thought nervously, looking up at the tall curtained windows; she could still change her mind. Then she forced herself to open the gate. She must go through with it; she must!

Decisiveness helped; she felt her spirits lift a little as she mounted the steps to the wide porch, and pressed the bell. Luke was probably right; she was being foolish to judge Julius by childhood memories. After all, he was a man now, he must have changed; surely, if she could only explain, he would help them?

'Miss Valway?' The door was opened by a manservant in a dark suit, who ushered her into a wide, brilliantly lit hall. 'Mr Morrell will be with you in a moment. If you would like to wait in here. May I take your coat?'

He led her into a huge drawing room, and withdrew, silently, the closing door making hardly a sound. Nervously Luisa looked around her. Julius must be a very rich man, she realised with surprise, her eyes taking in the rich Chinese carpets, the antique furniture. The room was painted a deep red, one wall was flanked from floor to ceiling with books; dark velvet curtains the colour of blood masked the tall windows that over looked the park. She stood uncertainly, near the door, and then—when no one came—she moved reluctantly into the room and stood near the fire. A clock ticked; the room was perfectly ordered; not a cushion, not a book or newspaper was out of place. On a table by the fire was a huge Chinese bowl, planted with white hyacinths which were just coming into bloom. She leant towards them, looking at the tight buds just flushed with green, just beginning to unfurl; their scent rose up to her powerfully on the warm air, heady, clear, the scent of spring in midwinter.

'Miss Valway.'

She spun round, words rising to her lips. Then she froze, staring in disbelief across the room.

The man who spoke had come in quite silently, had shut the door behind him. He was standing perhaps twenty feet from her, his hands in the pockets of a dark formal suit, his eyes grey, cold, even at that distance. Dark auburn hair fell slightly forward over his forehead, and as she looked at him he brushed it back with an impatient gesture. She felt the blood rush to her face.

'I ... I don't understand,' she stammered finally. 'There must be mistake ...'

'There's no mistake.' He crossed the room to her, his face unsmiling, and came to a halt some five feet away. 'We met this morning. Or have you forgotten so soon?'

'I know ... but ... there must be some confusion ...'

'No confusion.' He smiled grimly. 'Perhaps we should introduce ourselves again. I'm Julius Morrell.'

Luisa swayed, and he made no attempt to steady her. Instead her hand found the smooth polished surface of the table behind her, and she leaned against it for a moment, staring at him, as the seconds lengthened. Of course: how could she have been such a fool? she thought bitterly. If she hadn't been so nervous, so keyed up, she could never have made that mistake. Kit's eyes were grey too, but they had never had that coldness; his mouth had always been slightly weak, almost girlish; not cruel, almost savage, like this man's. And the voice—how could she have forgotten the voice, so incisive, clipped, beautiful but harsh—a prosecutor's voice, even then. He was looking at her now, she realised, rather as he might look at a witness in the box that he was about to tear to shreds before a jury, and the dislike in his eyes, uncompromising, undisguised, foreshortened ten years to a few seconds. He had looked at her like that, just the same way, once before ...

The memory gave her courage; she straightened and stepped forward.

'I'll go, then. There's no point in my staying now.'

'You think so? I should say, from your sister's point of view, that there's every point in staying, wouldn't you?'

He moved, lazily, without haste, so that he was blocking her path, and she was forced to look up at him.

She stopped, her mind confusedly jumbling the events of the past day, trying to make sense of them. She must not act hastily this time, she thought, in a flood of desperation. Perhaps there was some misunderstanding. Perhaps, this morning, it had all been some kind of cruel game ...

'You want an explanation, I suppose? Women usually do.'

He crossed and sat down on a chair by the fire, his eyes never leaving her face.

His words stung her, and she turned to him defiantly, keeping her voice low. 'Don't you think you owe me one?'

He shrugged. 'Perhaps. Then we both have a debt, don't we?'

She stared at him, not understanding, but he said nothing more. There was a long silence; Luisa clenched her hands. She was not going to be outfaced, she thought suddenly, her courage returning to her. If she left now, she was throwing away her last chance. Slowly, taking her time, she chose a chair opposite him, and sat down. It was covered in red velvet; her dress was black. As she sat, the skirt swirled out in an aureole of shadow across the vivid colour, and he smiled grimly.

'Did you choose that costume specially?'

'I . . . I don't know what you mean . . .' she stammered.

'I think you know exactly what I mean.' The grey eyes flashed. 'So demure, so chaste. All in black, like a nun. Did you think I'd be impressed?'

'I didn't think about it at all.'

'I'm sure you did. After all, you must have thought about this meeting quite carefully.'

'I thought about the meeting. Not my appearance.'

'Really?' The narrow lips curved briefly in a cold smile that never reached his eyes. 'What a paragon of your sex! Not the way they usually operate.'

'I came here purely for your help.' Her voice sounded stiff, and as she spoke she met his eyes. Not even pride, she knew, could hide the pleading in her own.

'For my help?' His voice was deeply sarcastic. 'This morning you told me I wouldn't help a dying man in the street.' He stood up. 'A vivid phrase, I thought, that. Over-coloured, perhaps, but still revealing. Will you have a drink?'

'No, thank you.'

'As you like.'

Ignoring her, he crossed and poured himself a tumbler of whisky and water, then he stationed himself in front of the fire—deliberately so, she thought; now she was forced to look up at him.

She swallowed nervously; since he clearly was not going to help her, she had better begin, she thought. She leaned forward.

'This morning . . .' She hesitated. 'Why didn't you tell me
who you were?'

'Because I didn't choose to.'

'It would have saved time. And a lot of misunderstanding.'

'Possibly.'

'I should have recognised you, of course.' She looked at
him, forcing herself to remain calm. 'It's . . . a long time
since we met. But you're nothing like Kit.'

'No.' He looked at her coldly. 'You chose to go to him,
however.' He paused. 'But then you were always fond of
Kit, weren't you, Luisa? Even as a girl . . .'

She felt the blood rush up her neck, crimsoning her
cheeks. She looked away, ignoring his remark.

'I went to Kit . . . as I thought,' she said slowly, carefully,
'because Claudia had already spoken to him. Because she
thought he would help us.'

'And when—as you thought—he wouldn't, then you came
running to me. What were you proposing to do, tell tales of
my brother?'

'If necessary.' She met his gaze levelly. 'I don't care what
I do. My only concern is to help Claudia, and wipe out what
she's done.'

'That's not true, for a start. As we established this
morning, you do care what you do. Your concern—your
laudable concern—for your sister has its limitations, does it
not?'

The grey eyes met hers unwaveringly, and Luisa felt the
panic start up again inside her. Surely, now, he was not
going to resurrect *that*!

She clasped her hands nervously together in front of her,
forcing herself not to flinch, not to look away.

'It has one limitation, if you want to call it that. Yes.'

He smiled, and very deliberately raised his hand,
running it down his cheek where she had hit him that
morning.

'How prim!' He put down his glass. 'You imagine I'm
taken in by all that? By that dress . . . by your behaviour this
morning? Oh no. As acts go, it was quite a good one. But it
doesn't convince me.'

'That is irrelevant.' Luisa stood up, confusedly fighting
the anger she could feel beginning inside her, fighting off the
faint but perceptible sense of fear he awoke in her. 'Julius,

please.' She saw him flinch at her use of his name, an expression of distaste crossing his mouth. Impulsively, she stepped towards him.

'Please,' she said earnestly. 'I know that you dislike us. I know there's no reason why you should help us. Claudia has done something wrong . . .'

'It's called embezzlement,' he cut in. 'It also involves forgery. I did some checking after you'd gone. After you'd so conveniently brought the matter to my attention.'

'I *know* that! I know she should be punished. But don't you see? She's already being punished, she's ill with worry and guilt . . .'

'Because she might be found out.' He laughed contemptuously. 'Don't be naïve, Luisa. If I hadn't turned up on the scene, do you imagine for one moment that this would have happened? No. Claudia would have happily gone on milking that poor woman's money for as long as she safely could. Claudia's not sorry—she's scared.'

'That's not true!' She stared at him wide-eyed, fighting the doubts his words raised in her own mind. 'She wouldn't have done that. It was done on an impulse, she already regretted it, long before you ordered the audit . . .'

'On an impulse! Cashing cheques for two thousand pounds, over a period of three months, at carefully calculated intervals? You call that impulse!'

'She . . . she needed the money . . .'

'What for?' The grey eyes blazed at her angrily. 'She was starving, was she? She had some child to support, couldn't pay the rent to the council, couldn't afford food? Don't give me that! I've seen women in just that position sent down for three months for shoplifting, and you try and get Claudia off scot free? Why the hell should she? You call that justice?'

'No.' She dropped her gaze. 'I don't.'

'Then what do you call it?'

'I don't know!' she cried desperately. 'Forgiveness, mercy, call it what you want . . .'

'You know what I call it?' He glared down at her. 'I call it buying your way out. Claudia happens to have a sister with enough money, who's a soft touch, who she thinks can get her off the hook, wipe out everything she's done, make the slate clean. One system for the rich, another for the poor. God damn it, it's sick-making!'

'So.' Luisa looked at him calmly, feeling the tears start to her eyes, and fear and concern for Claudia swelling up inside her painfully. 'What would you like to see happen?'

'I'd like Claudia to have to face the consequences of her actions, just like anyone else.'

'And ruin her life. She's only twenty! Please, Julius, can't you see?' She stepped closer to him, all fear of him wiped out now, and raised her hands to him pleadingly. 'Claudia has done wrong, but she does see that now. She'll never do it again. She's . . . she's got the chance now, with someone, to try and make something of her life. To make up for . . . for all the mess in the past.' She hesitated. 'It's partly *my* fault all this has happened. If Claudia had had a normal childhood . . .'

He laughed sarcastically.

'Don't laugh!' she cried sharply. 'You talk to me about deprivation. About people who . . . who have no means, who are desperate. Well, there are other kinds of deprivation too! Claudia hardly knew our mother, hardly saw our father. She never had any love as a child . . . if she's stupid and irresponsible sometimes, there are *reasons* for it. Can't you see that?'

'No, I can't,' he said roughly. 'Don't give me sob-stories about Claudia. She never wanted for anything!'

'She wanted for love!'

She cried the words, and there was a sudden silence. Julius made no answer, and her words rang oddly in the air between them, echoing and re-echoing in Luisa's head. Their gaze was locked together so strongly that it was as if an invisible thread held them, and the rest of the room, the world outside stopped, quite suddenly, just for a second. She saw his expression change, fleetingly, and briefly thought she saw something different, something reachable, a kind of compassion in those cold grey eyes. But it was gone as quickly as it came. His mouth twisted, and he stepped towards her.

'She wanted for love.' He repeated her words mockingly, throwing them back in her face. 'The eternal cry in our indulgent age. The eternal all-purpose, built-in, ever-useful excuse. The eternal cry of your whole goddamned family!' He reached across and gripped her arm hard, wrenching her towards him. 'I'll tell you something, Luisa.' He forced her face up to him, his voice low, his eyes blazing with hatred. 'You know who you remind me of, just at this moment?

Who you reminded me of this morning, when you leaned across my desk with precisely that same expression of hope and pleading you've got on it now? You remind me of your mother, that's who.'

'Of my mother?' She stared at him in bewilderment, taken aback by the sudden vehemence, the passion in his voice. 'But I don't . . .'

'Oh, I know you don't look like her.' He spat the words at her contemptuously. 'But you are like her, aren't you, Luisa? Inside, where it doesn't show except in your eyes. God, I hate your eyes! I can't bear to look at them.'

He pushed her violently away.

'I've seen your mother look just like that, just the way you do now. When she came crawling to *my* mother with her excuses and her prevarications and her barefaced goddamned lies. God!' He covered his face with his hands. 'I'll never forget that look as long as I live. "Forgive me, forgive me. I'm sorry I broke up your marriage, I'm so sorry for your sons, for your husband, for what I've done to your life," ' he mimicked her mother's voice, the odd lilting Italian accent, with extraordinary vividness, so that Luisa recoiled; it was as if her mother were in the room with them. He stepped closer towards her, suddenly reaching out and gripping her wrist, wrenching it up painfully between them.

'That was her plea too. She wanted to use it, just the way you do, because it suited her purposes. God, we had it all— the childhood in the slums, the lovers who had never understood her, and then the one man who had come along and finally helped her, given her the love she'd been craving all this while in her poor forsaken life. The man who just happened to be my father. Whom she walked out on six months later, when she'd finally achieved all the mess and destruction she'd set her heart on . . .'

'Stop!' Luisa tried painfully to free her hand. 'That's not true! It wasn't like that, you're twisting everything . . .'

'What do you know?' With a sharp gesture he released her. 'You were just a child!'

'And Claudia was a baby!' she countered, her eyes blazing at him angrily. 'She had nothing to do with all that. She's not responsible for it! All you're doing is . . . is revenging yourself on Claudia. And you talk to me about justice. That's not justice, that's hate!'

There was a silence, and for a moment she thought she

had reached him, that her words had got through the shell of memories, the store of anger. Certainly he appeared, for the first time, discomfited. This time it was he who turned away.

'Maybe,' he said shortly, his back to her now, so she could not see his face. 'Maybe.'

She hesitated, letting the silence lengthen, listening with half a mind to the shifting of the coals in the fire, the subdued ticking of the clock. Then, timidly, she plucked at his sleeve.

'Julius.' He did not turn. 'Please!'

Her voice sounded odd to her ears, slightly choked, and she spoke with difficulty.

'I ... I can only speak for what I feel. For what I remember.' She let her hand rest gently on his arm, and he stiffened at her touch. 'I ... I never hated you, and I'm sorry, truly sorry, that you should feel as you do. But now, please, can't you put that aside, just this once, and help us?' She sighed. 'If you don't ... I have nowhere else to turn. Please. I can only ask ... beg ...'

He turned.

'You asked this morning,' he said coldly.

'I'm asking you again.' She looked up at him, feeling the tears well into her eyes, not just for Claudia, she realised, but for him too, for the pain and anger in his face, for the past. He brushed her hand from his arm.

'And I told you this morning. There's a price.'

'*What?*' She stared at him, recoiling instinctively. 'You can't have meant that! I ... I thought it must be some kind of ... of game.'

'It's not a game. I told you.' His mouth had set in a hard line, and his eyes glittered at her strangely. 'Either your sister pays the price, or you do. It's time someone in your family paid off their debts.'

'But ... I told you. I can pay back the money ...'

'I'm not talking about money!'

'You can't mean it!'

'Oh, but I do.' He moved towards her again, and she saw his lips lift in a mocking smile. 'Call it rough justice, call it what you will. I think it ties up a long equation very neatly, don't you?'

'A long equation?' Something in his voice, in his eyes, held her.

There was a silence, and they stared at each other. Luisa felt something lift and stir in her heart, something so old, so powerful, it frightened her.

'I don't know what you mean . . .'

'You know exactly what I mean. Don't you, Luisa?'

She tried to back away from him, but before she could move his strong arms came round her, holding her effortlessly, drawing her towards him. He didn't force her, but just held her so she could not move, and then with a gentleness that took her by surprise, tilted her face up to him, so he could look down into her wide scared eyes.

'Is there some man in your life now, Luisa? Does this involve you in some betrayal?'

'No . . . I . . .'

'Don't lie.'

'No, it doesn't!'

'Well then.'

Her lips parted to answer him, and as they did so he bent his head and kissed her. His lips were warm, firm, and the first touch of them sent a violent wave of shock through her whole body, so sudden, so unexpected that she had no time to resist. His arms locked behind her, drawing her to him, pressing her soft body against the hardness of his own. She felt her hands, trapped between them against his chest, flinch, and then relax. Julius sighed, oddly, harshly, in a way she had never heard before, and she could sense a man's urgency growing in him, pulsing in him, communicating itself to her like an electrical current, its force seeping irresistibly into her, demanding a response. She heard herself give a little moan, and he deepened his kiss, running his hands up her back until they were laced in her long thick hair, and cradled her face up to him like a flower while he sought the honey of her mouth.

Pleasure, edged with fear, sharpened by it, welled up inside her unbidden; it flowed through her veins irresistibly, and undeniably. She felt her body begin its betrayal of her mind, going limp, pliant, in his arms. She should have compressed her lips, wrenched her head away, but somehow she could not. Something had awoken in her, something she had buried so long she had believed it dead—a compulsion of terrifying force surged up inside her, coming from deep within the womb of her body, like a message at one moment in her blood, her heart, the next in her arms, her lips, her tongue.

She heard him, as if from far away, give a low groan, as his lips moved down to her throat, sending a piercing pleasure right through her, and his hands, moving with a new urgency, as if they had no enemy but time and all delay, moved down to her breasts, full under the black dress, cupping their weight in his palms.

'Luisa ... don't you remember?' She felt rather than heard his voice; his skin was rough against her cheek, and she knew she arched her throat back instinctively, arched it for his kisses, in a way she had seen once somewhere, sometime. The portrait. Even as he touched her, it came back, the memory, the image, and with it her heart seemed to stop. As instantly the pleasure was gone; her whole body stiffened, flooded with shame. She heard herself give a low strangled cry, her hands clenched, knocking his away, pushing him aside with all her force.

'No!'

She broke from him, and they stood, like two combatants, each breathing fast, their eyes locked in a look that cut off the rest of the world. His were now pleading, demanding, hers suddenly cold, furiously, uncontrollably, cold. She was shaking.

'I will not!'

'Luisa ...' He reached for her, and she hit at his hand, feeling her heart grow small and tight and vengeful inside her.

'Get away from me. Never touch me again!'

He drew back, and she saw his face harden, the guardedness come back.

'Next time ...' she forced her voice out, 'next time you stand at the bar in court, Julius—God, I hope you remember this, I hope you never forget it as long as you live! You have no right to be there. You hear me? No right!' She heard her voice rise, saw him flinch from her accusation. 'There's no one you could be prosecuting much worse than you. A blackmailer, a liar, taking advantage of someone's weakness ... you're despicable. Loathesome. You repel me, do you understand that? You ...'

To her fury, she saw his mouth twist in a half smile.

'Do I?' His voice was low, tight, and she could see he was restraining his temper with difficulty. 'I shouldn't have said that, and I've a good deal of experience in these matters.'

'That's a lie!'

'No, it isn't.' He reached for her arm and held it. 'Whatever I wanted then, Luisa, you wanted it too. So what does that make you? Where's your sanctimonious purity now?'

'Damn you, Julius, let me go!' She tried to wrench herself free, but his grip tightened, and suddenly fear flooded through her, an old blind unreasoning fear, and she lost all control. On a pure animal instinct, she bent quickly, so her mouth was against his skin ... she tasted blood warm against her lips, and heard him give a cry of pain. He let go of her instantly, and she stepped back, shuddering, appalled at what she had just done. As she did so, he laughed.

'What a little vixen!' He rubbed his wrist ruefully. 'What are you going to do next, go for my eyes with your nails?'

Luisa backed away from him jerkily, quickly, unconscious of her movements, colliding painfully and clumsily with the small delicate table behind her. With a cry she turned, but it was too late. It tipped; the Chinese bowl, the hyacinth, crashed to the floor and shattered. After the crash there was a terrible silence, that seemed to ring in her ears. In numb dismay she stared down at the floor, at the shards of crimson and gold and white, the dry mould scattered, the white flowers crushed.

'Oh no!' Quickly she turned to pick them up, to do something, but he forestalled her.

'Leave them. It doesn't matter. Things get broken.'

'I'm so sorry...' The words faded on her lips; to apologise now was clearly ridiculous.

He turned away curtly, and pressed a bell by the fireplace. 'Myers will clear it up. And he can fetch your coat.'

'Julius...' Instinctively she reached out her hand to him, but he turned away. The door opened.

'Miss Valway is leaving, Myers.'

'Very good, sir.'

'Oh, and Luisa...' His tone was light, perfectly normal, as if nothing had happened, Luisa thought bitterly. 'Consider my proposal, will you? I'd like a definite decision. Shall we say in the next three days? Then I shall know what to do.' He gave her a brilliant icy smile. 'One way or the other.'

She didn't answer but went quickly into the hall. Impassively, formally Myers helped her on with her coat. If he saw she was shaking, he made no sign.

'Good evening, Miss Valway.'

'Good evening.'

The door shut.

Luisa walked home. It was over a mile, and the air was now bitterly cold, but she knew she could not bear to face the bright lights of buses or tubes, the company even of strangers. The sky above her was quite clear, the moon not quite full and white, the stars each distinct. The windscreens of the parked cars she passed were just beginning to film with a pale frost, and the pavements glittered. Behind her the sound of her own footsteps echoed along the empty streets. She walked fast; then, just before she reached Haverstock Hill, she suddenly stopped, staring ahead of herself, seeing nothing. She let herself think the thought that reverberated in her mind. She said to herself, enunciating the words silently: I loved him once. So much. So much.

To confront at last what she had known so long calmed her. She held the thought in her mind for a moment, then, very deliberately, she discarded it, made it leave her. She would let it go, she thought, like a coin tumbling into deep dark water, glimpsed for a second and then gone for ever. She gave a little involuntary cry of pain, then she began walking again.

As she walked she made plans, busying her mind, occupying it. She did sums in her head: the money must, regardless of what happened, be paid back. Then, when it was all over, if the publicity was bad, perhaps there would be just enough to take Claudia somewhere, to go abroad, somewhere neither of them knew. Where they could both forget.

# CHAPTER FOUR

As she reached their flat, Luisa saw Harry's car just disappearing at the end of the road, and—glancing up—saw that their windows, at the very top of the tall old house, were still lit, uncurtained, light streaming out into the night sky.

Tiredly she climbed the stairs, and let herself in. Claudia was sitting hunched over the fire, wrapped in a rug. The table was littered with the remains of the evening's picnic; a champagne bottle, dirty plates, a Fortnum's hamper that must have been Harry's surprise treat.

She hesitated in the doorway, and Claudia looked up at her, a curious expression compounded of excitement and fear glittering in her eyes.

'Would you like something to eat?' She spoke not ungraciously, and Luisa knew it was her method of declaring a truce.

'No—I'm not hungry, thanks.' She came across and kissed Claudia gently. 'Are you feeling better?'

'Sort of. You look awful—where have you been all this time?'

Before Luisa could answer, she stood up.

'Is there any champagne left? And maybe I'll have a bit more salmon. I'm starving!'

'You sit down, I'll get it.' Quickly Luisa carried the dirty plates to the kitchen, fetched clean ones, poured Claudia the last of the champagne . . . All the time phrases pulsed in her head, how she should tell her, what she should say. But none seemed right; her mind froze over with cowardice and indecision. In the end, she just handed Claudia the glass and then sat down quietly opposite her. She would count to ten, she thought, resorting to an old childish method, and then she would speak . . .

But Claudia gave her an odd smile and raised her glass.

'You'll have to drink this after all. One can't drink a toast to oneself, can one? Isn't it unlucky?'

'A toast?' Luisa stared at her.

'I'm engaged. I'm going to get married.'

49

'Married?' Luisa stared at her blankly, and Claudia laughed.

'Well, you might look a bit more pleased! Here——' she held out her glass, 'to the happy bride and all that . . .'

Hesitantly Luisa took the glass and sipped; it nearly choked her and she put the glass down. Claudia was watching her carefully.

'Have you . . . have you told Harry?'

'No.' Claudia smiled and stretched like a pretty cat.

'But then . . .'

'I've told him something else.'

'I see.'

'Oh, I don't think you do. I'm pregnant.'

'*What?*' Luisa stood up quickly, feeling all the blood drain from her face. Claudia continued to look at her with a maddening unconcern.

'Two months. The doctor confirmed it this morning. I must have missed out some pills.' She laughed gaily. 'Isn't it exciting? I was pretty sure, of course, and then when I started feeling sick . . .' She stood up, and patted her slim figure. 'It doesn't show yet, does it?' She turned sideways, and surveyed her own figure critically in the long glass that hung by the door. 'Of course Harry didn't hesitate. And we can't delay too long. I've no intention of going down the aisle trying to conceal the bulge under my bouquet! He's going to tell the old battleaxe tonight.' She smiled. 'One in the eye for her, don't you think?'

'But, Claudia . . .'

'Harry was so *sweet*. So kind. And so happy. I can't tell you, Lou. I mean, I've always been absolutely sure, because you are, you know, when you meet the right one, you just sort of feel it, here.' She pressed her hand to her heart. 'And tonight—oh, I love him so much, Lou! I shall be such a good wife to him. I . . .'

'Claudia,' Luisa cut her off, knowing she must speak now, or it would be too late, 'why didn't you tell him?'

'Tell him about what?'

'About the money, about . . .' Her voice trailed away, and Claudia turned to her, her eyes wide with incomprehension.

'Oh, *that*! I couldn't tell him about that, not now.'

'But you'll have to tell him. Claudia—if you marry— you can't begin with a lie . . .'

'It isn't a lie. And I will tell him—afterwards. I will, Lou, of course. But not now, when he's so happy and when we're making all these plans, and . . .'

She broke off and took Luisa's hands impatiently, her face irradiated with happiness.

'Don't you see, Lou? It's got to be all right now. *You've* got to make it all right! You can't let me down. Not now. Not with all this.' She took her sister's hand, and placed it gently on the soft swell of her stomach. 'Don't you see, Lou? Everything's different now. There's the baby.'

Luisa stood absolutely still, not moving. She did not move her hand, but let it rest gently where it was. Claudia's stomach was still as flat as her own, warm to her touch. It was too soon, of course, for the baby to stir, to move; but as she stood there, it was as if she felt something beneath her hand, something shifting, pulsing, with a mysterious life of its own, asserting itself the more powerfully for being invisible. She caught her lip, feeling tears start to her eyes. It was awesome, that tiny thing, that tiny force, locked in Claudia's womb, and she herself felt as cold and barren as the moon.

Gently she removed her hand and kissed her sister.

Claudia sighed, and settled herself back in her chair. 'Of course, I shall demand lots of cossetting,' she said, smiling at her own smugness, her new maternal role. 'Dr Ramsay says I'll need lots of rest and no worries . . .' She broke off and raised her eyes to Luisa's face with a look of mute enquiry.

A glance of perfect understanding passed between them.

'You won't need to worry. I promise,' Luisa said softly.

Claudia lowered her eyes. 'Thank you, Lou,' she said gently. 'Lou——' she looked up again, uncurious, detached, her eyes slightly misty. 'Thank you for leaving us alone tonight. You can be very clever sometimes.' She paused. 'Did you go anywhere . . . special?'

Luisa shook her head, and began to busy herself tidying the room.

'No,' she said quickly, lightly, and saw the relief flood back into Claudia's face. 'Nowhere special. I . . . just went to see Luke, that's all.'

'So it really will be all right?'

'I promise.'

Claudia smiled and blew her a kiss.

'You're an *angel*,' she said.

'Not a very efficient one.' Luisa smiled wryly.

'You are!' Claudia curled her legs up under her with an easy grace, and hugged them to her, resting her chin pensively on her knees.

'Are you happy for me, Lou?'

'Very happy.'

'And you'll be his godmother? Harry and I want you to . . .'

'His?' Luisa smiled down at her.

'Certainly his!' her voice was indignant. 'I can tell already. Will you, darling Lou? Please say yes.'

'Yes,' said Luisa, and dropped a light kiss on her sister's lowered head.

'I knew you would,' said Claudia.

The next day was a Saturday; Claudia was up early, and brought Luisa some tea in bed.

'Come on,' she said cheerfully. 'Rise and shine!'

She drew back the curtains, and sunlight flooded into the room. Luisa shut her eyes, she had slept no more than a couple of hours and then wretchedly, uneasily. She opened them again, forcing herself to appear cheerful.

'This is an unusual honour.' She took the cup and sat up.

Claudia grinned. 'I think I might become an early riser. I was up at six-thirty being as sick as a dog. Isn't it wonderful?'

'Are you all right?'

'Oh, I'm fine *now*. I don't mind being sick in a way. Dr Ramsay says it should only last a couple more weeks at most, and it sort of—well, confirms things. Reminds me.' She smiled. 'I slept like a log, and as long as I don't see food before midday, I'll be fine.'

In spite of herself Luisa smiled. Claudia had always had this capacity for recovery, the ability to rebound from disaster; she was like a child, she thought sadly, still—the end of the world one minute, all problems forgotten the next.

Claudia watched her closely as she sipped the tea.

'I'm going out this morning . . .' She hesitated. 'You know what Harry wants to do? Go and buy baby clothes! Isn't that ridiculous? I thought men were supposed to hate all that side of it, but I think he'll be wonderful—I can see him now, changing nappies . . .' She broke off, her face suddenly sobering. 'Lou, did you mean it last night? Will it really be all right? Do you think you can . . .'

'It'll be all right.' Luisa stopped her. Their eyes met, Claudia's nervous, still uncertain. Luisa drew a deep breath.

'I've got three days,' she said haltingly. It would be better, she thought, not to mention Julius. 'At the end of that time, Clou, it'll all be fixed, I promise.'

'You mean you're really going to . . .'

'Don't ask me.' She leaned forward. 'That's the only thing, Clou. I swear it will be all right, but I just can't bear to . . . well, to talk about it. Do you understand?'

Claudia lowered her eyes; she sighed.

'I thought you might say that. You're always so secretive. It might help, you know, if you did talk about it . . .'

'No, it wouldn't,' Luisa said quietly, finally. 'I know what I've got to do, and I'll do it, and then I never want to talk about it or think about it ever again. It can be our secret. All right?'

Claudia nodded silently.

'And Clou—in the meantime, it would be better if you stayed out of it. Don't speak to Kit—or anyone. Just leave it. You ought to leave the office, I think—you ought to rest now anyway, and they can perfectly well get a temp. Will you promise me to do that?'

Claudia smiled impishly. 'That's not difficult! The very thought of going anywhere near Morrell & Kennedy makes me feel ill anyway. Shall I resign—by letter or something? I could do that . . .'

'Yes.' Luisa forced herself to sound businesslike. 'The sooner the better.'

Claudia stood up. She hesitated awkwardly by the door, her fingers nervously pleating the skirt of her dress.

'Lou—you know how much I love you, don't you? And I'm sorry for all those awful things I said . . .'

'It doesn't matter.' Luisa smiled. 'You were probably right in a way.'

Claudia gave her a long silent look.

'It might turn out for the best,' she said finally, hopefully. 'You never know, Lou . . .'

'All's well that ends well?' Luisa kept her voice light. 'Perhaps. Now. You go, and we won't talk about it any more. All right? Oh—and Claudia.' Her sister paused in the doorway. 'Buy some pink things. You don't want to tempt fate too much, do you? And if you buy everything blue . . .'

Claudia laughed.

'Wait and see,' she said happily. 'I *know* how things are going to turn out.'

When she had gone, Luisa got up and washed and dressed slowly. She felt better now, better than she had last night, calm at least. In a way it was easier, knowing there was no way out, knowing there was no time for indecision, no possibility of compromise. She must steel herself, that was all, blank out all the pain and the fear. That was unimportant now; she was unimportant. All that mattered was Claudia. And the baby. Instinctively she touched her own stomach, clasping her hands across it. Her own skin felt like ice, all her muscles were taut.

If only the past would go away, if she could forget, treat the whole affair coldly . . . But even as that thought came to her, she felt her blood quicken its pulse; memory shot through her body like a dart; last night—she had not felt cold, or unaffected or distanced last night. Was that why she was consenting to this now, making promises to Claudia so quickly, because this was what she secretly wanted? No. She slammed the doors of her mind to the thought. It was *not* so. She would go out, she thought quickly. Go for a walk, do anything. The worst thing would be to sit alone, to think.

But even as she made the resolve, the door-bell rang. She jumped, startled, and went quickly to answer it.

Standing in the hallway was a woman, a stranger. Luisa stared at her in surprise. She was short and square, somewhat mannish in her appearance, dressed in heavy tweeds, with an unbecoming tweed hat pulled low over short iron-grey curls. Her face was square too, powerfully formed, almost ugly, but dominated by the eyes—sharp, alert, intelligent blue eyes.

'You must be Luisa.'

'Yes. I . . .'

'I'm Harry's mother.' The woman took a step forward, and for one absurd moment Luisa thought she was going to put one heavy brogue shoe in the door.

'Oh, Lady Warrender.' Luisa collected herself quickly. 'Would you like to come in?'

'Thank you, my dear. Claudia's out, I gather? Good.' She spoke briskly, already inside the door. 'I thought she would be, and I didn't telephone, which is very rude, but you see, my dear, I want to talk to you.' She turned with a quick smile. 'Through here? Good.' She marched ahead into the sitting room. 'How very charming.' She looked around her approvingly, her eyes missing nothing, then turned back, her sharp eyes running over Luisa's pale face, the tumbled thick hair, the slightly old-fashioned grey wool dress.

'Now,' she smiled, 'from what I gather, you're the sensible sister. You certainly don't look like Claudia . . .'

Luisa looked at her uncertainly, wondering anxiously why she had come.

'Can I get you some coffee . . . sherry perhaps?'

'No, thank you, my dear. I'm not staying long.'

She parked her bulky frame uncompromisingly in the middle of the sofa, and reluctantly Luisa sat down opposite her. Lady Warrender's eyes never left her face.

'Well, my dear,' she smiled, 'here's a pretty kettle of fish. What *are* we going to do about it?'

Luisa felt herself blush.

'Look, Lady Warrender,' she said awkwardly, 'I know this must have been a shock, but . . .'

'A shock? It certainly was!' She produced a packet of cigarettes from a large untidy handbag, inserted one into a short holder, and made odd stabbing gestures with it to emphasise her words. 'Oh, we knew Harry was mad about Claudia, of course. And his father and I weren't terribly pleased about it. I may as well say so—no point in beating about the bush. However,' she lit the cigarette and inhaled deeply, 'there we are. Now all this has happened.'

'I think . . .' Luisa hesitated, 'I think they're very happy, Lady Warrender. I'm sure that, now . . .'

'Well, yes. Don't let's indulge in platitudes, though.' Lady Warrender cut her off. 'The point is, I'd hoped Harry would see sense given time. As it is—well, clearly they're going to have to get married. No other way for it. Don't approve of all this modern abortion business, never have. Impossible in my day, and a good sight too easy now. People have to face the consequences of their actions. Much the best thing.'

Luisa felt her heart give a sickening lurch; Julius's words, last night.

'Far too young, of course. Didn't marry myself until I was thirty, and I hoped Harry would have the sense to do the same thing. However, you can't live your children's lives for them.' She paused. 'What I want to know is, what do you think? Is it all going to be a disaster, or what?'

She spoke so directly, so brusquely, that Luisa could not repress a smile.

'I think Claudia's too young,' she said gently. 'Harry—well, I don't know. He's . . . he's been very good for Claudia. But I think that when she has a baby . . .'

'She'll grow up, you mean?' Lady Warrender compressed her lips. 'Well, maybe. Could happen. Does sometimes.'

She looked at Luisa closely.

'She loves him, does she?'

'Very much.' Luisa met her eyes and spoke levelly.

'Not just a flighty thing—you know, here today, gone tomorrow?'

'Lady Warrender, please. I know what you're trying to say.' Luisa stood up. 'I know how Claudia must seem to you—impulsive, very young and—well, perhaps changeable.' She hesitated. 'But she's not really like that. Underneath . . . she's a person of very strong feelings, strong attachments. She loves your son. She wants very much to be a good wife to him. She told me so herself, last night.'

'I see.' Lady Warrender's sharp blue eyes looked at her closely. 'We don't know your family, of course.' She paused. 'Your mother's dead, I believe.'

'She died about ten years ago. Our father is still alive . . .' Luisa paused, and Lady Warrender looked at her curiously. 'He . . . he lives abroad mostly. He's a poet.'

She didn't expect that to go down very well, and it clearly didn't. Luisa repressed a quirk of amusement. If she told Lady Warrender about her father's politics, his Marxist leanings, membership of the Italian Communist Party, what would she say then? She'd think she was taking on the daughter of some dangerous revolutionary, Luisa thought with amusement, whereas in fact, her father's politics consisted mostly of a fondness for reminiscing about the Spanish Civil War, and writing lengthy, bad odes to the overthrow of capitalism in Europe.

'A poet?' Lady Warrender's tones suggested blank amazement. 'Have I heard of him?'

'I shouldn't think so,' Luisa smiled. 'As poets go, he's not a very successful one.'

'I see.' She paused. This clearly didn't please her much either, and Luisa felt nettled at her tone.

'Are you saying you think our family's unsuitable, Lady Warrender?' she said sharply, and the older woman smiled.

'Odd, my dear.' She put out her cigarette. 'I know what you're thinking—that I'm a terrible old-fashioned snob. Well now, I don't think, on the whole, that I am. Debrett— all that nonsense. No time for it myself. No. Harry will have to run our place in Norfolk one day, and Claudia will have to help him do it, that's all. And very feudal and old-fashioned, not to mention ridiculously costly, it is. Of course I can see Claudia's very decorative. But how's she going to cope with all that? And children? Harry's always wanted a big family, masses of children about the place. Frankly, my dear, I can see you dealing with all that. But Claudia?'

'Claudia loves him.' Luisa met her eyes levelly. 'She will try and be—do—whatever Harry needs . . .'

'That's not such a good thing either. No good a woman bowing and scraping to a man, trying to fit some damn stupid tailor-made image he might have. Half the time they don't know what they really want anyway. In my experience . . .'

She broke off, and Luisa looked away. Julius Morrell knew what he wanted, she thought dully, unable to keep the memory at bay. She felt nervousness rise again in a tide within her, and thought Lady Warrender sensed it because she looked at her keenly.

'Look, I might as well be frank.' Lady Warrender stood up. 'I don't give a toss about your family, one way or the other. Our family's as dull as ditchwater, and to my mind it could do with a bit of livening up. My brother Freddie's the only remotely artistic one, and when he finds out who Claudia is, he'll be in seventh heaven, silly man. But is Claudia flighty—that's what I want to know. Because I want to see Harry happy, and I don't want us all being dragged through the divorce courts three years from now.'

'Lady Warrender, please.' Luisa stepped forward, the colour rising to her cheeks. 'Claudia and I were brought up in a family with no . . . no emotional security at all.' She hesitated. 'Our parents' marriage was disastrous—they . . . they hardly lived together, though they never actually divorced. But . . . don't you see?' she looked at her pleadingly. 'All that makes Claudia and me *more* aware of the importance of marriage, of love, of commitment to someone—not less.'

Lady Warrender looked doubtful; her keen eyes rested on Luisa's face.

'I can see that in you, my dear,' she said quietly. 'I don't doubt the truth of what you say as far as you're concerned. But Claudia? Well—' She stood up briskly. 'Only time will tell, I suppose. I feel better now, though, now I've met you.'

She turned to the door, pulling on a pair of heavy sheepskin gloves. Then she paused.

'You see, my dear,' she spoke more warmly, 'I am probably very old-fashioned. But marriage is the most important step a woman ever takes in her life. Everything, children, other people's lives, her happiness, her future husband's, depends on her making the right decision. The big question, of course, is how you judge? How do you know? Well, if I could answer that one no doubt I'd be one of those famous agony aunts in the newspapers, not a middle-aged woman just worried about her children. So——' she paused, 'I just hope Claudia knows her own mind, and won't change it later. That's really what I came to ask.'

Luisa felt the doubts crowd into her mind, and she lowered her eyes.

'I . . . I think she does,' she said softly. 'I . . . I could talk to her, if you think it might do any good. But I don't think I need to say . . . well, anything I haven't already said to her——' She broke off.

Lady Warrender smiled. 'The "sanctity of marriage"— that's the phrase, isn't it?' She gave a laugh. 'Well, that sounds a bit pi, doesn't it? Altogether too Roman for my taste. But one knows what it means. I'm sure you know what it means.'

It was a question, Luisa realised, and she looked at her in surprise.

'Yes, I think I know what it means,' she said gently. 'And so does Claudia. In her heart.'

'I hope so.' Lady Warrender opened the door. 'Have a talk to her, my dear. I'd feel a lot happier if you would.' She paused. 'You're not thinking of getting married yourself, by any chance?'

'No, not at all. Why do you ask?'

Lady Warrender smiled. 'Nothing, my dear. Just something in the way you spoke, that's all.' With a sudden awkward gesture she turned back and planted a rather leathery kiss on Luisa's cheek. 'Don't see me out, my dear, and thank you for your patience. Will you come and dine with us, one evening, when you're free? With Claudia, of course?'

'I'd like that very much. Thank you.'

'Good.' She turned. 'And now we'd better get on with arranging this wedding, hadn't we?' She gave something very like a wink. 'Lots to do and somewhat unseemly haste, eh?'

Then, with a quick, dismissive wave, she was gone.

Luisa watched her go from the window, a small determined figure, striding across the square and heaving herself into an old battered Daimler parked on the opposite side. She rested her forehead tiredly against the cold panes of glass. The sanctity of marriage; she wished heartily that Lady Warrender had not used that particular phrase, not just then. How stupid, she thought rebelliously, that she, who went rarely to church, was not overtly religious, should care so much about the meaning of that phrase, the long implications of those words! Yet she did, she knew she did, and always had done, ever since she was a child. In Scotland, that summer, lying in bed at night, thinking of marriage, thinking of her parents, of their ugly weak approximation to it. When she had thought of marriage, it had seemed to her so remote, so strange, almost a place; a great carved cathedral—perfect, impregnable, a private place where two people pledged something to each other, and defied time. Where each gave themselves to the other, without lies, in a state of purity. The sanctity of marriage; the sacrament of marriage . . .

Quickly she turned away from the glass; now, that was not for her. She put a record on the gramophone, *The Marriage of Figaro*, and listened to the Countess's great aria, her lament for the infidelity of men, of her husband; to the gaiety and joyousness of Susanna's wedding march. Then she turned off the music, found the directory, picked up the telephone.

Julius answered; she recognised his voice at once.

'It's Luisa Valway,' she said. 'I'm calling to say that I agree to your proposal.'

There was a silence.

'I see,' he said finally.

She hesitated, feeling the blood rush to her face, even though she was alone and there was no one to see her. He said nothing more; even now, she thought bitterly, even now he would not help her, even with a word.

'When would you like me to . . .'

She could think of no suitable words, and expected him to

laugh, but there was only silence.

'I think tonight, don't you?' He spoke flatly, quite casually, as if they were making a business arrangement. 'Come here. It's Myers' night off but I can give you dinner.'

'I don't need dinner,' she said sharply, stung by his audacity, his insolence.

'Come at eight,' he said, and rang off.

That afternoon she walked. Miles around London, on her own, following no set direction, letting her feet lead her, letting the cold winter air numb her body and her mind. They led her eventually, as she had known they would, irresistibly, and with a will of their own, to the park near his house. She thought of going to see Luke; but knew that was not why she had gone there. Instead she sat on a seat in the park, on a low hill, where one way she could look out across the darkening skyline of London, the other across the railings and grass to his house. There were children playing; people taking their dogs for walks; she hardly saw them. At four, as it began to grow dark, she saw lights in his house, in the upstairs windows. Then, as she rose to go, his front door suddenly opened; she could see it quite clearly from where she stood. Julius was standing in the doorway, lit by the light behind him. Beside him was a woman, tall, dark, wrapped in furs. As Luisa watched, the woman turned to him and put her arms around his neck, reached her face up to be kissed. She turned away quickly, fear, anger and bitterness rising up inside her like bile. Then she went home.

She washed, bathed, changed; but she could not make herself feel clean. She wore the black dress she had worn the previous evening; out of perversity, she knew, so that he would see she had made no special effort to appear alluring; perhaps in the half hope that it might persuade him to change his mind.

He opened the door himself in a silent house brilliant with lights, and as he took her coat, she saw him note what she was wearing instantly.

He looked at her, his eyes running over her tall slender body and back to her face, just as they had done that first day in his office.

'Same costume?' He raised an eyebrow in an ironic smile.

'Same play,' she answered sharply.

He touched the long full aureole of her hair lightly, so she flinched.

'You look very beautiful.'

'Please,' She looked at him scornfully. 'I don't need compliments. You don't need to woo me.'

He shrugged.

'What if I want to?'

'Don't bother.'

'As you wish.'

Formally Julius led the way back into the drawing-room where she had been the previous night. It looked just as it had before; tranquil, warm, without threat. The table where the hyacinth had been now held a bowl of red roses.

He caught her looking at them, and gave that odd twisted half smile he had, which never seemed to warm his eyes.

'Appropriate?' he gestured in their direction.

'I don't like hothouse flowers.'

'No, I'd imagine you wouldn't,' he said coolly. 'Let me get you a drink.'

He didn't bother to ask her what she would have; he took no notice of the quick denial that rose to her lips, but poured champagne into two long glasses, and then held one out to her.

'This is ridiculous!' Luisa ignored the glass. 'You're turning this into some absurd ceremony!'

He shrugged. 'Call it a ritual. I like ritual.' He thrust the glass into her hand. 'What did you expect me to do?' he went on, eyeing her with a cold amusement. 'Catch you by the hair as you came in, and have you on the hall carpet? Or drag you upstairs to my bedroom straight away?' He paused. 'Perhaps you'd prefer that.'

She felt the quick colour rise instantly to her cheeks.

'I didn't expect anything,' she said, as coldly as she could. 'And I'd prefer there to be no hypocrisy.'

'I see.' With complete composure he sat down in the chair by the fire where he had sat the previous evening, and sipped his champagne.

'Well,' he said slowly, 'I think we'll do it my way, if you don't mind. We'll have dinner together, in a civilised manner; we can talk about old times...' He smiled mockingly. 'That will be nice, don't you think, Luisa? We'll have some good wine, and the excellent food that Myers has kindly left. And then...'

'And then you can pretend that all this is perfectly normal. I suppose?' Her eyes blazed at him. 'That it's just another routine seduction, that I came here willingly, and . . .'

'You never know.' The cold grey eyes travelled languorously and insolently over her body. 'It may be willingly. These things can happen.'

'I don't think so!'

'Well, in the meantime, don't you think you could sit down? This is beginning to remind me of a bad play, and you look extraordinarily melodramatic standing there in that dress, clutching that glass as if you'd like to smash it in my face.' He smiled. 'You've wounded me already, twice. I'd rather you didn't do it again.'

'Not a very deep wound, in either case!' she flashed.

'No,' he said silkily, and his eyes met hers. She caught the implication in his instantly, and her eyes widened. Suddenly she felt terribly afraid. He must have seen her expression change, because he spoke more gently.

'You needn't worry,' he said softly. 'I shan't hurt you. I'm not a sadist, Luisa.'

'Julius, I . . .'

'Here.' He crossed to her quickly, and took the glass from her hand. With a surprising gentleness he put his arm around her, and tilted her face up to him. He looked into her eyes, as if searching for something in them, and she knew he could feel that she was trembling uncontrollably. 'You're afraid,' he said softly, as if her reaction took him totally by surprise. 'Luisa.' He half drew her to him. 'I don't want you to be afraid. Listen . . .' She wanted to resist, but something held her back. He rocked her very gently, slightly, in his arms, as if he were comforting a child. 'If it helps, I want you to know that I've taken care of everything.' He hesitated. 'The money has been repaid; I've instructed the auditors to make no mention of the . . . inconsistencies . . . in the accounts. I've told them how and why I'm dealing with the situation as I have. There'll be no further problems. Claudia must leave, of course. But beyond that, there are no . . . business, or legal, repercussions.'

'Is that true?' Luisa lifted her face to him in amazement. His lips tightened.

'In spite of what you think, I'm not a liar.'

'But the money . . . I haven't given it to you yet . . .'

'We can talk about that later.'

She stepped back, disengaging herself from his arms, the implications of what he said coming to her slowly, as if her mind, her senses, were dulled by his nearness.

'When did you do this?' Her lips were dry, her voice little more than a whisper.

'This morning.'

'But then . . .' She stared at him in confusion. 'Why did you . . . why am I here?'

He looked at her searchingly. 'Only you can answer that.'

'But I wouldn't have come . . .' She broke off, and saw him tense.

'Go on.'

'I wouldn't have come!' She stared at him, her cheeks flushed. 'I only came because everything is changed. I found out last night. Claudia is having a baby. She's getting married. That's why I came!'

There was a silence, then Julius shrugged, his eyes suddenly like ice again.

'I don't much care for what altruistic reasons you came,' he said finally, carefully. 'You're here. As far as I'm concerned that's all that matters.'

'You mean that's enough?' She stared at him in disbelief. 'You mean I can go now, without . . .'

'I didn't say that.'

'You have no hold over me now . . .' She cried the words without thinking, and they came out like a taunt. Instantly his mouth tightened.

'Oh, but I do.' His voice was sarcastic. 'We had an agreement. Are you going to try and wriggle out of it? How typical of your family!'

'I wouldn't put it like that.' She glared at him, feeling tears begin to prick behind her eyes. 'Why not be honest, Julius? This is all an attempt on your part to make this whole ugly business a bit more acceptable, isn't it? What do you expect me to do, fling myself into your arms out of gratitude?'

'It might be interesting if you did.' He smiled insolently, and she felt anger rise up in her unchecked.

'This is just a cheap trick on your part! A way of conning me into doing something . . .'

'Possibly.' He spoke seriously.

'I hate you, Julius!'

'Do you, Luisa?' He looked at her coldly. 'Well, perhaps I

shall be able to change your mind. Now—shall we stop this wrangling? It's very tedious. I think...' he paused, and gave her a dazzling smile, 'I think we'll go in and have some dinner, shall we?'

Before she could protest, or push him away, he took her arm. Forcefully, so she could hardly resist, he led her out of the drawing-room, past the dining-room, to the back of the house. There, she saw to her surprise, they *were* obviously meant to have dinner together, in the kitchen. It was a beautiful room, with a stone-flagged floor and a tall pine dresser. A table had been laid, with blue and white plates, candles; it looked pretty, warm and inviting. There was an Aga stove and two tortoiseshell cats curled asleep in front of its warmth.

'Now,' he said, almost forcing her into one of the chairs, '*isn't* this nice? I thought we should have dinner here together, like an old married couple.'

The obvious sarcasm in his voice cut her, and she looked away. How carefully he had worked it all out, she thought bitterly, all the best ways to protract her torture, increase her humiliation. He turned away from her to the stove, and Luisa dug the nails of her hands deep into her palms. For a moment then, back in the drawing-room, she had thought he would relent; but she had been wrong; now... She straightened her back proudly; she was damned if she was going to let him see how afraid she was again. If he wanted to play out this ridiculous charade, then she would.

'Do you like claret?' Julius turned back to her.

'Thank you, yes.'

He raised his eyebrows, but said nothing. Carefully, quietly, he uncorked the bottle and placed it on the table. Then he poured a little more champagne, and brought her the first course, a fish mousse of some kind. He sat down opposite her, and Luisa tasted it; it was delicious.

'Myers did this?' she said lightly. 'He's a very good cook.'

'He takes care of all my domestic needs.'

'How lucky for you!'

He smiled. 'I do work quite hard, you know.'

'Oh, I know.' She smiled at him. 'I've read accounts of some of your more famous prosecutions.'

He let that pass, and they ate for a while in silence. Luisa had no appetite for the food, delicious though it was, but she forced herself to eat it, to drink the champagne, and doing so made her feel better. She felt her courage return.

'So, Claudia's getting married.' He looked at her speculatively. 'She's a little young, I'd have thought.'

'She's twenty. And very much in love.'

'And who is she marrying? May I know?'

'His name is Harry Warrender,' she said stiffly. 'Perhaps you might know him ... or his father. He's a judge, I believe.'

He smiled. 'Luckily I've never encountered the father. One of the grimmer members of the senior bench. I remember Harry, though. He's much younger than me, of course, but we went to the same school. With a very formidable mother, as I recall.'

'Lady Warrender?' In spite of herself, Luisa smiled. 'I met her this morning.'

'Did you cope? Her bark's worse than her bite, I believe.'

'Just about.'

He looked at her carefully. 'And your father,' he said. 'Does he know about ... about the marriage and everything?'

Luisa glanced away.

'No,' she said softly. 'He doesn't know yet. We haven't seen him for some years. He's in Rome at the moment.'

'Still devoting himself to the liberation of the masses through verse?' His tone was sarcastic.

'He's still writing poetry, I believe,' she said stiffly.

'How loyal.' He stood up and took away her plate. 'Really, Luisa, if it weren't so absurd, your devotion to the rest of your feckless family would be quite touching.'

'I don't want to discuss my family with you.'

Julius registered the coldness in her voice, and made no answer. Solemnly, as if it were the most normal of meals, he poured out the claret, and brought her more food.

'Do you like pheasant?'

She nodded.

'Good.'

Again, it was delicious, perfectly cooked, the vegetables were crisp, light. Every mouthful she took nearly choked her, but she managed to eat a little, keeping her eyes firmly fixed on her plate. She knew he was watching her closely, as a snake might watch its prey, and his hard-eyed gaze made her nervous.

'You haven't changed much, you know.' He spoke so

suddenly that she almost knocked her glass over, and looked
up startled to see his face was closed, thoughtful.

'I remember when you were born.' The cold grey eyes
never faltered. 'I was seven then, home from school. My
mother took the call. The families were still friends then, of
course. It was before . . .' He shrugged. 'I watched you grow
up, Luisa.'

'I don't recall . . .'

'I do.' He looked at her coldly. 'We went to visit you once,
my father and I. You were staying with some aunt . . .'

'Aunt Con. She's dead now.'

'That's right. Your mother was still alive then, I think.'
He paused. 'You were up in the nursery with Claudia, but
you came down to tea. I remember you sitting in the corner,
never saying a word, watching everything. A funny pale
quiet child, with this extraordinary hair.' He broke off. 'You
were twelve, I think.'

'I don't remember.' But she did, she thought. She
remembered every time she had met him, and certainly then.
The embarrassment among the grown-ups, the veiled
allusions. And a tall dark proud boy, sitting to one side
watching them all with contempt.

He gave a sudden harsh laugh.

'Of course, it was Kit you took to, wasn't it? Quite an
adolescent flirtation. We spent a summer together once, all
four of us, do you remember that? The year before your
mother died. In Scotland.'

Luisa put down her knife and fork; she knew she had gone
pale.

'I don't want to talk about all this.'

'Too many memories?' Julius looked at her coldly. 'As you
like.'

'And I don't want anything else to eat.'

'I see.' He smiled mockingly. 'Coffee?'

She stood up quickly, almost knocking over the chair in
her haste.

'Will you please stop this! It's unbearable!'

'Perhaps I should have continued to let you think I was
Kit.' His words cut across her harshly, and she swung
round, startled by the venom in his voice. 'Would that have
been more bearable, Luisa?'

'No, it wouldn't!' she cried. 'I . . .'

'Shall we go upstairs?'

He moved towards her, and she knew he was about to touch her again, to take her arm, but she forestalled him, moving quickly out of his reach. She turned to the door, and he drew back, opening it for her with insolent courtesy. Not looking back, she went ahead of him, along the passage, and back to the hall. But there her nerve deserted her. She turned into the drawing-room.

'In here?' His voice was heavy with sarcasm.

Instinctively she had moved towards the warmth of the fire, and he stood just inside the room, watching her. She was shaking all over, but all she was conscious of now was that she had to get it over with, had to get out of his house, away from his words and the memories they conjured up out of the darknesses of her mind, away from him and his cold clever appraising eyes. Trying to steady her hands she moved them impatiently to the neck of her dress, fumbling with the catch, the long zip that snaked down her back. Julius made no move to help her, and said nothing. The catch had tangled in her hair; impatiently, aware that her cheeks were burning, her eyes vivid with tears, she struggled to free it. For a moment he seemed to hesitate, then he crossed quickly to her.

'Let me.'

She felt the catch give; felt the glancing touch of cold hands against the skin of her back as he undid the dress with one easy movement. For a moment she paused, clutching the black folds of the dress to her throat. He stepped back, his arms folded, and watched her, as if he were looking at something inanimate, a statue in a gallery, and the coldness in his manner suddenly filled her with a terrible anger. It was he, not she, who should be ashamed at all this, she thought. And she would make him feel that shame.

She loosed her hands, and the dress, with its wide sleeves, slipped from her body to the waist. She was wearing nothing underneath its top, and her small high rounded breasts were naked to his eyes. She heard him give a sharp intake of breath.

# CHAPTER FIVE

FOR a moment neither of them moved. Curiously anger had taken her beyond modesty, but it had not given her detachment. Her breath came quickly, lifting her breasts; her hands trembled, and the silence of the room seemed immensely loud to her ears. Their eyes met for a long moment, and she was unsure what she saw in Julius' face—desire perhaps, but also something like pain, perhaps anger. The grey eyes were shadowed,, and his hands did not move from his sides. The silence lengthened, beat in on her, until she could bear it no longer.

'Well?' The words came out like a taunt, and he moved.

He stepped towards her, and without touching her he bent his head and kissed her lips. She kept herself rigid, unresponsive, but her control was not needed; the kiss was brief, cold, dismissive. He stepped back, lifted his hand, and then let it fall again.

'Cover yourself,' he said harshly. Luisa stared at him, transfixed.

'God damn it, you heard what I said!'

His eyes met hers with a look of such dislike, such hatred, that she wanted to hide her face from it. But she steadied herself, drawing a deep breath, staring at him in confusion. For a moment she was aware of something else within her, another emotion, akin to disappointment or want, and she felt colour wash up her neck and across her face. Silently, slowly, she gathered up the folds of the dress.

'Shall I go, then?' Her voice sounded forced, near to breaking.

He crossed and dismissivily helped her arms into the sleeves, did up the zip, hardly touching her, as if proximity to her filled him with distaste.

'No,' he said facing her once more. 'Sit down. I want to talk to you.'

'I wouldn't have thought there was anything to say,' she cried bitterly.

'Well, there is.'

Suddenly he looked terribly tired, exhausted; all vitality had left his face. Something in his voice, not just the imperative of its tone, but the fierceness of it, stopped her arguments. As quietly and calmly as she could, she sat down, and after a moment Julius crossed and sat next to her. They sat in silence for a few minutes, he staring into the fire, his face averted. Covertly she looked at him, at the harsh profile of forehead, nose and chin, the eyes shadowed by the dark straight brows. Something near pity moved within her for a moment; he was a man now; when he was a boy there had been something in his face, an openness, a vulnerability—surely she remembered that? But it was gone now, and she did not want to think of the past. She looked away.

On his left hand he wore a plain gold signet ring—it had the crest of some bird of prey on it, she remembered its being given him for his twenty-first birthday. Now he circled it upon his finger with his long, curiously beautiful hands; his knuckles were white with tension.

At last he spoke, his voice light, cold, dismissive, professional: as if he were summing up to a jury, Luisa thought sadly.

'If you'd given me the chance I should have explained.' He paused. 'I'm not interested—in all that. Not with you.'

Pain shot through her like a knife, and her eyes widened. Julius saw her reaction and smiled bitterly.

'Obviously you're relieved.' He paused, and when she didn't answer, went on, never looking at her. 'I don't need another woman, or another mistress, and seducing unwilling girls isn't something that gives me a particular kick.' He smiled coldly. 'In spite of all the literature devoted to the subject, in my experience it's time-consuming, tiresome, and generally unpleasurable. For both parties. I prefer . . .' he hesitated, '—well, shall we say I prefer women of experience.'

'I see.' She could feel the pain behind her eyes, knew it was close to welling into tears, but she kept her voice flat and dull.

'In short. You're very beautiful, Luisa. But not my type. There's a certain mixture of heat and ice in you which is initially intriguing, but . . .' He shrugged and broke off. 'Please don't cry,' he said coldly, as the tears spilled silently from her eyes 'There's no necessity to get emotional about this, is there?'

'Maybe not for you!' Luisa stood up, and stared down at him accusingly, brushing the tears angrily from her cheeks. 'No doubt you're enjoying this very much. Setting me up, playing me along, letting me think ... putting me through all this! And for what? So that you could—extract every last variation on the situation, humiliating me, shaming me ... God, Julius, I hope you're satisfied!'

'Yes, well, I'm sorry to have put you through such a range of maidenly emotions,' he said sarcastically. 'However, I've changed my mind. And I should have said so earlier, if you'd given me the chance.'

'No, you wouldn't!' She stared down at him angrily. 'Because then your nasty little revenge wouldn't have been complete, would it, Julius?'

'Revenge?' He smiled up at her mockingly. 'Well, I must admit that it was all quite entertaining, watching you wrestle so hard with your conscience. I admit to being quite intrigued to see how far you would actually take all this, Luisa. And at what point you might or might not admit to yourself that your motives were not entirely as altruistic as you'd like to believe ...'

'How dare you! You mean you think I ... I *wanted* to go through all this?'

'You showed a remarkable alacrity in undressing.' He paused, looking up at her insolently. 'In fact, I'd have said you were quite practised at it. No...' he moved with amazing grace and speed, catching her hand even as she raised it to strike him, 'we won't go through all that again, I think.' He paused, holding her tightly and painfully. 'You'll listen to me for a change.' He smiled coldly down into her flushed upturned face. 'I have an alternative suggestion to make.'

'Oh, have you? Well, I'm not interested!'

'You'd better be. As far as I'm concerned, our bargain still stands. It's just that I'd like to suggest an alteration of the terms. You could be extremely useful to me, Luisa.'

'*Useful?*'

'Oh yes.' He smiled at her coldly. 'As I said, I have no need for a new mistress. I do, however, have need for a wife.'

'*What?*' His words stopped her struggles to free her wrist, and she stared at him, frozen with disbelief. Julius let go of her, and sat down composedly, as if daring her to walk away, to turn from him. As he had known she would, she thought bitterly, she stayed, mesmerised, watching him.

'May I explain? It's quite simple really.' He paused, his voice crisp now and businesslike, devoid of emotion. 'I'm thirty-two. As it happens quite rich. I'm considered successful at what I do—for what that's worth. Up until now I've had no inclination to marry and considerable success at avoiding the intrigues of those women who sought to persuade me to do so. However, I find it increasingly tiresome. If I married . . .' he hesitated, 'I should be free of all that.'

She stared at him. 'Are you saying you'd marry . . . to give yourself an . . . an escape clause, an excuse?'

'Something like that.' He smiled. 'It would be an extremely convenient way of ending any other relationship that threatened to become too involving, don't you think?'

'I think it's the most evil, horrible suggestion I've ever heard! You can't mean it!'

'Oh, but I do. What's marriage, after all? A contract, a legal contract. If you doubt that, you should work on some of the divorce cases I've handled, and see what happens when people decide to disentangle it. Do you think they talk about love, responsibility, need, then, Luisa?' He laughed bitterly. 'I can assure you, they don't. They talk about money and property. About *possessions*. Maybe you don't believe me—you're a romantic, of course.'

She stared at him, all the anger slowly seeping away, and made no answer.

'So—it's always seemed to me that if one married it would be much more honest to regard it as exactly what it really is—a contract, one engaged upon by both parties, clearsightedly, without hypocrisy; a business agreement. No more, no less. And certainly free from all those inherited notions of true love and eternal truth that happen to be so unfortunately locked up in most people's consciousness.'

'How can you *say* that?' she interrupted him passionately. 'It . . . it isn't true! Of course . . . things go wrong. It doesn't always work out. But at the beginning, the promises people make, the words they say . . .'

'Oh, that?' He laughed. 'Well, if they say them and they mean them—and I agree that the ritual aspects of the marriage ceremony are most poetically expressed . . . but if they make those promises, then they have to stick by them, don't you think?' He looked at her coldly. 'It really won't do, Luisa, to talk so ingenuously about things going wrong, about change. Either marriage is immutable, or it isn't. And as—in our society—it clearly isn't, then I think one has a duty to say so, to invent a new kind of marriage. As I say— no poetry, no high-flown vows. A business and legal arrangement.'

'That isn't a marriage!'

He shrugged. 'It's an alternative.'

'I don't think it will catch on!' Luisa laughed at him scornfully.

'Possibly not. People have an endless capacity for self-deception. Look at your own family.' He stood up. 'However, it's what I'm proposing.'

'To me?'

'Certainly.' He gave her a long cold look. 'You could be extremely useful to me, Luisa, in innumerable ways. This house would benefit from a woman's presence; a hostess is a role Myers can't, alas, fulfil. It would enable me to live my private life . . .' he paused, 'as I want to live it. And I think we might get on together perfectly well, don't you?'

'Of course I don't!'

'Why not?' He looked at her calmly, as if her vehemence did not convince him.

'I . . . I don't love you!'

'I see.' His mouth tightened, and there was a brief silence. 'Well, I see you cling to your romantic illusions. Perhaps I should spell it out for you. I'm suggesting a purely platonic arrangement.'

'Platonic?'

'But of course,' he said smoothly. 'You would have no need to fear any advances from me. You can have your own room—and you needn't worry, Luisa, about locking the door. I have no liking for forcing myself in where I'm not wanted.'

'I shouldn't have said so!' she said sharply. Julius gave her an odd glance as if her words pained him.

'Perhaps I just wanted to be sure on that point,' he said lightly. 'Now that I am . . .' He broke off. 'Well? Perhaps you'd be good enough to give me an answer. And—before you speak . . .' He lifted his hand, and touched her hair with a surprising gentleness. 'You might remember, we still have an agreement. Now we're just negotiating the terms.'

Something in his voice made her hesitate. 'An agreement?'

'Yes.' He looked directly into her eyes. 'You might call it a long-standing agreement.'

'Long-standing?' She stared at him.

He turned away suddenly with a gesture of impatience.

'Do you think you could stop repeating my phrases in that idiotic fashion? It's extremely irritating. You know exactly what I mean. I know you now find it difficult to distinguish me from my brother, but presumably your memory for the past hasn't totally been wiped out?' He paused. 'I find it revealing, to say the least, that you're so unwilling to talk about Scotland . . .'

Their eyes met. There was a long silence. Luisa felt her blood pound in her ears, felt the years slipping away before her eyes, saw his face changing, growing younger, gentler, so different from the way it was now. Scotland. She put her hand to her eyes.

'I *see* . . .' she said softly.

His eyes registered her words at once. Recognition, and something like triumph came into his face.

'Then you haven't forgotten?'

She stared at him silently. Suddenly the room seemed infinitely still beyond the clamour of her heart. The shapes of the furniture in the room blurred; she saw only his pale intent face, the watchfulness of his eyes.

'Well?'

'It was so long ago . . .' Her voice faltered, and broke off.

'Well now,' he smiled coldly, folding his arms, 'perhaps we could refresh your memory. You remember the house, for instance?'

'Of course I remember the house!' Suddenly she could feel sweat begin to bead on her forehead.

'And you remember the loch, perhaps? And the moors behind the house?'

He was leaning against the chimneypiece, his cold eyes never leaving her face. As he said the words an image of the place was conjured up in her mind; instantly she felt her pulse quicken, and a feeling of sick unease lurch in her stomach.

'Well, do you?'

'Stop this!' She rounded on him angrily, something like fear giving her voice strength. Julius registered her reaction—it seemed to surprise him, but obviously he chose to ignore it.

'And you remember our being there, presumably? Your Aunt Con. Claudia and you. Myself.' He paused. 'And Kit.'

'That's enough!' Violently she turned away from him. 'You're not in the court room now. You can't cross-examine me. Leave me alone. I don't remember!'

'Don't remember, or don't *want* to remember?' With a swift sudden movement he was beside her again, reaching urgently for her arm. 'Which is it, Luisa?'

She managed to evade his grasp, and turned her face angrily towards him. Somewhere at the back of her mind she could feel other, darker, memories start to crowd in on her, and she knew only, blindly, that she must keep them at bay.

'That's a ridiculous suggestion!'

He stopped, regarding her narrowly and intently.

'Is it, Luisa? I'm not so sure. You'll have to face up to the past sooner or later, you know. Why not now? What are you afraid of?' He paused. 'Of what happened, or of what you felt?'

'Be quiet! You're obsessed by the past—you've talked of nothing else since we met . . .'

'Perhaps because it was important to me,' he said quietly, cutting across her words, but she rushed blindly on, ignoring his tone, knowing only that he must never know what she felt, that all she wanted to do was forget, forget what she might have felt, forget everything.

'Well, it wasn't important to me,' she cried sharply. 'Not in the least. It was just a holiday, that's all. Like any other. I was fifteen years old. The time we spent there—I've never given it a second thought, not until now . . .'

'Is that true?' His eyes burned darkly into hers, but even the coldness in his face, the scorn in his mouth, could not stop the flow of words. All she could think of, suddenly, unreasoningly, was that she wanted to hurt him, as much as he hurt her . . .

'Of course it's true!' Her eyes blazed at him. 'Surely you, Julius, of all people, never imagined anything different?'

'Then what happened?' He spoke levelly enough, but she saw his breath came a little more quickly.

'Nothing happened.' She cut him off, and then stopped. She was lying, she thought suddenly, with an odd lightheaded detachment. Yet her voice carried the ring of conviction. Instantly she felt ashamed, and turned away. 'I don't know,' she said haltingly. 'Maybe I flirted with you a little.' She laughed, an ugly little controlled laugh. 'Maybe I'm my mother's daughter after all.'

He would stop her now, she thought, he must. He would tell her she was lying, make her admit the truth, tell her it wasn't true, what she said, tell her that once . . .

He didn't move, and he said nothing. In the end it was Luisa who turned back, but now she could not meet his eyes.

'And you?' she said finally, her voice catching in her throat.

'Me?'

'Yes, you.' She met his eyes. 'This seems a very one-sided inquisition. If we're going to talk about the past, Julius, you tell *me*. What did you feel then? In Scotland?'

Her voice nearly broke on the last word, and his face hardened.

'Oh, don't you know, Luisa?' He spoke very deliberately. 'I thought I'd made it clear. Just like you, I felt nothing at all.' He smiled icily. 'Perhaps a passing attraction, as you suggest. I wasn't very discriminating at that age.'

There was a silence that seemed to Luisa to go on for ever; she would never forget this moment, she thought. No matter how often she had told herself that that was how it had been, that he had never cared for her, the confirmation now caused her terrible pain. It was as if some last tiny hope, one which had never quite gone away, had suddenly been trampled and destroyed. There was nothing left; it was like stepping into a void. *I lied*, she wanted to cry out. *It's not true*. That she should assert the truth of what she had felt suddenly seemed imperative, but she could not speak. Fear held her back, and—worse than fear—a horrible sick suspicion. Perhaps he was right; perhaps, all these years, she had clung to belief in a lie. She turned away.

'Then I don't understand you,' she said shakily. 'We have no long-standing agreement, you and I.'

'Obviously not.' His voice was sullen. 'I was imprecise. Perhaps I should be more exact. It seems to me, in view of what happened between my father and your mother, that this would be a neat conclusion . . .'

'A loveless marriage?' She turned on him fiercely.

'Shall we call it a marriage of convenience?'

'Call it what you damn well like! Dress it up in any

phrases you choose! It's a kind of revenge however you put it
...' She broke off, and set her mouth, determined, now, that
he should not see her cry. 'And I'll have nothing to do with
it.'

'All right.' He stepped a little closer. 'Then we'll revert to
my original suggestion.'

'*What?*' She stared at him in horror. 'After what you said
to me earlier? I thought you said you preferred—
experienced women?'

He shrugged. 'So I do. Generally.'

He gave her a lazy mocking smile, reached up and flicked
her hair back from her shoulders, and caressingly laid his
hand upon her neck.

'I'll just have to make do, shan't I, Luisa?' he said softly.

'No, you won't!' Angrily she knocked his hand aside. 'I
... I've had enough of this. Of these games ... these
threats.' She drew in her breath. 'I ... I shall do what I
should have done in the first place. I ... I shall go to the
police. To the Law Commissioners. I shall tell them exactly
what has happened ...'

'Oh, do, Luisa.' He interrupted the tumbled flow of
words. 'After all, your family has never been averse to
scandal, has it? There's every possibility Claudia will get a
suspended sentence. Harry's very loyal—no doubt he'll
stand by her ...'

He let the threat tail away, and there was a silence.

'You wouldn't do it!' She stared at him defiantly. 'You
couldn't. Julius, *please*! You're not that kind of man. I
always believed ...'

She broke off and she saw his eyes grow intent.

'Believed what?'

'That you were ... *honourable*.' As she said the word, with
its curiously old-fashioned ring, she suddenly knew it was
true. She *had* always believed that. The worst part of all this,
she thought, suddenly calm, was not the threats but the
destruction. It was as if Julius were destroying himself in
front of her eyes. 'Please.' She turned to him and reached for
his hand. 'I know you hated my mother. I know what you
think of my family, but please, Julius. This is not *you* ... it
can't be ...'

'Perhaps I've changed.' He drew back so she could
not touch him. 'You're changeable enough, Luisa, God
knows ...'

She stared at him, frightened by the cold hatred in his face, not understanding what he meant. Then, quickly, she turned on her heel.

'I've had enough of this! I'm going . . .'

'No, you're not.' He reached out and grabbed her arm, and his voice was low, fierce with repressed anger. 'I've had enough of your goddamned prevarications and lies to last me a lifetime. You don't leave this room, Luisa, until you make up your mind. One way . . .' he paused, and then very slowly, drew her towards him, 'or the other.'

His arms tightened around her and he pulled her against him, so his lips were against her hair. 'Luisa,' he said softly, venomously, 'is it so hard? Why not just close your eyes? Why not pretend I'm my brother?'

The sickness and revulsion that instantly rose up in her gave her the strength to push him away.

'No!' She stared at him. 'I'll marry you.' Her voice broke, and she knew she could not keep back the tears much longer. 'Do you think I could bear to let you touch me, knowing how much you hate me, knowing you despise me, that . . . that I'm not to your *taste*? I'd rather die . . .'

'Don't be melodramatic.'

'All right, if that's what you call it, I won't.' She forced her voice not to tremble. 'I'll treat this your way, Julius. Coldly. As if I were a machine. That's what you like, isn't it? So—I'll marry you. On your terms. Just never touch me, that's all. And I hope that makes you as miserable as it makes me.'

To her fury, he only laughed.

'Is that your final decision?'

'Yes, it is!'

'Good.' He looked at his watch. 'Well, that's settled, then. We'll get married in a week's time, by special licence. I've already checked and it's quite easy to obtain. And we'll go to Venice, I think, for our honeymoon. I have some business affairs that will take me there anyway, and we should keep up some appearances, don't you think? Now . . .' he turned away, 'as we've reached an agreement at last, perhaps you'd like me to call you a cab?'

Luisa stared at him in disbelief as, with total composure, he picked up the telephone and ordered a taxi. He turned back.

'Fine. It will be here in a few minutes. Let me get your coat.'

'Julius, you can't do this!'

'Oh, but I can,' he said drily.

He fetched her coat and handed it to her, his hands ostentatiously avoiding all contact. Luisa stared at him, rooted to the spot, dry-eyed, beyond tears. Her voice choked in her throat.

'I believe you planned all this, from the first! This was your revenge, wasn't it, Julius? All along.'

'Possibly.'

'I hate you!' she cried. 'This marriage is a farce, a hideous lie. It will be hell on earth for both of us, and you know it!'

'Don't worry, Luisa,' he said softly, moving to the door. 'It will be hell in separate rooms. Now, let me show you to your cab.'

The wedding veil was old; it had belonged to her mother. It was made of Valenciennes lace, creamy with age, and it fell over her thick heavy hair in soft folds. It was held in place by a coronet, exquisitely worked in silk flowers and pearls. Luisa put it on, and looked at herself in the glass. The flowers were less white than her skin, she thought wryly; the pearls hung like tears. Her own eyes looked back at her from the glass, anxious, fearful, questioning, and she looked away quickly. It was nearly time.

Across the room, Claudia was sitting on the bed, sobbing softly into a handkerchief. Luisa felt suddenly a wild desire to laugh. This wasn't like a wedding at all, she thought savagely. It was more like a funeral.

'Claudia, please.' She stood up. 'You're not supposed to cry until later. Do stop.'

'I can't.' Claudia sniffed pathetically. 'It's all so awful. I still don't understand why you're doing it.'

Luisa sighed. 'Why do most people get married?'

Claudia's head jerked up. 'Don't pretend, Lou! You can't hide it from me! You don't want to marry him. You don't love him. You've always hated him . . .'

'That's not true,' Luisa said quietly.

'But why so suddenly? And like this? No one's going, no proper party . . . it's horrible, Lou!'

'Julius . . .' Luisa hesitated. She had to force herself to speak his name. 'Julius wanted it to be as quickly as possible. It had to be like this.'

'Lou, you're lying to me. It's something to do with the money, isn't it?' Claudia stared at her accusingly.

'Only indirectly.' Luisa looked away. That was true, she thought sadly. It wasn't the money, or Claudia's actions, that had brought her to this point. It was the past. And a man who could nurse revenge for ten years.

'It's all my fault!' Claudia gave a wail. 'If I hadn't involved you in all this, you'd never have met Julius again. This never would have happened. Oh, Lou, I'm sure you're making a terrible mistake!'

Luisa smiled at her gently. She had given Claudia only a very carefully edited account of what had happened; just that she had, as a last resort, gone to Julius, that he had helped them, that that meeting, and subsequent ones had led—quite suddenly, romantically, she had said, to this marriage. This o'er-hasty marriage, she thought bitterly. Claudia looked at her closely, and she quickly erased the bitterness from her face.

'Lou,' Claudia reached for her hand, 'just tell me one thing. I have to know. This isn't . . . well, it isn't some kind of recompense for what I did, is it? Please tell me it isn't, I couldn't bear it if it were!'

'Clou,' Luisa knelt down beside her sister, and met her gaze levelly, 'I promise you, it isn't. It . . . it goes back much further than that. To when Julius and I knew each other before. Now, are you satisfied?' she smiled at her coaxingly. 'You'd better be, you know. We have to go now.'

'All right.' Claudia stood up, and quickly kissed her. They looked at each other, and then Claudia laughed unhappily.

'And I thought I would be the first at the altar!' she said lightly. 'Now you're going to beat me to it by weeks.' She took Luisa's hand. 'You will be back in time, won't you, Lou? You promise?'

'Of course—I told you. Just promise me you'll rest, and look after yourself. All right?'

'All right.' Claudia looked nervously at her watch, and met her sister's eyes again with a look of despair. 'We have to go.'

'Don't look so tragic, you'll upset Luke. Now, come on.'

Julius had arranged the cars, and outside the house a long sleek brown Rolls-Royce was already drawn up. Luke was waiting for them, resplendent in a somewhat raffish morning suit. He kissed Luisa warmly, and helped them both into the car.

'Do you know, my dear . . .' he smiled at Luisa as the car accelerated smoothly away, 'I've never given anyone away before. Haven't been to a marriage, come to that, for—oh, a good ten years.' He touched her hand lightly. 'It ought to have been your father, you know, my dear. You could have wired him.'

Luisa squeezed his hand gratefully.

'I'm glad it's you,' she said.

The church Julius had selected, a small private chapel, was half an hour's drive. To Luisa it seemed like an eternity. After the first few minutes both Luke and Claudia lapsed into silence, leaving her to her thoughts. She stared out of the windows of the great silent car, watching the streets of London speed by. Snow had fallen in the night, and the pavements and houses were pale, white, ghostly in the thick grey light. The snow already fallen, and the threat in the sky of snow to come, gave an air of unreality to the streets. Luisa felt as if she passed through them in a dream, just as the last week had passed. She felt unreal, distanced, and yet also trapped. Events since that night at Julius's house had succeeded each other with a dreamlike mad inevitability; they had met again only once. He had been polite, considerate, businesslike. She had agreed to all his arrangements without argument, and left him feeling like a dead thing. She looked down at the bouquet she held in limp hands. Julius had sent it. It was beautiful, delicate, composed of pale spring flowers, narcissus and hyacinth, with a clear sharp scent. The flowers had tiny wires through their necks, she saw, looking down. Tiny, almost imperceptible wires, but they were speared by them, nonetheless; they would die, she thought, very shortly.

'Oh, Lou!' Claudia gave a muffled sob. The car was stopping.

Luke took Luisa's hand gently, and placed a light kiss on her forehead. His eyes, so sensitive, so all-seeing, met hers.

'Be quiet, Claudia,' he said. 'Luisa knows what she's doing.'

Claudia left them, going in ahead of them, and Luisa leaned weakly on Luke's arm. She hesitated, and then lifted the veil forward, so it covered her face. Then, leaning on Luke, she entered the chapel. An organ was playing softly; it was shadowy, lit by candles with a wavering smoky light, and it was almost empty.

But Luisa saw none of the empty pews; the few figures on either side of the aisle were invisible to her. From the moment she came in the door she saw only one person— the tall dark man who stood with his back to her at the altar. She moved down the aisle to him like a ghost, dreamingly, unaware of taking any steps. As she approached he suddenly turned, and those cold grey eyes met hers.

'*Dearly beloved, we are gathered together here* ...' The priest was Welsh; he intoned rather than spoke the words, and they seemed to Luisa to come from a great distance. Try as she would she could not take her eyes from Julius's face. His eyes seemed to burn into her, never leaving hers for an instant. His face was serious, expressionless, intent.

'... *therefore is not by any to be enterprised, nor taken in hand, unadvisedly, lightly, or wantonly* ...' The priest's voice sang in her ears. '... *First, It was ordained for the procreation of children* ... *Secondly, It was ordained for a remedy against sin* ... *Thirdly, It was ordained for the mutual society, help, and comfort, that the one ought to have of the other, both in prosperity and adversity. Into which holy estate* ...' The words swelled and softened, seemed to move in the air around her. Luisa drew in her breath sharply. She could not go through with this. She knew it suddenly, fearfully. It was a kind of damnation, a lie she would never escape. She tore her gaze away from those eyes, half turned, and Julius's hand, quite suddenly, as if he knew what she thought, read her mind, reached out and caught hers. He held her gently, without compulsion, and if the priest noticed this departure from the prescribed ritual, he chose to ignore it. Her eyes met those of Julius again.

Apart from the taking of her hand he had made no movement. His face was still as it had been, impenetrable, guarded, harsh even in this uncertain shifting light. But suddenly the edge of anxiety in her was gone. Some force seemed to pulse through their linked hands, from his body to hers, and she felt at once a great quietude, an extraordinary peace. It flowed through her veins like blood, and she was still.

The priest turned, his vestments rustled softly; there was a fleeting glimpse of gold, as his collar caught the light.

'*Wilt thou have this woman to thy wedded wife, to live*

*together after God's ordinance in the holy estate of Matrimony?*
*Wilt thou love her, comfort her, honour, and keep her, in*
*sickness and in health; and, forsaking all other, keep thee only*
*unto her, so long as ye both shall live?'*

Still Julius's eyes did not leave her face; there was a long
cold silence; all the blood seemed to drain from Luisa's
heart. He was going to lie, she thought suddenly,
desperately, and she must stop him, before he perjured
himself. Words rose to her lips, involuntarily she pressed his
hand. The silence wheeled . . .

'*I will.*' His voice was private; just audible.

The words died on her lips. She stared at him, pale with
horror. The priest was turning back to her.

'*Wilt thou have this man . . .*'

Still she clung to Julius's hand, kept her eyes fixed on his.
He could not see her face clearly, she realised, through the
thick lace of the veil, though perhaps he could see her eyes,
dark with anxiety. He seemed to sense something, for—just
for a second—she thought his face changed. A shadow came
to it; doubt flickered and then was at once suppressed, wiped
out. How proud he was, she thought, and in that instant
some shutter in her mind lifted, and the old knowledge
flooded back. Suppressed, shut off, denied so long, it
suddenly reasserted itself with a power she would have
thought impossible, informing and filling her heart. How
much she had loved him, once. Silently she stared at him,
and the world slowed. The priest's words came to her, each
separate, with a great clarity, marking time with her
memory, swelling into a great cadenza in her mind, its
rhythms taking possession of her, seeming to dictate the
pulsing of her breath, her heart. It was all so simple, she
thought suddenly; not complicated at all. Once long ago,
when she was almost a woman, not quite a child, she had
wanted this, in that other country of the past. And now. She
felt as if she were poised, high on a cliff, and the air was
intoxicating, clear and free.

'*. . . forsaking all other, keep thee only unto him, so long as ye*
*both shall live?'*

Julius let go of her hand.

She turned and looked directly at the priest.

'*I will.*'

It was done. A sigh like a cool breeze passed through the
tiny congregation, and the candles wavered. For a moment

she closed her eyes. It was her voice; she had spoken; she had made the oath. But she had not willed her lips to move, could not, a second later, recall the impulse of articulation. The words had come, out of that silent music in her heart perhaps, or from the past; a woman stood there, but a girl had spoken. It was done.

Haltingly, both their voices sounding unsteady, they were taken through the responses.

'*With this Ring I thee wed, with my body I thee worship . . .*'

It was a wide gold band; quite plain. As Julius fitted it upon her finger his hands were shaking; the knuckles white. His hands swam before her eyes; his touch felt cold, indistinct. The music had fled, and her mind hurt with a dull ache. *He lied*, she thought dully, distantly, gazing at his hands, and the knowledge frightened her; she had never felt so close to another person's sin. She raised her eyes to his face, half curiously, still distanced, wondering if he would show something now—knowledge of what he had done, regret, fear. But his eyes were lowered; his face told her nothing.

They knelt, and were blessed. The tide of the priest's voice swelled in the air above their bowed heads. Then they stood.

The organ was playing again. Mozart, she thought, from the far recesses of her mind, where she watched all this as if it were happening to someone else. Yes; it was Mozart.

Julius was turning to her, reaching to her. He lifted back her veil and their eyes met once more, locking out the rest of the world in a complicity that excluded thought. Tears started to her eyes, and she felt as if her heart would burst; hope had sprung, out of nowhere, as he had touched her veil. It died, extinguished like a flame by the look in those cold grey eyes. He leaned towards her.

'I should kiss you, I think, Luisa.' His voice was awkward, almost inaudible.

Wordlessly she raised her face to him.

His lips brushed hers, very lightly, hardly touching them, and she swayed. His arms steadied her; he kissed her forehead, and her heart burned. He kissed her as one might kiss a child, she thought, dismissively; in consolation. It was over.

Julius had arranged everything. They went back to a small

house not far from the chapel; it belonged to a friend of his, she thought he had said, but she did not care who, hardly saw the rooms they entered. There was a fire burning in a long bright drawing room; the air was sharp with the scent from the baskets full of white lilies and narcissus. There was food, canapés, smoked salmon, all exquisitely arranged on a long table; Myers, aided by another silent, discreetly efficient manservant, was handing people glasses of honey-coloured champagne. She looked at it all with dull eyes, feeling she moved even with difficulty, as if the pain in her mind numbed her limbs. There was only a small group of guests, and they stood in an embarrassed huddle by the fire, their voices lowered, their conversation punctuated by awkward silences that not even the copious champagne seemed to ease. Luke was there, of course, talking to Lady Warrender, who had come, without any sign of embarrassment, at her own insistence. Harry was there, and Claudia, looking pale and tense. There were a couple of men she did not know, friends of Julius's, she supposed, standing together looking desperately ill at ease. Looking at them, Luisa suddenly felt an hysterical wish to laugh; it was ridiculous, this charade that Julius had insisted upon, and she could see no reason for it unless it was a wish to make her more miserable still. If the thing had had to be done, she would have expected some hole-and-corner affair—a small register office; witnesses persuaded in from the street.

'My dear!' Lady Warrender had crossed to them. She said a few words of conventional congratulation to Julius, some reference to his schooldays, to friends they shared. Luisa saw her keen eyes look at him appraisingly, curiously, and Julius answered her, politely enough, but stiffly and then turned away. Lady Warrender kissed Luisa's cheek. She smiled.

'You *are* a dark horse, my dear. I thought you told me you had no thoughts of marriage?'

Luisa felt her cheeks burn. 'I didn't then,' she said lightly. 'It . . . this was rather sudden.'

'Was it?' The sharp eyes, the humorous plain face, regarded her intently. 'But you've known each other since you were children—I think Claudia mentioned that . . .'

'Oh. Yes—we have.'

Lady Warrender pressed her hand.

'Well, I wish you both every happiness, my dear. Now,

drink your champagne. You look so beautiful, but a little colour in the cheeks might not be amiss . . .'

After that exchange, time seemed to slow. The minutes passed in a daze. The warmth of the fire, the excellence of the food, the copious champagne did gradually begin to have an effect, Luisa could sense it. Gradually the atmosphere in the room lightened; people lost their selfconsciousness; all around her voices became more animated; conversation was punctuated by laughter, not silence. Religiously she did what was expected of her; she talked to Claudia, to Luke, to Harry, to the two friends of Julius. Afterwards she could not even recall their faces, let alone their names. Julius himself appeared quite at ease; he circulated among his guests, returning periodically, briefly, to her side, with every appearance of attentiveness. Now he was talking to Harry, in the far corner of the room; drifts of their conversation came to her, phrases about their schooldays, merging with some long story one of Julius's friends was telling her. She nodded her head at his words, did not allow her eyes to waver, kept her face intent, but she heard him with impatience, as if he spoke nonsense, a foreign tongue. The story finished; clearly it was meant to have had a punch line of some kind, and she laughed dutifully. The young man's face widened into a smile.

'Anyway,' he said, 'all my congratulations and best wishes to you both. I'm so pleased for Julius. This is the best thing that could have happened to him, you know . . .'

Luisa was suddenly attentive. He was about to turn away, and she wanted to stop him, ask him what he meant. But before she could do so, she felt a hand on her arm.

'Luisa? Well, well, well. *What* a way to meet again after all these years!'

She swung round, and froze. She was looking into a pair of pale grey eyes, set wide in an alert tanned face. The auburn hair was lighter than Julius's, she saw now, and the mouth still had the old droop to the corners of the lips, giving the handsome face a slightly childish, petulant look.

'Kit,' she said softly, and he smiled.

Before she could prevent him, he had drawn her to him, and kissed her on both cheeks, his lips lingering against her skin, his breath smelling of whisky.

'And I thought you might have forgotten me!'

'Not at all.' She disengaged herself quickly, and a mocking

expression came into his face.

'Oh, Luisa, don't look at me like that.' He opened his eyes wide, boyishly, favouring her with that look of apparent frankness she had never trusted. He lowered his voice conspiratorially. 'I'm not supposed to be here, you know. Most definitely not invited. Now, isn't that shocking? The bridegroom's own brother, and *such* an old friend of the bride's . . .'

'You mean Julius didn't invite you?' She stared at him curiously.

'Quite the opposite, darling. Strict instructions to take myself off. Go elsewhere. Now I wonder why Julius should have done that, don't you?'

Luisa looked at him coldly.

'If that's the case then, don't you think you ought to leave? You could. Julius hasn't seen you, I think.'

She glanced nervously over her shoulder, but Julius had his back to them. He was talking to Harry, and Claudia had joined them. Kit followed her eyes. He smiled impishly.

'I'm sure you're right, Luisa dear. Frightfully good advice. I *never* take good advice, though, it's against all my principles . . .'

'I didn't know you permitted yourself principles at all,' she snapped, but Kit ignored the hostility of her tones.

'In any case . . .' he swept on as if she had not spoken, 'I *had* to see you, Luisa. Looking so lovely, so ethereal. And Claudia, of course.' He glanced sharply across the room to her sister. 'How *is* Claudia? That little *contretemps* of hers . . . all smoothed over, I gather?'

'You'd better ask Julius.'

'*Really?*' He turned back to her. His voice was still lazy, as affected as ever, and his expression was bland. But there was something in his eyes, Luisa thought, with a sudden wariness—an alertness, a sharpness. Instantly she wished, though she did not know why, that she had kept silent, said nothing. His eyes scanned her face.

'Well now,' he said softly, 'this was all rather a surprise to me, you know. Frankly I thought Julius would never marry. Might cramp his style too much, you know? And this was all so *sudden*, wasn't it? I wonder what could have happened to make Julius change his mind? And you too, of course. From what Claudia has always said, you were more likely to take vows of quite a different kind . . .'

He broke off, suddenly dropping the artificial bantering tone he had adopted, and his eyes met hers. Something flamed in his eyes, briefly, like a dart of light, an urgency, a rapaciousness. Luisa saw it, and something tugged at her memory. Nausea suddenly churned in the pit of her stomach, and she felt her blood rush to her face, pounding in her temples. Quickly she tried to turn away, but Kit caught her arm and drew her to him. Unwillingly, fearfully, she looked into his face.

'Luisa.' His voice was quite different now, urgent, lowered. 'You look exquisite, do you know that? But you're not happy, are you? How can you do this? You should have let me see you, before, when I asked Claudia to arrange it. You could have given me a chance, you know—to talk, after all this time. If we could have met, just once . . .'

She could feel his breath warm against her skin, sweet with its overlay of alcohol, and it sickened her. She met his eyes stonily.

'There was nothing to say.'

'I shouldn't have needed words.' He said it silkily, suggestively, and the dart of light flared in his eyes again, then was gone. His hand on her hand felt too hot, clammy; she was stifling, and the room felt suddenly crowded, airless. It was as if his hand were not on her arm, but across her mouth, shutting out the air, suffocating her . . . she swayed against the black material of his jacket, saw blackness before her eyes, and some part of her welcomed it, the blackness of obliteration that was coming down over her mind, over her memory, like a thick tide of blood.

'Get out!'

It was Julius. His hand was on Kit's, prising his brother's fingers from her arm, and as the dark receded and Luisa looked up into his face she saw it masked with a terrible anger. His eyes blazed at Kit with an undisguised hatred, but his voice was low. Julius's back blocked the scene from the rest of the room; no one else witnessed the exchange except the three of them. Kit stepped back, then recovered his nerve. Their eyes met.

'Make me.'

For a moment none of them spoke. She saw Julius clench his fist, and for one moment thought he would hit him, that the two of them would fight, there and then, in the middle of the room, among the guests, the champagne, oblivious to everything but the hatred that crackled like electricity in the air between them.

Then Julius broke the moment. He glanced at Luisa's white face, then back at Kit, who was breathing heavily, with a look of murderous contempt. He took her arm brusquely, and without further word let her away. His mouth had set in a tight line, his face was white with anger, and at least one of the guests, Luisa saw, noted it. Luke stepped quickly forward, a look of concern on his heavily lined face, and raised his glass. People turned, and there was a sudden silence. Luke smiled.

'There should be no speeches, I think,' he said quickly. 'I abominate speeches. But I think we should have a toast. To Luisa and Julius. And to their future happiness . . .'

Glasses were raised, clinked together. There was a murmur of laughter and conversation, amidst which, to Luisa's horror, Myers suddenly appeared, majestically, bearing before him on a huge tray a most amazing cake, an exquisite edifice, tier upon white tier, latticed and scalloped with glistening white icing, its top decorated with white roses. She saw Julius stiffen; clearly he had been unprepared for this. But the pride and pleasure on Myer's face was unmistakable. He had made it himself, Luisa did not doubt it, and it was magnificent, a labour of love. She stepped forward quickly, as she saw Julius's brows draw together in an ominous frown.

'It's beautiful!' Shyly she kissed Myers' withered cheek, and he flushed with pleasure. 'Thank you.'

'It's nothing, madam.'

Carefully he laid it on the table before them; people crowded round them, laughing and talking, and Luisa forced animation into her face and her voice. She made herself look up at Julius, smiling, apparently happy. Next to the cake a long silver knife glittered on the white cloth.

'We must cut it, Julius.'

With difficulty, Julius collected himself.

'But of course.'

Her hands shaking, she fumbled for the knife, picked it up and held it poised, feeling ridiculous, an actor in a black farce, forced to play her part. Julius's cold hand came down over hers and gripped it. He guided the point of the knife into the very heart of the first tier, then, his fingers gripping hers tightly, pressing them painfully against the cold metal, he forced the knife in. It cut deep, and Luisa saw that his eyes turned at once from the mess of crushed white sugar and dark fruit before them, to the back of the room. He was looking at Kit, who was standing nonchalantly there, leaning against the door. As she looked Kit raised his glass in an ironic salute. Quickly she looked away.

After that first cut, Myers had taken over the dispensing of the cake. Expertly he was passing it to his helper, who was handing it to the guests. Julius was watching the scene coldly, with an expression of boredom. He looked at his watch.

'We should leave soon.'

'I should go and change,' she said stiffly.

'Yes, you should.'

Miserably Luisa turned away. Kit had gone, she saw with relief, and Claudia was making her way across to her, also indicating her watch, and nodding her head to the door of the room in which she would change.

Luisa went across to join her. She felt better at once when they were alone, when the door was shut on the babble of voices, when she could sit in a stranger's room, in front of a glass, and slowly unpin the veil from her hair. Claudia helped her, busiedly, excitedly.

'It wasn't so bad, was it?' she exclaimed. 'Quite fun— much better than I expected. And the church looked so beautiful; you looked so beautiful, and when you and Julius . . . Oh!' She broke off with an expression of concern, and reached for Luisa's right hand. 'Darling!' she cried. 'Look! Whatever's happened to your hand?'

Dully Luisa looked down at her hands. The left was pale, unmarked, the third finger banded in gold. The right, also pale, was bruised. In the short while since she had picked up the knife and Julius's hand had covered hers, the marks had begun to stain her skin like stigmata. A livid violet badged the pale skin; subcutaneous blood.

She rubbed at it gently; it did not hurt. The stain deepened at her touch. Claudia kissed it, and laughed with sudden comprehension.

'Julius doesn't know his own strength,' she said lightly. 'You'd better watch out, darling.'

Luisa smiled. She was glad to see Claudia restored to happiness.

'It's nothing,' she said quickly, and folded up the white veil.

The same great silent car that had taken her to the church took them both to the airport. As they left, Claudia tossed rice after them, and Lady Warrender, unexpectedly, a handful of brilliantly coloured paper bells and hearts. Tiny fragments of colour, pale grains of rice, still clung to her hair. The plane took off just as darkness fell, and as it wheeled and banked over Heathrow, the lights of London lay spread out below them like a pattern of stars.

The dark man at her side had hardly spoken. Now he said, 'I thought we would arrive by night. We shall have to go up the Grand Canal. Venice is always beautiful, but for the first time, I think, one should see it by night.'

Luisa did not understand what he meant, and his words made her obscurely nervous; she nodded and looked away, making no comment, clasping her gloved hands tightly together. Julius watched her, also silent, for a few moments, then turned away. He looked quickly at the Italian newspapers the stewardess had given them, then folded them away without offering them to her.

'If you have your passport, I'll fill in the immigration forms.'

Silently Luisa opened her bag and handed him the shiny blue document. Julius had arranged that too; a friend in the Home Office, he said, so it had been obtained within three days, not the usual month. Luisa Morrell, it said on the cover. Luisa averted her eyes from it, and turned her face to the glass.

*Luisa Morrell:* the sight of those words suddenly brought the reality of her situation home to her. She was his *wife*; his name was on her passport, his ring was on her finger, and in the church she had made a solemn promise. *To have and to hold from this day forward, for better for worse, for richer for poorer, in sickness and in health, to love and to cherish, till death us do part* . . . The words sang in her head, and she felt cold beads of sweat start to her brow. It was no good, she realised suddenly, speculating on why this had happened, on the obscure and ugly motives that had led Julius to this course of action. No good thinking how she might have behaved differently, avoided all this. It made no difference, either, in what spirit he had made his vows, or how lightly, contemptuously he might regard them. None of that altered one jot what she had done, and what she had promised. Yet at that thought her heart recoiled within her. She could *not* love him, she told herself dully. How could you love someone who looked at you with a cold contempt, who was using you . . . She felt nothing for him now, nothing, except sometimes hatred or those odd lurches of pity that would twist her heart unawares that any man could so systematically set out to destroy another person—and never realise that he might, in the process, be destroying himself.

The pain started up behind her eyes again, and she knew that if she let herself go on thinking, the memories would start to come back . . . of an old remote house, sited at the neck of a narrow glen; of long hot summer weeks, and two brothers. In the evenings, in her room, she had left the windows open, and lain there on her narrow white bed, listening for hours to the soft lap of the water at the loch's edge; the air had smelled of peat, dry grass, gorse and heather. '*Your hair smells of the heather*,' Julius had said to her once . . .

'What are you thinking of?'

She started; he was looking at her curiously.

Of you, she wanted to say. Of the person you used to be. But the colour rushed to her cheeks, and she shook her head. 'Of nothing.'

His eyes narrowed slightly, but he merely glanced at his watch.

'We'll be there in half an hour.' He paused. 'It's about an hour from the airport to the Danieli. Shall you want dinner when we arrive?'

She felt the panic start up again.

'No,' she said quickly. 'I'm not hungry. I'm very tired, I . . .'

He shrugged. 'As you like. I'll get them to send something up to our rooms in case you change your mind . . .'

*By night. Our rooms.* The two phrases coupled in her mind, and she felt her heart lurch; her eyes widened in anxiety, but he had turned away from her already, he was signalling to the stewardess to bring them a drink. Silently she stared at him, this man she had once known so well—or thought she had known; this stranger; this man who was now her husband. He was wearing a black suit, one more suited to a funeral than a wedding day; his long, finely shaped hands lay in his lap, perfectly composed. Surely, after what he had

said, that night at his house, he could not intend ... Luisa
drew in her breath and forced herself to be calm. She was
being ridiculous, she thought bitterly. He had made his
sexual tastes only too plain; and at the memory of his
rejection she felt again a deep shame. She felt bloodless,
awkward, gawky, unattractive, and for a second ached to be
the kind of woman who could wrap herself so elegantly in
furs, who, when she wanted to kiss a man—this man, would
just reach up casually, and draw his mouth down to hers,
certain of his response, assured of his arousal. But as swiftly
as that thought came to her she put it from her mind. It was
mad to think like that; in her unattractiveness to him was her
only surety, perhaps almost her only sanity. She could bear
all this, she thought coldly, just; so long as Julius never
touched her.

The landing was smooth. There were few other
passengers and they passed through Customs and
Immigration swiftly. A car picked them up, travelling fast
through dark streets in the direction of the lagoon. Then,
when it pulled in beside the small landing-stage and they
climbed aboard the motorboat that was waiting for them,
Luisa saw what Julius had meant. Suddenly, out of darkness
and mean streets, they had come to a magic city, a city of
silence and lights. Beyond the soft purr of their boat's
engine, the city lay silent under the stars; water lapped
against other boats, against old jetties, against the old stone
of houses dyed gold and iridescent green by the tides of the
lagoon. Their wake arced white behind them over the dark
water, and ahead of them the wide canal reflected gold. The
houses, the palaces that lined the canal were lit up, rich,
various and stately under the darkness of the sky. The way
ahead was wide, clear, a long triumphal curve round to what
she knew must be the square and basilica of St Mark's, the
great dome of Santa Maria della Salute, that, shadowy now,
seemed to float without support except from stone angels
under the clear sky.

Luisa stood up in the boat, letting the breeze from the sea
beyond blow against her face, and felt her heart suddenly
break free of all its fears, and lift with a wild exhilaration.

'Julius! It's so beautiful!'

He smiled, warmly enough, as if amused at her response.
She felt him take her elbow, half turning her, gesturing to
her to look not just ahead, but also to the sides, to the tiny

canals as they sped past. And she did so, noticing them for
the first time, tiny snaking necks of black water, unlit,
disappearing between the high walls of the houses,
mysterious slightly sinister.

But even they had no power to affect her mood now. She
turned to him impulsively.

'Oh, Julius, I'm so excited! I want to see all of it—
everything, the whole city. I can't believe . . . May we? Will
you take me?'

He laughed, and for the first time she felt no fear of him.
His eyes seemed warmer in their expression than she had
seen them all that day, and she touched his sleeve, without
thinking, excitement and happiness ridding her of all
wariness. Instantly she felt the warmth of his hand over
hers; the little boat gave a sudden lurch and a swerve as they
rounded the last bend of the canal, and for a second the
movement threw her sharply against him. He caught her and
steadied her, and she turned her face up gratefully to his.
They were closer than she had realised; as their eyes met and
his hands tightened around her she felt suddenly a wave of
extraordinary feeling pass like a shock through her whole
body. She caught her breath at the force of it, so sudden, so
unexpected, a demand that came straight from her body that
her mind had no time to fend. It was as if her blood, her
womb, thought. She felt herself sag against the hard lines of
his body; his breath was against her skin, his mouth close,
but not close enough, to her own.

Then the moon, full, high in the sky, passed behind a
cloud. His face fell into shadow, and instantly she tensed.
Formally, embarrassed, she drew back, and equally formally,
as if nothing had happened, he released her. She could not
see his eyes; they were in shadow. He spoke quite levelly.

'We're almost there.'

Confusedly Luisa looked ahead to where he indicated.
The square of St Mark's opened up on their left. From the
cafés the music of violins drifted across the water. Beyond,
over the masts of larger ships, and the black hulls of the
gondolas she saw the fretted walls of the Danieli.

It faced out to the sea; plain, not immediately beautiful,
unless you knew its past perhaps. She stared at it, thinking
of all the people who had stayed there once, in its long
history. Henry James, George Eliot, Ruskin, Robert and
Elizabeth Barrett Browning, beginning the long years of

Italian exile there together.

'Browning spent his honeymoon here,' she said, then cursed herself for sounding so stupid, so gauche.

But Julius seemed not to mind. He smiled.

'There could be worse omens,' he said lightly, and helped her down on to the landing-stage.

# CHAPTER SIX

As they arrived in the quiet lobby of the hotel, there was a sudden flurry of activity. Luisa blinked in the bright warm lights from the chandeliers, so vivid after the soft darkness outside; porters appeared as from nowhere, and a small man, dressed in a tail-coated suit with striped trousers, hurried towards them, both his hands outstretched in welcome.

'*Signor Morrell, e la signora! Bienvenuto a Venezia* ... many congratulations, *signore*, and the beautiful *signora*. This is an honour, Signor Morrell ...'

Julius replied in fluent idiomatic Italian, and Luisa tried to follow the rapid-fire phrases. She had spoken a little of the language once—picked up from her mother, from a short visit once to her father when he had been living in Milan. But that had been so long ago: now, she realised, she remembered almost nothing. The manager was gesticulating, his tiny hands moving in the air like a conjuror's, his face bright with pleasure; he seemed to know Julius well, she realised, and to be talking about their rooms, for she caught the word *camera*. Then Julius interrupted the flow with a sharp question, and she saw the manager's face fall. He paused, looking doubtful.

'*Questo? Ma no! Non è possibile* ... we received a telegram—yes, yesterday.'

He turned back to the reception desk, and produced a piece of paper. Julius looked at it, and Luisa saw his mouth set in a tight line. There was more rapid conversation, none of which she could follow, except that obviously the manager was suffering from a million regrets, but it was impossible, impossible.

Julius turned back to her, taking her elbow and leading her a little aside.

'Luisa?' His voice was tense.

'What's happened?' She stared at him in sudden concern. 'Haven't they received the booking ...'

'The booking has been changed.' He spoke grimly, then glanced quickly back over his shoulder to where the manager

95

hovered, looking nervous and upset. He moved so his tall body blocked Luisa's face from the manager's view and lowered his voice. 'Luisa—please. You must trust me and believe me. I didn't arrange this.' He hesitated, and she saw a dark flush stain his cheekbones. 'I reserved two rooms for us.' He paused, and lowered his eyes. 'Somehow that booking has been changed. The hotel received a telegram, yesterday. They've put us in the honeymoon suite . . .'

Luisa stared at him in dismay, and incomprehension.

'A telegram? I don't understand . . .'

'Someone's idea of a joke, I think.' His mouth set in a hard line.

'But who?' She broke off, gazing at him pleadingly. 'Can't they change us?'

He shook his head.

'Apparently it's impossible. Half the hotel is closed off until April. A large party booked in this morning. The original rooms won't be available for three days. The hotel is full.'

His distress and his anger were so clear that she doubted him only for a second. Quickly she drew in her breath, and touched his sleeve lightly.

'Please, Julius. It . . . it doesn't matter. Tell him it's all right. We . . . we can manage. Please.' She smiled at him more bravely than she felt. 'He must think we're mad . . . I'm sure the room is very beautiful . . .'

Julius hesitated, and she saw his eyes darken.

'You don't think that I . . .' He spoke stiffly and left the sentence unfinished.

'No,' she said firmly, 'I don't. Of course not. Now, tell him I'm delighted. Go on.'

For a second she saw something like admiration in his eyes, then he turned back to the manager.

'*Va bene* . . .' she heard. 'My wife is delighted . . .'

Instantly the manager's face cleared, and his pale features spread wide in a delighted smile. Quickly he turned to the porters, gesturing them to the lifts, picked up a key and made an odd, theatrical bow in Luisa's direction. Julius took her arm lightly, and they all set off up the great staircase, in a solemn procession.

In the room Luisa stood quietly to one side as the porters left the bags, the manager effusively opened doors, spread wide the shutters, and had a brief conversation with Julius.

She stared around her in wonder. The room was one of the most beautiful she had ever seen, panelled and painted, its great arched ceiling a triumph of gilded rococo. At the far end were tall windows opening on to a balcony that looked out across the lagoon to the sea. There was a huge marble-topped carved chest, a wardrobe almost as big as a room, with tall rosewood doors inset with mirrors. The carpet was old, pale rose, wreathed with flowers, and the room was bathed in soft light. Off it was an enormous bathroom with a cool marble floor, and a huge bath with claw feet; through another door was a small sitting room, with a table laid with a white cloth, food laid out, champagne cooling in an ice-bucket. Everywhere she looked there were flowers, as if there were no such thing as winter. Gardenias and tuberoses, iris and freesias; the air was soft with their scent. Then, at the far end of the room . . . she looked, turned away, and then looked again. There was the bed, It dominated the room, and she felt colour rise to her cheeks as she looked at it, and the nervousness start up again, constricting her chest. It was wide, covered with an embroidered white linen coverlet, piled high with great square pillows decorated with lace. Its headboard was old, carved wood; two cherubim, holding swathes of cunningly carved wood in tiny pudgy hands peeped coyly from its corners. It was tented, and two curtains of white brocade were looped and draped over its head. A marriage bed; a bed for lovemaking, not sleeping. Miserably Luisa turned away her eyes and stationed herself by the windows, waiting impatiently for the manager, the porters, to leave, yet also willing them to stay.

They had gone. After the flood of Italian the room was suddenly silent, and she heard the door close softly. She stiffened; she could see Julius's reflection in the glass of the windows, and he had paused, irresolute, gazing in her direction.

She turned and their eyes met. For a second he hesitated, then he gave her an odd, ironic smile.

'I had planned something altogether more discreet. I'm sorry, Luisa.'

'Please. It doesn't matter.' Her mouth felt dry, and she held his gaze with difficulty. 'It's just that I don't understand—how it could have happened. Was there some mistake with the telegram—could it have meant someone else's room?'

He shook his head, his face set once more.

'Oh no, there was no mistake. I know who's responsible for this.'

Something in his face, the tone of his voice, told her. She stared at him.

'Kit?' She stared at him, her eyes wide. 'But how could he have . . . why would he . . .?'

'Innumerable reasons.' He cut her off. 'I'd rather not talk about it.'

'But . . .'

'Please, Luisa. Kit likes to cause trouble. Shall we leave it at that?' The tone of his voice was final, and the anger banked like fire in his eyes made her bite back any further questions, although they started up instantly in her mind. She dropped her eyes, and Julius crossed to her. He took her hand gently, and raised it to his lips, his eyes searching her face. When he spoke his voice was quite different, softened, more gentle than she had yet heard it.

'Was it so very bad, today, Luisa?'

She looked up at him, and again, as she had on the boat, she felt a dart of something like pain, a weakening, shoot through her body.

'No. No, it wasn't . . .' she said hesitantly, trying to read the expression in his eyes. 'The church and . . . it was very beautiful.' She broke off. 'You'd gone to so much trouble . . .' she finished stiffly.

He smiled. 'I told you, I like ritual.'

Even empty ritual? she wanted to say. Ritual without any underlying truth, ritual that was there to disguise lies? But she bit the words back. There was no point in reproaches now; she had agreed to all this. Bitterness, argument, could only make it worse. Besides she could feel something else rising up in her heart, a desire to explain to him, to tell him at least something of what she had felt in the church, of the memories it had brought back, of the past which every second he was near her seemed to grow stronger, asserting its hold and its presence. She was about to speak, when she saw his face change.

'Your hand.' He stared at it. 'What's happened to your hand?'

'It's all right.' She tried to withdraw it quickly, but he held it tight.

'How did it happen? It's covered with bruises . . .'

The sudden concern in his voice, so uncharacteristic and so unexpected, touched her. Something of the happiness, the gaiety she had felt on the canal, came back to her. She smiled at him teasingly.

'You did that.'

'I did?'

'When we were holding the knife . . . for the cake. At the reception . . . It's fine, really. It doesn't hurt . . .'

Her voice trailed away. Their eyes had met, his dark and questioning, and in that second something arced between them like a current, a knowledge beyond words, a fierceness of need and want so forceful it seemed to pulse in the air between them, extinguishing distance.

Memory of his quick easy strength caught at her heart, and their mutual knowledge of it, of his power, her frailty, beat in on them both, opening something up between them, a great dark cavern of space into which she felt herself sinking, sinking. Yet he was vulnerable too; she could sense it, see it in his eyes, in the sudden gentleness and uncertainty that darkened them.

'Luisa, I . . .'

With a low sigh he lifted her hand again to his lips, covering it with kisses. She half moved, was hardly conscious of taking a step, but the next moment she was in his arms. They tightened around her, and in that instant the want, and the need, exploded inside her. It was so violent, so sudden that it blotted out all thought, the need to feel his warmth, his skin against hers. Urgently his lips sought hers and she arched her face up to him. As his mouth touched hers and her lips parted, she heard herself give a low moan, and his hold on her, as she trembled in his arms, tightened. Her eyes closed. She knew nothing, saw nothing, was conscious of nothing but the warm pressure of his mouth on hers, the hard pressure of his thighs against hers. All her senses seemed to bond in one, so she heard through her body the pounding of his heart, tasted his want with her lips, saw him, this man who was her husband, saw him though her eyes were shut, and saw down to his very soul, to a place in which they were at one, beyond questioning, beyond uncertainty.

Julius kissed her gently, deeply, as if they could never break apart, his hands running through the long strands of her hair, clasping her against the hardening of his body, so she could feel the urgency of his want, his hunger for her naked, terrifying in its force, willing her, as if she were the only one who could assuage it.

When they broke apart at last, they stood close, their eyes locked together, that want and their knowledge of it palpable between them, knotting them together into a communication deep beyond words. Their breath came quickly; Luisa was shaking. She could not speak; her mouth felt dry, her lips were bruised from his kisses, her breasts burned for the touch of his hands.

He would touch her, take her. He must. But he did not. He stood very still, his eyes shadowed, still holding her hand tightly. Then at last, very slowly, he raised the hand with her wedding ring to his lips, and kissed the gold band lightly. Luisa felt tears start to her eyes and a flood of conflicting thoughts and feelings rush through her. There was so much she wanted to tell him, so much she wanted to explain. But he let her hand fall, and stepped back a little from her, as if deliberately cutting them off from what had just taken place.

When he spoke at last his voice sounded uneven and harsh, as if he were controlling it with difficulty.

'I didn't plan this, Luisa. You must think...' He gestured to the room, and then shrugged. Once again he seemed completely in control of himself. 'I'm very sorry.'

She looked down at her hands, lowering her face from his eyes.

'I ... I am your wife.'

Silenty she cursed herself. It was not what she wanted to say, and the words came out flatly, without apparent feeling, with a tone of resignation she had not intended.

There was a brief silence.

'Yes. Well——' He paused, but she did not look up. He turned away suddenly, brusquely, and she felt her heart cry out in silent pain. 'Up to a point. As we agreed and you carefully stipulated. I have no wish to coerce you into anything more than that. Particularly in the present circumstances.' He laughed bitterly. 'I'm sure you imagine I set all this up.

'No, I don't.'

'Then you're commendably trusting.'

It might have been a compliment; it sounded more like an

accusation. Miserably Luisa turned away. She moved to the window, where she could look out to the open sea, and rested her forehead against the glass. Suddenly she felt exhausted, ill with tiredness. She wished she were alone. At least then she could cry; perhaps she could sleep. Confusion and pain welled in her heart, but she said nothing.

'Tell me,' she knew he was still watching her, though she did not turn her head, 'was it you who invited Kit this afternoon? Had you told him where we were coming?'

The question so took her by surprise that she whirled round to confront him, her eyes wide with incomprehension.

'I invite him? No.' She stared at him questioningly. 'I haven't seen Kit, haven't spoken to him—not for years . . .'

'Until this afternoon? You were quick enough to talk to him then.'

'*What?*'

Julius shrugged. 'It doesn't matter.' He turned away in the direction of the small sitting room. 'Would you like something to eat? Some champagne?'

'I'm not hungry,' she said in a small flat voice. 'I . . . I should like to go to bed.'

'Then by all means do so.' His voice was cold now, bitingly curt. Luisa hesitated, and he laughed.

'You'll be quite safe. I shan't touch you. You needn't look so worried.'

'But where will you . . . I mean . . .'

'I don't intend to sleep. I intend to get drunk. Goodnight, Luisa.'

Without a backward glance he went into the small sitting room and shut the door. A few moments later she heard the sound of champagne being opened, the clink of a glass. Then silence. Miserably, hardly knowing what she was doing, she unpacked the small overnight case she had brought with her on the plane. Like an automaton, she washed and brushed her long hair. Then, her hands trembling a little, she put on the nightdress she had brought with her. It had been a present from Claudia; she would never have bought such a thing, a confection of white lace and silk that curved over her breasts and floated, loose and semi-transparent, around her legs and thighs. She had intended to hide it, to leave it behind, but then, at the last moment, on some impulse—it was so beautiful—she had packed it. The silk felt cold and soft against her skin. Shivering slightly, she slipped between the white linen sheets and lay back on the pillows. When she turned out the light she could just see a thin band of gold light under the door to the sitting room; she heard the sound of a glass, a muffled phrase that sounded like a curse.

She closed her eyes. Her wedding night. Tears, warm against her cold skin, coursed down under her shut eyelids. She thought of the moment on the boat, as they arrived, when for a brief time all questions had seemed irrelevant, when happiness had taken possession of her. In her exhaustion she felt now as if the boat, the waters of the lagoon, rocked her still. Julius would break her, she thought confusedly. It was only a matter of time. And she fell asleep.

She dreamed of Scotland. Of a day with the sun high in the sky, cloudless. They were on the moor, up beyond the house, where the peaty soil was starred with thousands of tiny flowers in midsummer; where you could see the long line of the loch, the point where its waters flowed out to the sea. No one went there; they were alone, she and Julius, and the air was infinitely still. But then they were always alone that summer, even when the others were there; their eyes and the knowledge in them excluded all others.

She had not seen him for years, not since that day at Aunt Con's. Then he had been a boy; now he was a man; he had left Oxford that summer. He had met her and Claudia at the station in an old Wolseley car, and as she climbed down from the train, lifting out suitcases, making sure Claudia had left nothing behind, confused, urgent, nervous, because she knew he would be meeting them, and though she didn't understand it all she understood one thing, that he hated her family, he had suddenly been there. His hand, over hers, lifted the suitcase she had been lugging. She had straightened up, dazzled a little by the sun which shone full in her face, and their eyes had met, and she had *known*.

They had said nothing then; just the usual polite banalities. Later that afternoon they had met again, just as if it had been arranged, in the cool echoing hall of the old house. 'We're going for a walk,' Julius had said, as if they had already agreed it. They had gone, and it had begun. Something had lit in Luisa's heart that day; a glorious secret knowledge, a sureness. She saw the same knowledge in his eyes whenever he looked at her. She had felt, that day, that summer, as if her life had suddenly begun. It stretched before her, sunlit, golden, glittering. Her future was Julius. There were no doubts, no darknesses. And now she lay back, on the grass cropped short by the sheep, feeling the warmth of an eternal afternoon warm on her eyelids. Julius was stroking her hair. It fanned out, over the grass, the heather, the vetch, the periwinkle.

'Your hair smells of the heather,' he said. It was the last afternoon they had been happy.

She was not sure when she wakened. The edge of the dream was so sharp, so strong, that it stayed with her, pulsing in the darkness of the strange room. For a moment she did not know where she was, then slowly memory came back to her. She felt the happiness ebb away from her heart like sand sifting through the fingers.

Slowly she stretched her arms out, across the wide cool expanse of the bed. It was empty, and the room was still dark, but beyond the shutters she could see a thin band of light. It was day.

She lay there quite still, quite calm, her mind suddenly alert, willing the past away. She did not want to remember; it was all too long ago, and too painful. She thought: I'm married to him now. And under the white sheets her fingers touched the wide gold band, cold against her skin.

She had married a memory, she thought suddenly. Once Julius had seemed so close to her that each had known the other's mind without speaking; it had never occurred to her before to question that understanding, to dismiss it, to think how young she had been, and to find, by way of erasure, words that would diminish the truth of what she had felt. First love; adolescence; infatuation. They came to her mind now, but still she knew they were curiously irrelevant, inexact and timorous. No. She had loved Julius, she thought. But now he was another man: cold, remote, unapproachable and unpredictable. When she looked in his eyes now she saw hate, or a sensuality so naked it frightened her. It was like a black fire, beyond all moral boundaries, and she flinched from it.

She sighed, and crumpled the cool linen sheets nervously between her fingers. It was no good, she thought, thinking about the past, no good letting events go so out of control that they took the course they had the previous night. And it would do no good to be bitter or distrustful. They were here; Venice was beautiful. And at that thought she felt an odd rebellious optimism lift her heart. She did not, she realised, surprised, wish she were anywhere else. The day and the city waited outside the windows, and in spite of herself she felt a quickening, an excitement.

She got up swiftly and crossed the room, pulling back the heavy curtains impatiently, pulling aside the tall shutters. Outside the sky was misty, pale, lit a soft rose by the veiled sun. Across the water the great basilica of Santa Maria rose, softened by the mist, shimmering, as if compounded of water. There was no sound from the next room.

As she looked out, there was a light tap at the outer door, and a maid entered, carrying a tray.

'*Buon giorno, signora!*'

She laid the tray by the bed, and turning, Luisa realised that she was ravenously hungry. There was breakfast for one, she saw—fresh orange juice, a tall pot of steaming coffee, warm milk, bread, croissants, honey. She thanked the maid, who withdrew as silently as she had come, hesitated for a moment, and then climbed back into bed. She ate her breakfast quickly, a little nervously, glancing occasionally at the door to the little sitting room. But she heard no sound beyond it, and suddenly she felt a dart of contrition. She had slept and dreamed and wakened refreshed. And Julius?

At that moment the door from the corridor opened, and he stood there. She stared at him confusedly, instinctively reaching for the sheets and pulling them a little higher around her. He smiled and came into the room. He looked fresh, she saw, cleanly shaven, immaculately dressed. He was carrying an armful of boxes which he tossed on to a chair. Without hesitation, as if it were the most normal thing in the world, he closed the door, came across, lent down and kissed her hair very lightly.

'You slept well? I've been up for ages.'

Cheerfully he helped himself to some coffee, then perched himself on the end of the bed, just as if the events of the previous evening had never happened, as if they were the oldest, most intimate of married couples. She stared at him for a moment, and then something in his eyes made her lips lift. She smiled.

'I think I probably slept better than you did. What

did you do—was it one of those little armchairs, or the floor?'

He laughed.

'The armchair. If it makes you feel any better, it was damned uncomfortable.'

'And did you get drunk?'

Julius shook his head solemnly. 'Unfortunately not. I tried, but it eluded me. You slept disgustingly well, I take it?'

Luisa coloured, the memory of the dream stealing back into her mind.

'I know you did anyway.' He looked at her intently. 'I came through this morning, fell over the furniture, had a bath, unpacked. You never stirred once.' He smiled. 'I watched you, for quite a long time.'

'How unfair!'

'Not in the least. You looked very beautiful.'

His eyes met hers, lazily, mockingly, and Luisa felt something stir at once within her. She looked quickly away.

'If they really can't move us . . .' she hesitated, then met his eyes candidly. 'You can't spend every night in a little gilt armchair designed to sit down in for five minutes to take tea or write a letter . . .'

'You mean I could join you in that bed?' Julius raised his eyebrows mockingly, and stretched. 'We ought to have a sword to put between us, like Lanceelot and Guinevere— isn't that the solution? Would pillows do, do you think? of course . . .' he paused, his eyes intent on her face, enjoying, she thought, the embarrassment he caused her, 'it is a very *wide* bed . . .' He broke off, teasingly, then stood up abruptly. 'Well, anyway, no doubt we'll find a solution. Now——' He put the coffee cup back on the tray, and stood looking down at her, tall, dark, curiously formal in his impeccably cut black suit and crisp shirt. The formality of his attire made her feel all the more naked. But he smiled, and she relaxed; the tension was all in her, she thought quickly, meeting his imperturbable gaze.

'You wanted to see Venice, or so you said yesterday. When the mist clears it will be a beautiful day. A little cold, but clear, I think. So—when shall we begin?'

'A guided tour, you mean?' She smiled at him. 'You obviously know Venice very well.'

'Well enough.' He looked away. 'I've always been here alone before. I shall enjoy having someone to show it to.'

He spoke stiffly, and Luisa looked at him in surprise. Somehow she had never thought of Julius as being alone. In her imagination, she realised, he was always with someone—another woman, the kind he had said he preferred, experienced, sophisticated—everything she was not.

'So? Shall we begin? Today I thought we might walk around the city, have lunch ... tomorrow I could take you to Torcello ...'

'Torcello?'

'It's one of the other islands in the lagoon,' he said shortly. 'Very beautiful, few people go there, especially at this time of the year. You might like it.' He turned away. 'I'll leave you so you can get dressed. Will you meet me in St Mark's—in the square? The first café ... an hour, half an hour? It's just around the corner from here.'

Luisa felt her heart lift again, with excitement, she told herself, with an odd happy dart of anticipation.

'Half an hour.'

He smiled, his hand on the door.

'Oh—by the way, I think we've had a problem with the luggage. How many cases did you bring?'

She stared at him in surprise.

'Two,' she said. 'And an overnight case I took on to the plane. But apart from that, two old ones. Rather battered.'

'I thought so.' He looked down at her, the grey eyes cool. 'In all the confusion last night I didn't check. But they seem to have sent only one; I've rung the airport—I shouldn't worry. It'll probably turn up—it often happens. You didn't have anything valuable with you?'

'No. Just a lot of rather old clothes. It doesn't matter.'

'Well——' he hesitated, looking suddenly awkward, 'I thought you might need some things meanwhile, so I went out this morning and bought you some. They're probably all wrong, of course, but they're over there. If you need them.'

With a quick, careless gesture he indicated the pile of boxes he had brought in with him. Then, before she could speak, he had opened the door.

'Don't worry if there's nothing suitable. I'm sure the case

will turn up later today. I'll see you in the square, in half an hour.'

As soon as the door shut, Luisa pushed back the sheets and slid quickly from the high bed to the cool wooden floor. Swiftly she crossed the room and looked down at the boxes; there were several of them, large, tied with ribbon, and she stared at them in amazement. What an extraordinary man he was—and what an odd thing to have done. He was quite right. The larger of her two other suitcases was nowhere to be seen, and the one there, she knew, had been the second case she had packed. It was full of oddments, the fruit of indicisive packing, of nervousness. Inside it were a few old skirts—some thick jumpers because Claudia had started insisting it would be cold. Meanwhile . . . she looked at the beautiful white new boxes, their lids discreetly emblazoned with the names of famous shops.

She felt suddenly possessed with a stupid mad excitement, like a child's on Christmas Day. No one had ever given her such presents. With trembling fingers she undid them, pushing aside the layers of stiff white tissue. When she had opened them all she sat back on her heels wonderingly, dazed by what she saw. Unerringly, it seemed, Julius had chosen for her the things she might have chosen for herself, except that never in her life had she bought such things. There was a box full of shirts of the softest silk, another of jumpers of the finest, lightest cashmere. There was a bag of the most exquisite Florentine leather; a box spilling over with silk underwear all edged and embroidered with handmade lace, in another the most beautiful dress, of pale cream linen and silk, with a soft cashmere-lined jacket. Luisa stared at them in disbelief. One box remained, tinier than all the rest, made of leather. Now almost afraid, she opened it and caught her breath. Inside, laid on dark velvet, was the most beautiful necklace she had ever seen. It was old, of dark amber set in gold; it was the exact colour of her eyes, and when, with shaking hands she held it against her throat and looked in the glass, she saw the stones circle her neck with a mysterious beauty, ageless, soft, the colour of the water that lapped outside the windows.

Feverishly, on an impulse she could not explain, she suddenly turned back, and began to rifle quickly through the boxes. Julius must have put some message with this, she thought, agitation rising up unchecked in her. There must be some note some card ... something. But she could find nothing. Then, as she let her hand fall, she saw it tucked inside the little leather box which contained the necklace, a small plain white pasteboard card. It said: *To my wife, from Julius*. There was nothing else. No date, no sentiments, no mark or word of affection. Just all this.

Involuntarily she pressed the card to her lips, and looked around her, sudden joy starting unbidden to her heart. It was not just that the things were so beautiful, so carefully chosen, that he should be so generous now, and so carelessly so, after his harshness the night before, it was that they were from *him*. With a quick exclamation she picked up the folds of silk and lace and pressed them against her skin. They were lovely, lovely. And they were from Julius.

Then, quickly, realising the time that had gone past, she stood up; soon, very soon, she must meet him. She suddenly felt widly, inexplicably, uncontrollably happy. Her heart sang. Swiftly she washed, brushed her long thick tousled hair. With shaking hands she selected some of the tiny beautiful garments that foamed lace in the white box of lingerie—they fitted her exactly, as if they had been made for her, their silk caressed her skin, and she felt her cheeks colour deeply as she looked at herself in the glass. These were the kind of things Claudia might wear, the tiny bra, lifting her small rounded breasts, the silk stockings, the lacy camisole petticoat that brushed the tops of her long slender thighs. Quickly she bent and put on the cream linen dress, the light jacket that went with it, reverently her fingers brushed the label of the designer and for a moment she hesitated. All this must have cost so much; perhaps she shouldn't accept it, perhaps she should take them off, put them back in the boxes, refuse them ...

But the temptation was too great; and besides there had been something in Julius's eyes when he had gestured so casually, had left her so quickly. Just a trace, a hint, of a vulnerability she had thought he no longer possessed. If she refused these, she knew she would hurt him. Turning to go, she looked back once in the glass, and stared at herself in astonishment. The clothes were beautiful, of course—the dress a little paler than her hair, its soft texture glowing against her skin, the thick aureole of her hair. But it was more than that: she looked alive, she realised, she, who always looked to herself so bloodless, so dulled, so shut somehow. Her eyes danced at her reflection, and she laughed happily. The necklace of amber and gold sang in the light; its soft weight against her throat was like a caress. She banged the door carelessly behind her and sped down the stairs, her heels clicking against the pale marble.

He was sitting outside the café, just as he had said, and they saw each other in the same instant. He stood up, formally, and although he controlled it, tried to mask it, Luisa thought she saw pleasure light his eyes. His eyes travelled over her with a frank admiration, but he said nothing, merely drawing out a chair. He took her hand, briefly, lightly, as if in greeting, and then turned away to summon the waiter.

'Coffee?'

She nodded.

'Julius . . .' Summoning up her nerve, she laid her hand on his where it rested on the table. 'I've never been given such beautiful things in my life. I . . . Thank you.'

'Please, it's nothing. I'm glad you like them. They . . .' he paused, letting his eyes rest for a moment on her neck encircled by his necklace, on her lips, then back to her eyes. 'They suit you very well.'

She smiled at the dryness of the compliment, her eyes dancing.

'And they fit,' she said teasingly. 'As you can see. They fit extremely well.' She lowered her eyes demurely. 'Everything.'

She saw his lips curve into a smile; he shrugged.

'How did you manage that?' She looked at him challengingly. 'I'm sure most men have no idea at all about sizes, and . . .'

'Well now.' He leaned towards her, his eyes mocking her with that lazy, effortless sensuality that so perturbed her. 'I have an excellent memory. And in the shop I went into there was an assistant of about your height . . .' he lowered his eyes very deliberately to her small high breasts, her tiny waist. 'And *about* your build. Rather an attractive girl, I thought.'

'Oh, really?' She looked at him in mock sternness, and he laughed.

'Well, no, truthfully. She was something of a dragon and at least sixty. But when I explained the situation, she was very understanding, very helpful. I described you——' He paused. 'In considerable detail. *Et voilà!*'

The amusement in his cool grey eyes gave her courage. Quickly, impulsively, she leaned across and kissed his cheek very lightly. She expected him to stiffen, to recoil, but he did not. For a second the expression in his eyes clouded, darkened, then whatever it was she saw there, which might have been distaste, but which looked more like an odd, pained doubt, was gone. He smiled, the waiter brought the coffee, and when Julius next spoke his voice was brisk, businesslike.

'Now, I have to do some work, alas, while we're here. There are some people I shall have to see, next week. But not for long, and anyway we have two days without any interruptions. So, I'm at your command. What should you like to see? Art galleries? Churches? The market? The Lido? I don't recommend the Lido.'

Luisa laughed happily; a thought came to her.

'I think I should like to begin by just walking around, just looking—at the canals, the houses. Just exploring, and then—well, I should like to go to the Accademia. There's a painting there that someone once said I should look at.'

He raised his eyebrows, but asked no further questions. Her answer seemed anyway to please him.

'All right, agreed. We'll walk, and just see where our footsteps lead us. Then we can take the *vaporetto* across to the Accademia. Then we could have lunch . . .'

While they sat in the square, sipping their coffee, the sun began at last to pierce the thin layers of morning mist, bathing the great wide space before them in a light of extraordinary clarity. Delighted, Luisa looked around her. There were few people in the square, for it was too early in the season for many tourists. The famous, and, she thought, distinctly overfed pigeons wheeled and then settled in great shifting clouds of rose and grey. The cafés were still setting up for the day; across the *piazza* men in long white aprons were setting out little chairs, spreading table cloths. Opposite them were the two tall columns of St Mark and St Theodore, the golden lion of St Mark's glittering in the sun. Across the white marble chequerboarding of the paving a priest walked, his long black robes fluttering in the light breeze that blew across the *piazzetta* from the sea. Luisa let her eyes linger on the cathedral itself, that extraordinary, ebullient, eccentric building, with its fat Eastern domes, its soaring pinnacles. Julius's eyes followed her gaze and he smiled.

'Do you like it? I do—some people hate it. It's not pure enough, not classical enough for them. Mark Twain said it was squat—"like a vast and warty bug taking a meditative walk" . . .'

Luisa laughed.

'But it's nothing like that! It's so beautiful. Look at those arches on the roof—they're so delicate. They look like the crests of waves.'

Julius stood up.

'Come on, then, let's go and explore. We can go up on the roof of St Mark's if you like. The view is . . . well, you'll see.'

He took her hand, and led her across the wide sunlit space, and into the great echoing cavernous interior of the church. In the dim light Luisa stared around her, at the mosaics, the tall pillars of rose marble and porphyry. It glimmered with a strange, dark opulence, the colours of earth and gold and rubies and the air was thick with the smoke of incense and candles. Its magnificence, its size, their footsteps echoing on the ornate patterned floors, daunted her a little; the air was cold. Instinctively, looking down the great central nave, she reached for Julius's hand, finding reassurance in its quick warm touch. He led her up, up a maze of catwalks, stairways and passages, up and up, until suddenly, bending their heads through a low doorway, they came out on the parapets around the roof. Luisa caught her breath. After the darkness of the interior, the light was dazzling. On all sides the city spread and soared away from them, lapped and patterned by azure water; the stones of the city were gold, the roofs a deep terracotta; the light glanced, darted, danced on a million shapes and reflections. It was intoxicating, as if the whole world lay at their feet.

They stood there, side by side, their hands clasped, staring round them in silence. And as she looked Luisa felt start up in her heart that strange music of joy and certainty she had heard in the tiny church where they had married; it flooded through her again, with a wild obstinate certainty, and she turned to Julius impulsively, words rising to her lips. But he was watching her closely, she saw, with that odd shadowed gaze of his, and the words died on her lips. Without speaking they turned eventually, and made their way back through the darkness of the stairs, out through the nave to the *piazza*.

Then they walked—for hours, it seemed to Luisa, though she felt tireless. Julius was the best, the most considerate of guides. As they passed he pointed out some of the more famous of the buildings, told her something of their history. But he did not circumscribe her; when, delighted, she spied a little courtyard to one side, hung with washing, filled with old crumbling pots of ivy and geraniums, he let her explore. When she darted off down the small side canals, impulsively crossing and re-crossing the tiny bridges, peering through old, decaying iron gates at deserted boathouses, the abandoned rooms of a decaying *palazzo*, he let her go. Amused, withdrawn, but never impatient, he followed behind her, watching as she darted from sunlight to shadow, pleased, apparently, by the delight which she could not hide from her face.

Towards noon they crossed the Grand Canal in the *vaporetto* to the Accademia gallery, and passed, almost alone, through its long cool galleries. In the second room they came to the Bellini Madonna of which Luke had once spoken. Luisa knew it at once, among all the others. She stood still staring at it for a long while. The Virgin stood, looking down at the plump Child she held in her arms; on her face was an expression of concern, but of total tranquillity. Julius stood beside her.

'I think I see why this picture,' he said.

Luisa turned to him, her cheeks colouring.

'It was Luke,' she said quickly. 'He said I should look at this picture. I . . . all women should, perhaps.'

'Perhaps.' He turned, his face obscured from her, and after that seemed to withdraw back into himself, so that Luisa felt a return of her earlier nervousness. She followed him through the gallery, but he seemed to hardly look at the paintings. Except once.

In the fifth room he stopped, paused, then turned back again and studied for a long while one of the paintings she knew was most famous in the gallery. It was late fifteenth century, by Giorgione, the *Tempesta*. Silently Luisa looked at it. Luke had spoken to her of it once, she remembered, of its power, of its elusive mysterious qualities. 'Now there's a painting,' he had said, with some satisfaction, 'that has kept the art scholars arguing for centuries.'

It was smaller than Luisa had expected. A strange haunting landscape dominated by a fierce sky, livid with the threat of storm. Beneath a tree, in the foreground, was a man and a woman. The woman, one breast bared, was suckling a baby. All the figures were poised, threatened by the elements, and the connection between the man and the woman, their presence on the same canvas was obscure. They were near, yet disconnected. Luisa looked away quickly, feeling distress. The painting unnerved her, for some reason she could not explain. It reminded her of something she did not want to remember, and she was glad when they left the gallery and stepped out again into the clear light.

Whatever Julius had felt earlier, his mood now seemed to lift. Taking her by the elbow, he led her quickly, almost gaily through tiny side streets. They came out on to the Zattere, and walked along to its tip, where the two main canals of Venice divided. From there, in the shadow of the great Salute church, they could look back across the water to St Mark's and their hotel, and the other way across to the less populated shores of the Giudecca. Julius led them to a small sunlit square, lapped by water at its edge, and they sat down under a tall plane tree outside a small restaurant.

Their arrival seemed to cause a stir. A few of the other tables were occupied, and the Italians at them stared as Luisa and Julius sat down. She heard a murmur of conversation; one of the women there took out a camera and—when she thought Luisa was not looking—took their photograph. Luisa leaned across to Julius, who seemed oblivious to all this.

'That woman over there just took a picture of us.'

'Oh?' Julius turned round sharply.

The woman saw him turn, made a gesture with her hands, and said something in Italian that Luisa could not follow. Julius relaxed.

'What did she say?'

'Nothing much . . .' He picked up the menu and studied it intently.

'But why did she take the picture?'

The woman, plump, aged about sixty, was now smiling and nodding in their direction.

Julius met her eyes with an expression of veiled amusement.

'She thought we looked very happy. And that you looked ... decorative.'

Instinctively Luisa felt he was not telling her the truth, but he looked so unconcerned there seemed no point in pursuing the matter. Instead she leaned back in her chair, letting the sunlight wash over her face, and sighed. Peace and contentment rose up in her. Lazily she watched Julius as he consulted with the waiter, his hands moving quickly in the warm air as he gestured and explained, his voice so unlike his English voice, filled with a different softness, a liquidity, a gaiety, as he spoke Italian. The waiter seemed to know him; he was honoured by their presence, Luisa caught that. Then something Julius said made the man laugh; he looked across to Luisa with a glance of dark admiration, and brought them wine, bread, two tall glasses of Campari, their edges rimmed with sugar, the scarlet liquid glinting in the sun like ruby.

'You're very well known, in Venice,' she said teasingly.

Julius smiled. 'Not at all,' he said quickly. 'It's just that my work often brings me here.'

Luisa stretched. 'Isn't it lovely?' she said, feeling the sun on her arms. 'It's like spring. And it was so cold in England ...'

'It is spring—or very nearly. The weather now will be changeable. By April it will start to get hot ...'

'*April is the cruellest month* ...' she quoted at him lazily.

He laughed. 'Not in Italy.'

The waiter brought them food, delicious food—a salad of fresh crayfish, lightly roasted veal with rosemary; mounds of freshly made pasta smelling of butter and herbs. The wine was sharp, light; it warmed her like the sun. They ate and talked contentedly; Luisa felt all the tension of the gallery subside.

'Have you worked for Luke long?' Julius spoke suddenly, out of a long companionable silence, and she looked up to see those cool grey eyes watching her, as always, intently. Did he ever let go, or relax? she wondered. Probably not. She smiled.

'For five years. Your house is so close—it's surprising we never met.' She spoke without thinking, and a glint of amusement came into his eyes.

'Very surprising. But then I'm often away.' He paused. 'We have a lot to catch up on, I suppose.'

Luisa felt her shyness return. 'I haven't much to tell,' she said awkwardly.

'I'm sure you have.' He leaned forward intently. 'Ten years. Where were you, Luisa, what happened to you, in those years?'

She kept her voice light.

'Very little. After my mother died . . .' She paused, then went on. That was the last time she had seen him, before this new re-meeting, and the knowledge of that fact lay for an instant between them both, unstated. 'After that—we lived with Aunt Con for some years. My father went to Morocco for a while, then Italy again. We didn't see him very often.' She shrugged. 'I don't know. I left school. I did a secretarial course. Then—well, Aunt Con died, and she left me a little money. So I bought the flat in London—Claudia came with me. I went to work for Luke at the gallery. That's all.'

'You never thought of marrying?'

'No.' She spoke quietly and looked away.

There was a pause as if he were calculating something; he leaned back, sipping his wine thoughtfully.

'And my father's firm handled your investments, I think—the money your aunt left you?'

She nodded. 'Your father was always very generous, very kind. To Claudia and me.' Her voice faltered, for she knew they were on dangerous ground, but he seemed not to notice. Nervously she raised her eyes to his face.

'I was so sorry about your father. Is he . . . recovering?'

'He won't live long.' Julius spoke flatly, without emotion, but his mouth tightened. 'It's angina. The doctors have given him about six months.'

'Oh, Julius!' Instinctively she touched his arm in sympathy. 'I'm so sorry.'

Julius shrugged. 'It's better that way. Since my mother died—well, he didn't really want to go on living, I think. They were reconciled, you know, later.'

Luisa felt the blood start to her cheeks.

'Yes,' she said softly, 'I did know that. I heard. Aunt Con told me.'

'Such a waste. Such a stupid bloody waste!' He spoke suddenly with great bitterness, and she saw darkness and pain flare in his eyes.

'Were they very happy?' She hesitated, frightened that at any moment she might go too far, ask him something that released all the anger and bitterness he felt.

'Were who happy?' He looked at her abstractedly, as if not following her thoughts.

'Your parents. Were they, Julius? Before . . .'

'Before he met your mother, you mean?' The cold grey eyes met hers directly. He paused, then looked away, his eyes travelling across the water. He sighed, and the sharpness in his tone left it. 'I always thought so. But I was a boy, hardly in a position to understand these things. Unless something is wrong first, inside a marriage, I don't think adultery can happen. So . . .' He shrugged, and turned back to face her, his gaze dark, speculative. 'Besides, your mother was an unpredictable force, wasn't she? She attracted heartbreak. That was what made her so irresistible, I suppose, that quality of danger she had. The promise of so much, and just the smallest hint of destruction. And of course she was so beautiful. Beauty like that is always dangerous. My father was the gentlest of men. I don't think he had a chance.'

Luisa looked at him silently, feeling shame burn within her. She knew she ought to defend her mother; once, perhaps, she would have done so. But what was the point? She lowered her eyes. Everything Julius said was true.

'Your father survived it all, of course, admirably so.' His voice cut across her thoughts like a whip. 'But then he was always an incurable egotist. He could survive, because nothing really affected him.'

'Please, Julius—don't! I can't bear it.'

His eyes met hers, as she turned to him pleadingly, and his expression softened, momentarily.

'It's just odd, that's all.' He looked at her dispassionately, coolly, as if assessing her. 'How two such people could produce you.'

She felt her lip tremble; suddenly everything seemed to have gone very quiet, and a great silence echoed in her ears. Out of it, she heard herself say, flatly, without great hope,

'I'm nothing like either of them, Julius.'

The dark eyes burned into hers. Then he reached across, and lightly ran his hand up under her thick hair, so its touch caressed the soft skin at the nape of her neck. Involuntarily she felt a dart of pleasure, of desire, move through her; her lips parted. He smiled.

'Aren't you, Luisa?' he said lightly. 'I wonder.'

After that, the sun still shone, but to Luisa all warmth had gone from it. She felt something cold and black, a despair and a hopelessness, settle in her heart. Indignant words in her own defence rose up in her mind, but she pushed them down. She knew what he thought of her; pride would not let her argue. Silently she stood up. Julius paid the bill and without consulting her strode off across the square, back in the direction of the main island. Without speaking they crossed the canal on the *vaporetto*, passed back along through St Mark's Square, and on towards their hotel. By the time they reached the cool shuttered foyer Luisa's nerves felt at breaking point. Tension screamed inside her, tautening her nerves and her muscles. She felt if she didn't speak soon, if she didn't try and explain, justify herself, then she would go mad. It was unbearable that he should treat her in this way; that one moment she should feel so happy, so close to him, and the next ... *Why* had he married her, why? Why couldn't he leave her alone? Why did he have to go on tormenting her?

They went up in the lift. As they stepped into it, he brushed against her, and again she felt the sharp tug, the pull of a desire she could not explain, which seemed to defy all reason. Julius seemed to feel it too. As the lift mounted, he stood very close to her; the still languid air seemed tense with the feelings unspoken between them. She could feel his breath, soft against her skin; his powerful body, not quite touching her, seemed to pulse words, feelings, beyond language. Looking up, compelled, into his eyes she saw them darken, and she knew, in that instant, that no matter what he said, no matter how much he denied it, he wanted her, and wanted her violently. The doors of the lift opened. He reached out and caught her by the arm, drawing her quickly after him.

'Hurry,' he said, and his voice sounded strange, urgent, roughened. He drew her down the narrow corridor, his hand gripping her arm painfully, unlocked the door, and drew her inside. Just in the room, his back to the door, he leaned against it and slipped the lock. His breath was coming quickly, and Luisa could not release her eyes from the compulsion in his. Her pulse raced, her skin ached to be touched by him; want curved and arced up inside her, a wanting so urgent her mind had no time to control it.

'Come here.'

Roughly he pulled her into his arms; she caught her

breath with a sharp cry as she felt his lips against hers.

'Now, Luisa,' he said, against her mouth. 'Now, we mustn't talk, you and I. It has to be this way—first.'

# CHAPTER SEVEN

'YES?'

He had drawn her over to the bed. She nodded silently, unable to meet his eyes, and she heard him draw in his breath sharply. He was standing in front of her, close to her, loosening his tie. Impatiently, carelessly, he threw it aside, and his jacket. Want for him still sang through her veins, but she felt awkward, suddenly shy, desperately uncertain what she should do. Obviously he expected her to undress, and with shaking hands she reached for the fastening of her dress, slipped off her shoes. But her hands felt numb; her cheeks burned. Without looking up she sensed that he had paused, was watching her, and then suddenly he bent and drew her upright. Fiercely, possessively, he encircled her in his arms, forcing her face up so that she had to meet his gaze. He looked at her for a moment, his face grave, questioning, as if disconcerted by her hesitation. In that second Luisa hated herself for her inexperience; this was not how his women usually behaved, she could see it in his eyes. Was it so difficult, after all? Why could she not . . .

'Come here.'

His firm hands reached for the fastening of the dress. Calmly, surely he undid it, let it slip from her shoulders to the floor, helped her out of it. She shivered, the cool shadowed air suddenly cold against her skin, and Julius caught her against him. Their eyes locked for an instant; neither spoke.

Gently he pushed her back on to the edge of the bed, knelt, and undid her stockings, slipping the silk easily from her smooth skin. He bent his head, his lips brushing the skin of her thighs lightly, and she heard herself give a low moan. Then he pushed her back, so she lay stretched across the cool sheets, and she felt his hands, very softly, touch her neck, the silk that covered her breasts. She closed her eyes, and let him undress her. But then, when she was naked, she could not look at him. She heard him give a deep sigh, then he moved; she heard the quick impatience with which he took off his clothes, but still she could not force herself to look at him. She had never seen a man naked before; she was afraid.

She felt, rather than saw, him lie down beside her, felt his hands turn her face towards him, trace the lines of her face, his lips press themselves lightly against her eyelids. Gently he stroked the hair from her forehead, smoothing it away from her face, plaiting it, twining it through his fingers. He moved a little, and a shock ran through her whole body as she felt his skin, warm against hers. She opened her eyes. He was looking down into her face, with an expression so intent, so unfathomable, so dark it was like the sea. Looking into his face it was as if time contracted; the past ten years were gone in an instant, time stopped in the hush of the room.

'Julius,' she said softly, wonderingly, and at her voice she felt his hard body stir against her.

'Luisa, touch me.'

He took her hand, and she let him guide her. Timidly, wonderingly, she touched the lines of his face, his neck, his hair, and then down to his shoulders. He clasped her hand tightly, and held it against his chest, so that she could feel through her fingertips the thudding of his heart, and at that, involuntarily, she caught her breath, arched herself against him, felt, with a tremor that ran through her whole body, his flesh against her flesh, the long line of their bodies, pressed close against one another.

'Touch me.'

Her fingers curled tight in the soft hair of his chest, traced the hard line of his muscles. Then she let him draw her hand down, down, over the taut line of his stomach, the narrow hips, to the hard thighs pressed against her. She felt him shudder under her touch, and suddenly all fear left her. She let him guide her, and felt him alive, strong, hard, there at the core of his being, where his body flexed involuntarily at the touch of her long delicate hands. With a low groan he caught her to him suddenly, reaching for her lips. He muttered something she could not hear, and her lips parted under his, as he drew her arms around him in the lock of a tight embrace. Warmth flooded through her veins, the warmth, the infinite sweetness of his lips on hers; he kissed her fiercely, with a mounting urgency, a black tenderness that sucked her under in a swell of pleasure.

He laced their fingers together as they lay, and she felt her body begin to move under him, instinctively, intuitively, obeying a rhythm she had never realised she knew, arching her up, so that the soft curve of her belly, the long lines of her thighs pressed against him, felt his male strength, the hardness of him.

Then, very gently, moving so slowly she wanted to cry out, to beg him not to stop, to go on, on, he let his hands move up her arms, caressing the soft inner skin. Impulsively she caught his hands, trapped them, guided them to her throat, her breasts. And as they touched her there, she heard herself, as if from far away, give a little animal cry of want, felt his body flex, tense, move against her thighs.

'Oh now, Julius!' she cried out.

'Wait,' he said, and he lowered his mouth to her breasts. He was in control now; he would not let her hurry him, and slowly, feeling a liquid heat begin to pulse through her body, Luisa abandoned herself to him. She had no more control now, nothing, it was all gone, she was caught in a tide as powerful and implacable as the sea, and it was pushing her, pushing her, onwards, as his mouth sucked and kissed at her skin, and her own hands moved, wonderingly, more boldly, over the hard planes of his back, down the long curve of his spine, to the beautiful hard curve of his buttocks, his thighs.

His breath was coming fast; his heart, her own heart, seemed to thud together, to keep pace; their skins were wet, bathed in each other's sweat, so they moved together against one another like silk. Julius paused a moment, just long enough for want, desire, a new fierce impatience, to shudder through her. Then he touched her, there, where she craved him. He moved, roughly, quickly, and for a second she felt his weight against her, on her, though it gave her no pain to be crushed so, only pleasure.

'Luisa . . .' She felt him tense, lift, and he slid his hands under her back, lifting her up to the thrust of him. He moved against her, gently at first, but even so she cried out. Pain shot through her like the cut of a knife.

She felt him pause, and wanted to cry out something, anything, so that he would not stop now, no matter how much it hurt her. Oh God, let it be, her mind cried silently. Let it be now. And she opened her eyes.

He was poised above her, his eyes glittering, dark, intent, staring down into her face. For a second he seemed to hesitate, to draw back, and with a wild cry she pulled him down to her, arching her body up to him in offering. His eyes darkened, his face set.

He moved; she heard his voice cry out her name, once, as he entered her. They lay still for a moment, panting, their breath harsh, laboured in each other's ears; the pain flooded and ebbed.

'Yes,' she began to murmur softly, over and over, 'yes. Yes. Julius . . .'

Then, deep inside her, at the neck of her womb it seemed, she felt him move, and the miracle of that movement, the deep beating insistent pleasure it began pulsing through her veins, brought the tears starting to her eyes. With a moan she bound him to her in her arms.

'Give me your hand.' His voice was rough in her ears.

He took her hand, and led it down, over their damp skin, so that she could feel their closeness, and she cried out at the wonder of it, a strange harsh cry. Instant in response, his hold on her tightened, his body began to thrust against her with a new urgency; he was losing control. His hands moved, moved over her body; urgently his lips sought her breasts, her nipples hard, demanding, exquisitely sensitive under his tongue. His caresses were strange, maddening, arousing—at one moment gentle, the next fierce, the caresses of a wild animal. He was waiting for her, she could sense it, though when she looked at him her eyes were blinded by the violence of her feelings. He was taking her to some dark secret black place which she burned to reach, and she was so nearly there, so nearly . . .

He was speaking to her now, murmuring her name, words against her ear that quickened her flesh, made it molten under his. She felt his body tense, then shudder, his hands grip at her convulsively, so his nails bit deep into her bare skin with a climactic pleasure. He groaned aloud, and a shudder passed through his body that mirrored the sudden uncontrollable trembling of her own.

He cried her name once, as they came, and they clung together, bound in that last fierce release.

Then they lay still, their breath coming harshly. Slowly her body relaxed under him, gently, as the pulsing of her womb and her blood gradually ebbed. Such happiness, such peace, flooded up within her that it brought tears to her eyes. They coursed gently, warm against her cheeks under her closed lids. Julius kissed her again, kissed the tears away, kissed her lips, with a tenderness so profound she felt her heart could break from happiness. When he spoke her name, and he spoke it over and over again, his lips against hers, his voice was broken. After a little while he withdrew from her, and she cried to lose him, though she almost felt him within her still. He wrapped her in his arms, and as their breathing grew more steady, they slept.

She woke before he did, in the warm hush of the room. His head was against her heart, his arms wrapped around her, his chest rose and fell against her breast. One of his hands, in the abandonment of dreams, lay softly around her waist. She lay there for a while, half aware of the sounds beyond their windows, of the muffled cries from the *piazzetta* as the boats returned. It must be evening. Luisa looked down at Julius stealthily, afraid to move, to wake him, and as she looked down into his face, close in the impenetrable mask of sleep, her heart turned over within her. She loved him— loved him still, had always loved him. The knowledge of it was so fierce, yet so tender within her, that it gave her joy. She knew, she thought calmly, that he did not love her; but even that knowledge then, had no power to hurt her. She accepted it, without flinching. She thought, even so, we have this, and I love him so much. It is enough.

A little later, when still he slept deeply, she gently released her body from his arms, and slipped from the bed. She stood there, naked, in the cool shadows of the room, her body silvery, slight, her skin pale as the moon on water. She looked back at the bed, at the tiny complacent cherubim, at the man sleeping, his head dark on the pillows. The white sheets were crumpled. Where she had lain they were stained with bright blood. She went to the bed, and touched the mark delicately with her fingers, wonderingly; and as she did so, Julius woke, and his hand covered hers. Their eyes met, dark with a mutual knowledge.

'I hurt you.'

'A little.'

'And after?'

'You know after.' She smiled, the joy still secure in her heart. They looked at each other for a while in silence. She let her eyes rest, without shyness, on his nakedness, on the long powerful limbs, his skin tawny shadowed against the sheets. She saw his body move, stir, under her gaze, and his grip on her hand tightened.

'I want you, Luisa, Again—now. Oh, my darling!'

And he drew her to him.

Later he said, 'Do you want to go downstairs—go out for dinner?'

She shook her head, her eyes mocking him.

'No, Julius.'

'Neither do I.' There was a pause. 'Shall I ask them to send something up?'

'Yes, Julius.'

'Are you always this obedient?'

'Yes, Julius.'

'I shall test you, later.'

And later still, when the staff had brought food and champagne, and departed, and they had eaten a little, and the moon shone in, slanting through the shutters, and still they lay together in the wide bed, he said, his lips against her throat, his eyes suddenly dark, anxious,

'I always wanted to be the first, Luisa. And I thought . . .'

But she kissed his lips and stopped his words. He was right, she thought, it was better for them not to talk. When they talked things went wrong, the past came between them. It was better to stay here, she thought, touching him, in this dark secret world where they were beyond all words, did not need them. That world was so potent, it built walls around them, it locked out all misunderstandings.

When Julius took her again, sharply this time, quickly, with a passion that drained them both, she thought silently, I love you, Julius. She kissed the words against his lips, touched them against his skin, but she knew, somewhere in her heart, that it would be fatal to speak them.

And Julius seemed to sense that reticence, that refuge in her. Once, during the long night, when he was deep inside her, he forced her to open her eyes, to look at him.

'You are my wife now, Luisa,' he said, his voice roughened by desire. He shook her, holding her in a fierce grip. 'Say it to me. I want to hear you say it.'

'I am your wife, Julius,' she said.

She almost told him then; but she did not. She held the knowledge in her heart as she held him in her arms. It was better like that, safer; she welcomed the concealment.

In the morning, late, they had breakfast together. Luisa washed and dressed, and Julius watched her, as if he could not bear for an instant that she should not be in his sight.

'Shall we go to Torcello?'

'Yes.' She smiled at him gently. 'We can come back here, later.'

'You promise?' He laughed softly. 'Very well then, I'll get ready.'

Luisa stood as he had done, watching him as he showered, the water running over his lean tanned body, watching him as he dressed. In his clothes he frightened her a little now; she saw him again as she had before, formidable, distant, a man, not the lover who had lain with her all night. But she fought off the feelings; they were stupid, she told herself.

When they were almost ready to go, she hesitated. Unease took possession of her. She had a silly superstitious dread that if they left the protection of this room, this intimacy, something would go wrong, the spell would be broken.

But Julius crossed to her, as she waited, and drew her to him, kissing her deeply, as if sensing her fear. In his arms she at once felt it abate; it was all right, she told herself; they were all right, they took this secret world with them, it wrapped them.

As he was putting on his jacket, the telephone rang, and he cursed with exasperation.

'You go on down,' he said. 'I shan't be a moment. I'll meet you in the lobby.'

There the sun streamed in through the windows; it was a perfect day. Out in the bay one yacht curved over the water, its sails full with the wind.

'Signora Morrell!'

The name was so unfamiliar still Luisa did not turn immediately. Then she realised the manager had crossed to her. He smiled, made an ornate half bow, and she smiled too, happiness and surety returning to her.

'Isn't it the most beautiful day?'

'*Bellissima, signora.* But please—I have a telegram for you . . .'

She stared at him.

'For me? For Julius, surely . . .'

'No, for you, *signora.*'

He held it out for her, on a silver salver, and Luisa took it. It was from her father. Luisa stared at it. How could he have found out where she was? Claudia knew, of course, but she was not likely to have told him, not unless it was an emergency of some sort, and . . . She stared at the words. It was not an emergency. It was the same predictable appeal. *In need of funds urgentest. Canst help? Can meet you in Venice. Congratulations, Papa.* Suddenly she felt angry. She did not hesitate. Rapidly her mind calculated. She had repaid the money Claudia had taken, to Julius, before the wedding. He had taken it silently, coldly, without a word. There had only been a few hundred left after that, most of which was with her now, in travellers' cheques. She turned quickly to the manager.

'Can you telegraph some money for me, today, at once, to Rome?'

'But of course, *signora*, it will be a pleasure.'

Luisa rummaged in her bag, quickly signed the cheques and handed them over; she scrawled the address of his bank on a small card, and handed it to him.

'Please, it must go off at once. It's very urgent. And I must send a telegram.'

Wordlessly, he passed her a telegram form. She wrote: *Money following today. I have no more. Please do not come to Venice. Luisa.*

She read over the telegram, hesitated, then passed it across. It was no good making it sound gentler, fonder, she knew that. If she did, he might actually come here, and she couldn't bear it. She thought: Once I would have acted differently; not now.

'That will be all right? You're sure?'

'But no problem, *signora*. *Buon giorno*.'

He bowed once more and disappeared into the back office. As he went Luisa felt her heart lift. The money was gone; the inheritance was gone. It was finished. She felt as if she had laid the past, freed herself. By the time Julius joined her, she was standing outside in the sunlight, and her gaiety matched his.

'We're invited to a party,' he told her, as he led her along the quay to where the ferryboats between the islands were moored. 'A very old friend of mine—I acted for her husband once, years ago. The Principessa Guardi—she has a house on the Giudecca. And she wants to meet my wife.' Their eyes met, and the clarity, the happiness in his seemed to reflect her own. 'She's old now, but indomitable, and her house is quite amazing. I should like you to see it.'

'I should like to go.' She smiled at him. 'When is it?'

'Tonight. But it's a Venetian party, it won't begin until very late. So . . .'

He left the rest of the sentence unspoken, but took her hand in his. She felt again that familiar weakening, the pulse beat through her blood, and she saw he felt something too, he could not hide it from his face. Her heart lifted. There was nothing to worry about, she told herself. They were bound, they were safe.

'How did the Principessa know we were here?' she asked, as he bought their tickets, and they walked up the narrow gangway to the ferry boat.

'Oh, I don't know,' he said vaguely. 'Through the work I have here, perhaps. Word gets round.' He took her arm. 'Watch your step, the gangway's slippery.' On the boat, he changed the subject somewhat abruptly, pointing out to the yacht that circled the bay, remarking on its beauty. But there was nothing odd in that, she thought, relaxing against his side. Why shouldn't people find out where they were? And the yacht was beautiful.

Even as they watched, the sails of the boat fluttered, filled again, then hung suddenly limp. Its pace slowed, its wake now hardly rippling the water. The breeze had gone, she realised, and the sun beat down on them now with a sudden heat. As the ferryboat gathered speed, its engines churning, and they cut out across the lagoon, Luisa looked back. The little yacht was quite still now, becalmed on the wide flat water.

By the time they reached Torcello it was noon; the island was almost deserted, quiet, shimmering in the light, as if it were waiting for them. When they stepped off the boat and on to the tiny landing-stage, it appeared deserted; there was just one fisherman, dressed in black, mending his nets at the end of the quay. From inside one of the old peeling houses, shuttered against the sun, Luisa heard a child call to its mother—a sharp piercing cry of momentary distress, then silence. The heat was heavy, slumbrous; the land flat, fenced with vines, cut by a single canal.

'This was a great city once.' Julius stood still, dark in the brilliant light, looking around him. 'It's older than Venice, you know. The cathedral is seventh century.' He turned and smiled. 'As Venice grew and prospered, Torcello declined. Now there's almost nothing left.'

In silence they walked along the canal, took a white dusty path through the fields, until they came to the cathedral. There was no one there. Inside it was cool, shadowy. It was like going under the sea, Luisa thought, looking around her in the stillness. The walls and the thick pillars were a pale grey-green marble, as if washed for centuries by water; the light was glaucous. At the head of the apse the walls curved like a shell; they were decorated with a tall mosaic, the Virgin and Child, the Apostles, their figures indistinct, faded. With difficulty Luisa read the inscription underneath. '*I am God*,' it read, '*and the flesh of the Mother and the image of the Father; not slow to punish a fault, but at hand to aid those who waver.*' She turned away, shivering slightly in the shadows. Julius was at the other end of the church, he had his back to her. It was beautiful, she thought, but sad, a little grim. She was glad when they went out again into the sunlight.

There was a restaurant near the cathedral; it was very famous, Julius said. Now there were perhaps two or three other people there, and the waiters lolled, yawning in the heat of the sun. They sat outside, under a vine pergola, looking across the fields, talking little. Luisa let her hand lie on the smooth white cloth before them and after a while Julius covered it lightly with his own. When their eyes met, words seemed superfluous. Knowledge of each other, of the night that had passed, lay between them, unspoken, but linking them. From deep within her, as the sun warmed her skin, Luisa felt the beginnings, the flutterings of desire. As if he felt it too, Julius's hand tightened over hers. At once the need grew sharper; he raised her hand to his lips and kissed it gently, and want for him shot like pain between her thighs. The blood rose in her cheeks, and she lowered her eyes.

Julius spoke softly.

'Had you bargained for this happening, Luisa?'

She looked up again, knowing at once what he meant, and the cool grey eyes met hers gravely. She could not lie.

'I think . . .' She paused, steadying her voice. 'I think I always knew—that it might.'

'So did I—I think.'

They looked at each other for a moment, oblivious to the

world, to the other diners, the waiters. Luisa's heart gave a
lurch of pain. I love him so much, she thought silently, and
the desire to speak what she felt was consuming. But at that
moment Julius glanced away, letting his eyes travel over the
fields to the far horizon, his face closed and impenetrable.
The words died on her lips. What was between them
suddenly seemed to her so fragile, so delicate, that she must
put no weight on it. If she told him the truth he would recoil
from it; it was better to leave it be. He looked back at her,
and for a moment a want so palpable, so intense, pulsed in
the air between them that Luisa felt everyone in the room
must sense it. She was glad, then, that she had not spoken.

'I came here once before.' He was looking at her intently.
'About five years ago. I was alone. I had lunch here—at that
table.' He gestured across the room. 'I sat and looked at the
fields. It was a day like this—very hot.' He lowered his eyes;
his voice was very deliberate. 'I thought about you, Luisa.'

She drew in her breath sharply, but said nothing. His eyes
lifted, remained intent on her face, watching her, lazily, with
a half-mocking expression.

'But then there was nothing strange in that. I thought of
you constantly, these last ten years.'

'Charitably, or with ill-will?' She forced herself to keep
her voice light. His eyes darkened.

'I hated you sometimes, if that's what you mean.'

Pain shot through her again, and she looked away.

'You never tried to contact me, in all those years?' It was a
question, she realised, but also an accuastion. She met his
eyes reluctantly, hopelessly, thinking of the letters she had
written and torn up, the number of times she had, sitting
alone, reached for the telephone, and then replaced the
receiver.

'No,' she said softly. His mouth tightened.

'Did you think of Scotland? Ever?' He leaned towards her,
his voice low, but urgent. 'Luisa, don't look away. Answer
me, damn you!'

'I did,' she said quickly, brokenly. 'You must know I did.'

She felt her eyes begin to swim with tears, but his face
hardened.

'You thought of Kit, I suppose.'

'Of Kit?' She stared at him uncomprehendingly. 'Julius, I
didn't. Why should I have done?'

'Well, obviously it was not as I'd supposed.' His voice was

so cold she felt the blood drain from her face.

She stared at him. Why did he have this obsession with Kit? Why bring him up now—when they were so happy?

'I . . . I don't understand . . .'

'You understand perfectly well,' he cut her off sharply. 'Or are you suffering from some convenient amnesia? Don't play games with me, Luisa. You know what happened.'

There was a silence. Memories fractured, jangled in her mind; pain started up behind her eyes. Suddenly the heat felt oppressive, airless; she drew in her breath with difficulty; the room, his face, blurred for an instant. She passed her hand across her eyes. Kit. If only he had not mentioned Kit.

'Julius, please.' Her voice sounded strange to her, odd, slackly pitched, uncontrolled. Their eyes met, and she shrank from what she saw there, a blackness in which hatred and want were mixed. 'I don't want to think of . . . of all that. Please.' She paused, forcing her voice to sound calmer. 'If I think of Scotland, I think of you . . .'

His grip on her hand tightened momentarily. Then abruptly he stood up.

'We're going back.'

He paid the bill quickly, then holding her arm like a vice, he half pulled her back the way they had come. Luisa stumbled to keep up with him, but he never once slackened his pace, or helped her, though her breath was tight in her chest, and the stones of the road cut her feet through her thin shoes. The ferryboat was just leaving—it waited for them. On deck they stood, tense, under the canvas awning that flapped above their heads, his hand crushing hers against the rail of the boat.

'Please, Julius,' she said, trying to free herself. 'Please! Don't hold me like this. Let go of me.'

'I will not!' He turned to her, his eyes blazing dark in his face. 'God damn it, Luisa, if you won't talk then I'll reach you some other way!'

When they reached the harbour the sun was still high in the sky; the heat that hung over the square was now sulphurous. On the horizon clouds had begun to form, and the wide sky was streaked with a threatening liverish light.

'There will be a storm,' the ferryman said, as he lowered the gangway, and he spat into the thick metallic water.

'Walk faster, damn you!'

Julius half dragged her across the quay, through the

foyer, up the stairs. In the room he paused only to lock the
door. Then he pushed her roughly on to the bed. He stood
looking down at her for a moment, towering over her,
loosening the belt of his trousers with impatient hands, his
eyes glittering at her through the shadows of the room.
Luisa shrank back from him, but even so she could feel it,
starting to arc through her body, this fierce demanding pull,
sharpened by fear, given edge by it. Then Julius moved,
swiftly, and she felt his full weight on her, pushing her back,
his fingers grasping her long hair. She felt her fingers claw at
him instinctively, heard him give an exclamation of pain and
anger as she drew blood on his skin. He brought his thigh up
between hers, roughly parting her legs, his hands grappling
hers so she could not scratch at him again. He did not bother
to remove her clothes, or his; she heard the silk of her
underwear tear; he swore impatiently.

'Like this, then, damn you, Luisa!' he muttered, his voice
rough against her skin. His mouth came down on hers,
crushing her lips, drawing blood, and suddenly she felt her
body arch up under him, with a harsh sharp cry. She fought
him, and fought off the pleasure, but he was too strong for
her. He took her, like an animal, forcing himself into her
body, wrenching up her skirts with an urgency of lust so
forceful she could only cling to him, until, with a shuddering
groan like pain, it was over, quickly over, and he was spent.

Then, abruptly, he withdrew, rolled off her, and lay
beside her in silence, staring up at the ceiling, refusing even
to turn to her. Quietly, silently, Luisa watched him, without
recoil. She felt, to her own surprise, no revulsion, no hatred,
but only a profound tenderness, which stirred and moved in
the depths of her heart. She lay there a long while, her head
resting on her arm, watching him, letting her eyes rest on
the hard planes of his face, the muscles of his neck, taut with
tension. Then, suddenly, he moved, turning to her, his eyes
searching her face, his racked with a kind of self-hatred.

'Luisa,' he said at last, his voice low, intense, 'that has
never happened before. I've never treated ... anyone ...
like that before. Forgive me.'

She smiled at him gently.

'There's nothing to forgive. You were angry. If you
wanted me ...' She broke off.

'I want you all the time, damn you!' He gave a low groan.
Their eyes met again. There was a pause, then she saw the

corners of his lips lift in a slow smile. 'What have you done to me?' he said, more gently, his voice teasing her. 'What kind of siren spell have you cast, that I no sooner have you than I want you again?'

As he spoke he took her hand, and drew it down against his body; as if to prove the truth of his words, she felt it move, begin to harden again under the touch of her fingers. A sigh shook them both.

'I want you too, Julius.' She forced herself to meet his eyes as she spoke.

'Do you?' His face was suddenly grave. 'And yet I never feel as if I possess you, even when . . .' he lowered his mouth against her ear, speaking words she had never heard on a man's lips before, words that sent desire pulsing through her blood.

'Even then,' he said slowly, his eyes never leaving hers. 'When you're under me, when you cry out, when I feel you . . .' He broke off. 'Something eludes me, even then. Not your body, but your mind. I never know what you're thinking, what you're feeling. It's driving me insane. Luisa—why did you marry me?'

It was so hard, then, not to tell him. She paused, then smiled at him teasingly.

'We made a bargain,' she said gently.

'We haven't kept it.'

'No, we haven't.'

'But then we couldn't have kept it, you and I. Could we, Luisa?'

'We might have done.'

'Liar.' He kissed her lips, drawing them sweetly to his, clasping her gently in his arms, until she felt herself sinking again, drugged with his kisses. Her eyes were half-closed; their bodies slowly, languorously, wrapped themselves together, limb against limb, in a slow ecstasy of touching. The room was dark now, little light came through the shutters. Neither knew, nor cared, whether it was day or night. The world, the room, seemed to have shrunk to this bed, to their bodies entwined the one with the other. Julius undressed her, slowly caressing her body as he did so, lifting her breasts and cupping them to his lips; gently she helped him with his clothes, so that they could lie once again, their skin warm, moist, naked against one another. Her blood felt like honey in her veins; it beat with a languor that he could quicken with the smallest of touches. *There is only this world*, she said to herself, *no other*.

When, afterwards, they slept, she dreamed of Scotland; of an eternal afternoon, of sun, of heather.

They woke in the early evening, and went out. It was the hour of the *ambulente*, when the shops re-opened, when the squares filled with people, and lights shone out through the darkening sky. The air was still heavy with the threat of storm; it felt damp and humid against their skin. They sat in the *piazza* at Florian's and sipped long ice-cold drinks, listening to the café bands. They were playing Strauss waltzes. Then Julius took her to a shop; he was going to buy her a dress, he said, for the party. When she protested, he would not listen to her.

'The Principessa has very grand parties,' he said, laughing, drawing her inside the tiny shop, filled with exquisite silks and velvets. 'It's a Venetian party; you should have a Venetian dress.'

Among all the new dresses, the shop had a few antique Fortuny velvets, made of a cloth so fine, so delicate, it felt like the brush of a wing against the skin. Luisa touched them gently; the assistant, smiling at Julius, showed her how one was cut, lifting the skirt to one side so it spun out, a full circle, then letting it fall, so the million tiny, almost invisible pleats composed it again into a narrow column.

'They try to make the Fortuny velvet in Venice now,' she said to Luisa. She shrugged. 'They make the cloth on the old hand looms—it is almost right. The dyes—they are good, not as good as these perhaps, but good. But they cannot cut like this. This art—they have lost it.'

One of the dresses was black, a deep soft black like the midnight sky.

'It is tiny, this one,' the assistant said, showing them the narrow waist, the soft narrow bodice. 'But the *signora*, I think, could . . .'

'Do you like it, Luisa?'

'Of course. It's beautiful. But, Julius . . .'

'Try it on. If it fits, if you like it, we'll buy it.'

It fitted. Back in their hotel room she tried it on again.

'Look, Julius!' she cried with a childish delight. She spun round and the skirt, soft, clinging to her narrow thighs, spun out like a halo. 'Did you ever see anything more beautiful?'

'No,' he said drily, and caught her to him. 'You know why this dress?'

'No.' She shook her head.

'Because it reminds me of the one you wore when you first came to my house. Do you remember?'

'Yes, I do.' She met his eyes teasingly. 'And I remember what you said. That I was acting, in my black dress. That I was trying to appear . . .'

'Chaste?' He smiled. 'But I was right, wasn't I, Luisa? Oh, you cast your eyes down; you looked so pale, so delicate. But I wasn't deceived.' He stepped back, letting his eyes run over her body, to her flushed cheeks, her tumbled hair. 'The French . . .' He paused. 'As usual the French have a term for it. *Le diable au corps*—the devil in the flesh. You have that, a little, Luisa.'

She met his eyes frankly, surprised to see in them for a moment a shadowing, a kind of consternation.

'Then you have too,' she said challengingly.

'I do?' he looked at her with mock surprise. 'Hardly at all. The most restrained, the most celibate of men . . .'

'But you said . . .' She broke off. Out of nowhere the ugly memory came, not just of what he once had said to her, but of what she had seen, of the woman leaving his house, of that swift, casual intimate embrace.

'I said a lot of things.' He seemed to sense her change of mood, and took her hand lightly. 'Some day, soon, we'll talk about them. But not now. Now we're going to the Principessa's party.'

He smiled, his voice so carefree that his gaiety infected her, and she shook away all feelings of sadness.

'Come on.' He took her hand. 'You're about to have a true Venetian experience—crossing to the Giudecca at night, in a gondola. And not one of those ones the tourists hire, so they can be overcharged for a short tour of the Grand Canal and a bad impression of Mario Lanza. The Principessa is sending her own across. Come on, Luisa. I want Venice to see my wife!'

The gondolier was waiting, as Julius had said. He wore the Guardi livery of gold and black; his face was shadowed by his hat, and he never once spoke as, silently, expertly, he propelled them out from the *piazzetta* to the dark shores of the Giudecca. Luisa trailed her hand in the water, but it was ice cold, slightly greasy to the touch, and she withdrew it quickly. She leaned back on the deep cushions, and Julius put his arm around her. The air was still close, and as they rounded the point under the shadow of the Salute church, they saw the moon just rising. It was half full, stained yellow, its edges blurred with thick cloud.

'There'll be a storm, I think. The ferryman was right,' Julius said.

Luisa pressed herself against him, grateful for the warmth of his body.

'I don't much like this ferryman,' she said lightly, smiling up at him, and Julius laughed, glancing at the dark figure at the prow of the gondola.

'I don't either. Altogether too like Charon for my taste. But wait—you'll see the lights from the *palazzo* soon . . .'

They heard music first. The gondola glided between banks, down a narrow dark side canal, and then suddenly came to a landing stage. It was strung with paper lanterns, that rustled and glittered. Beyond them, Luisa could just make out the looming dark walls of a great house. The air was heavy with the scent of some flowers she could not recognise and as she and Julius made their way up the narrow path, she could hear the scratch of shrubs, creepers, against stone walls. A breeze was beginning to blow up. When they reached the house, it gusted suddenly, catching at the skirt of her dress and at her hair, like hands darting out of the air at her.

'Through here.'

Taking her arm lightly, he led her suddenly into light. A footman bowed; her eyes dazzled. They were in a huge room, pulsing with people, lit from high above by dozens of Venetian glass chandeliers. Champagne was brought to her, and she paused, staring around her in delight. The walls of the room were hung with great tapestries; every table was banked with flowers. Before her, people clustered, broke, re-grouped. The dresses of the women shone like jewels, emerald, ruby, sapphire, diamond. The scent of the women and the scent of the flowers mingled; pale shoulders brushed against the dark jackets of the men; the air was filled with the chatter of tongues. To one side Italian; on the other American, German, French. Luisa hesitated instinctively, timid in the face of such elegance, and Julius smiled down at her encouragingly. He was wearing an evening suit; its formality, the quiet elegance of its cut, emphasised his height, the effortless command of his features. He looked around him with composure, and she saw him again for a moment like an outsider, was aware of his containment, his hauteur.

'Giulio!' A man pushed through the throng towards them. He was small and dark, about fifty, Italian almost certainly, but when he spoke his English was faultless, hardly accented. 'My congratulations. It's so good to see you again—too long. The Principessa has been looking for you. So many old friends you must meet. Vittoria is here, but you must know that . . .'

He was clasping Julius's hands, seemed not to have noticed Luisa at all, and she shrank back, suddenly tense. Who was Vittoria?

'Lorenzo,' Julius interrupted him, drawing Luisa forward, 'you must meet my wife. Luisa, this is Lorenzo Cardinale, a lawyer, and an old friend . . .'

Luisa hardly heard the words of the introduction, she saw only the man's reaction. He was a sophisticated man, and it was momentary, tiny, scarcely perceptible, but it was there. A stopping, the briefest of hesitations before the slightly too effusive smile, the over-quick taking of the hands.

'But I had not known this. How charming! What a delightful surprise, Giulio. *Signora* . . .'

He bent over her hand. There was the briefest of silences, and Luisa saw the corners of Julius's mouth lift slightly in a wry smile.

'You know Venice well, *signora*?'

His eyes were benign, but appraising. They took in the Fortuny dress at a glance.

'No, I don't.' Luisa forced herself to smile at him. 'This is my first visit . . .'

'But this is wonderful! Come, there are so many people you must meet. We must find the Principessa. Out on the terrace perhaps . . .'

He was leading them through the throng of people; those nearby had overheard the conversation, and as they passed, Luisa saw heads turn curiously in their direction, heard a buzz of speculation spring up behind them.

Julius was propelled slightly ahead of them by the crush; Luisa found the lawyer taking her arm.

'Such a pleasure,' he was saying. 'In Venice Julius is a

famous man now. But you must know this. He is formidable,
your husband, is he not? Formidable? I should not like him
to be my prosecutor, but my defence, should the time come
... ah yes, that would be splendid.' He laughed, a little
nervously, watching for Luisa's reaction. 'And this is such
fine news. I had no idea. You have known each other long?'

The black eyes met hers speculatively.

'Quite long,' Luisa said with a smile, and if the answer did
not satisfy him he was too accomplished to show it.

'Through here, *signora* ...'

They passed out of tall glass doors and into a huge square
courtyard hung with lights. On one side a band was playing;
couples danced in the centre on a wide wooden floor laid
over the flagstones. On the other were long tables, white-
clothed, roped with flower garlands, weighted with the most
sumptuous food.

'Giulio!'

A deep rasping voice, heavily inflected, cut through the
noise of the music, the conversation. Luisa saw Julius stop;
the lawyer gave her a brief bow.

'The Principessa,' he said simply. 'I shall leave you now,
*signora*. We will meet again, I hope. Later perhaps ...'

He drifted away, swallowed up by the crowd of people, as
quickly as he had come. Luisa felt Julius take her arm, draw
her forward. She stared at the woman before her, and found
her stare returned with interest.

The Principessa was tiny. She was also very old, how old
it was impossible to tell. Perhaps seventy, Luisa thought,
but her face was such a patchwork of lines and wrinkles, and
so heavily encrusted with make-up, she could have been
much older. Once, obviously, she had been a beauty. It
showed in the high cheekbones, the arrogant, almost
masculine nose, the vitality of the dark eyes. Her hair was
white; her face deeply powdered. The eyebrows were drawn
in with two firm arched lines, the wide humorous mouth was
a brilliant scarlet. She was wearing more jewellery than
Luisa had ever seen on one woman; diamonds glistened in
her hair, at her ears, round her throat. The thin wrinkled
hand she held out now, imperiously, palm downward, was
encrusted with rings the size of birds' eggs.

'*Ma* Luisa. *È così bella!*'

She took Luisa's hand in a firm dry grip, and then—to her
surprise—drew her close and kissed her cheeks. Then she

held her at arms' length, the keen dark eyes searching her face.

'You approve?' Julius was standing back, arms folded, watching this little scene with amusement. At his words the Principessa gave a deep, throaty, almost peasant laugh.

'Approve? Of course I approve! She is a child still. But you'll make her a woman, Giulio . . .'

She turned back to Luisa with a wide smile.

'So,' she said. 'You take my Giulio from me. Now here is a thing.' She reached for his hand proprietorially, drawing him to them. 'I love this man, Luisa. He is an Englishman, of course, but still . . . After I am a widow, I think to myself, maybe now Giulio will notice me . . . I am not hard to notice, you know? But no. He has found you, it seems. I must resign myself to a lonely old age.' She gestured around her at the throng of people. 'You see how lonely I am.'

Luisa smiled, suddenly liking her, and the old woman's eyes warmed.

'You go away now, Giulio . . .' She gave Julius a firm push. 'I want to talk to this wife of yours. Oh, don't worry, I shall tell her what a paragon you are, how much we owe you. Now, go away. Leave us!'

Julius gave Luisa a helpless look, but it was clear that Principessa meant to be obeyed. Reluctantly he turned away, and was almost instantly drawn into a group nearby. The Principessa took Luisa's hand.

'But I know you already, my dear,' she ran on. 'I knew your mother, of course. Did Giulio tell you? Such a woman! But not like you at all. And I know you. I feel I know you from long back . . .' She paused, the dark eyes looking at Luisa's intently.

'From long back?' Luisa stared at her in confusion. 'I don't think that . . .'

'You misunderstand me. From Giulio. We are friends, you see, Giulio and I. For a long time—eight years, ten years maybe. Maybe more. I am his *confidante*. Oh, I know all about you, Luisa—Giulio told me. And so I am very happy for you now. *L'amore primero* . . . how do you say that? First love? The strongest and the best, and people say it never lasts, do they not? Pouf! Here today, gone tomorrow.' She laughed throatily. 'What do people know? Nothing! Sometimes it is like that, and sometimes . . .' She broke off, her face softening. 'I met my husband when I was twelve;

our marriage was arranged by our families. I fell in love with him—some time. Who knows when exactly these things happen? Who can catch the moment when the heart changes? After this, I do not look at another man, never. Not once.' She smiled up at Luisa impishly. 'Not even at your Giulio . . . not really.'

Luisa was staring at the Principessa in silence. The drift of her words was clear, yet they made no sense. Unless . . . Suddenly she felt a wild hope lift her heart. The Principessa had taken her hand, was pressing it painfully against the heavy rings, her old cracked, vital voice running on in a torrent of words.

'So I am happy for you, little Luisa. And for Giulio also. I am a stupid old woman, you see? A romantic. I like the happy ending. It makes me weep.'

Impulsively, Luisa half turned, searching the crowded courtyard for Julius's tall dark figure. The Principessa followed her gaze and laughed.

'You look for Giulio? It is only natural. Leave me now, my dear. We shall talk again. Over there perhaps . . .' she gestured across the terrace, 'you will find him.'

'Thank you.' Quickly Luisa turned, and pressed the old woman's hand. Their eyes met in a glance of total understanding, and Luisa felt courage, sureness suddenly charge her heart. She would find Julius now. She would tell him what she felt—now. No more hiding.

She lifted her chin, moved confidently through the press of people, her eyes searching. He had been beside her just a moment ago, he couldn't have gone far . . . She threaded her way through the crowd, circling the terrace, impervious to the curious glances that followed her. The band struck up a waltz, and then suddenly she saw him. She froze, stopped dead in her tracks, the blood suddenly cold in her veins.

He was there, at the far end of the terrace, leaning against a pillar, his face half in shadow. Beside him was a woman; she was tall; her thick dark hair was swept up in a heavy coil at the base of her long beautiful neck. She was wearing a white dress of thin chiffon that clung to every line of her perfect body. Their heads, both dark, were bent closely together, and as Luisa watched the woman suddenly laughed, reached up and touched Julius's hair, with a gesture utterly casual, yet curiously intimate. It might have been the woman she had once seen leaving his house. It might have been another. She couldn't be certain. All she knew was that a sense of bitter outrage, of betrayal, a bitterness so violent and cold gripped her heart that she was incapable of movement.

She stood still, telling herself she was being foolish, ridiculous. Then just behind her, she heard a man's voice; American. It sounded slightly drunk.

'Who's that guy with Vittoria?'

There was a pause, then a woman answered him.

'It's that lawyer, isn't it? The one who's so thick with the Principessa? What's his name? Morrell . . .'

'That's Morrell?' The man sounded as if he viewed Julius with sudden interest. 'I heard about him—he's all over the papers. But I thought Cardinale said he just got himself married.'

The woman laughed. She said something Luisa could not hear, and the man drew in his breath sharply.

'You don't say? That was him? You mean he and Vittoria . . .'

Quickly Luisa moved away, her cheeks burning. She slipped through the crowd, finding an empty space, a quiet refuge on the edge of the crowd. Looking back, she saw Vittoria say something to Julius. She gestured to the dance floor. Julius seemed to hesitate, looking round, then he laughed. Together they walked forward; his arms came around her.

As Luisa watched they began to dance, slowly at first, Vittoria's white dress spinning out around their feet, as they spun, glided over the floor. They looked beautiful; they danced perfectly, their two dark heads close together. One of Vittoria's arms, pale in the light, rested across Julius's dark shoulders. Luisa watched them, dry-eyed, as they circled, circled, to the beat of the waltz. The pain was so intense she felt as if her heart split in two as she watched them. Everything else was blotted out: the other dancers, the crowd on the terrace, the *palazzo* itself, the night sky, still heavy and leaden with the threat of storm. She saw only that tall dark figure, and the woman in white, moving together in perfect unison on an empty dance floor.

It was Julius's bargain, she thought. Exactly what he had said, exactly what he had predicted. And yet it was not, for the last two days, last night . . . this afternoon, in his bed, he had said . . . But what had he said? Dully her mind looked back: that he wanted her, never that he loved her. It was as simple as that. *Le diable au corps.*

And then suddenly she could bear it no longer. She turned on her heel and rushed blindly through the crowd, searching for a doorway for some escape, a way out, knowing only that she could not bear to be there any longer, to hear the sniggers, the innuendoes, the mockery.

At the side of the terrace she saw suddenly a dark passage. There was no one there, it was hardly lit. She turned down it.

Almost immediately the passageway turned a sharp corner, and branched off. Not thinking where it might lead, where she was going, Luisa rushed blindly on. It was leading her away from the dance floor, from the terrace, and the sounds of the music were growing fainter. The walls on either side of her were stone; the stone-flagged floor and the arched low roof made the sound of her feet ring and echo behind her. It was cold; the air was suddenly chill, and as her bare arm brushed against the walls she felt them clammy with damp. Then, suddenly, she heard water, and realised where she was. The narrow passageway opened out, and she came to an abrupt halt, leaning back against the cold wet walls, her breath coming sharply, painfully in her chest. She was in a boathouse; a few feet in front of her water slapped against stone; it was black, glistening like an oil slick in the thin light that filtered through the iron gates out to the canal. Tethered to rusty iron rings were two black gondolas; they rose and fell, silent on the slap of the water, their tall prows hooked and vicious. Their seat cushions had been lifted out; they were stacked neatly to one side of her, on a tarpaulin to protect them from the damp. Luisa shivered, suddenly, unaccountably afraid. She could still hear the music, just. But the wide dark space echoed more loudly to the dry gasps of her breath; her own heart thudded in her ears.

Then she heard the footsteps. They were coming down the passage she had taken; they paused, hesitated, then came on more swiftly. In a sudden unreasoning spasm of terror she pressed herself back in the shadows, feeling the cold damp stone chill through her thin dress. She forced herself to keep still, held her breath. The footsteps were louder now. They broke into a half run. Then suddenly they stopped. Whoever it was had reached the entrance to the boathouse; there was silence.

Someone was standing in the entrance; not moving, as if listening intently. Then a man spoke; his voice low.

'Luisa? I know you're there. I saw you leave. Where are you hiding?'

She felt her throat suddenly tighten, constrict with fear. She knew it was foolish, but she could not answer.

'Luisa?' His voice was little more than a whisper. It echoed eerily on the water. 'You'd better come out, otherwise I shall have to come and find you . . .'

She froze, desperately pressing herself to the wall. In that instant there was suddenly a low grumbling roar, as if the sky were falling in. It built, climaxed in a crash that seemed to shake the walls around her. After it, the silence was total. Then, outside, lightning arced. It lit up the boathouse, for a split second, with a brilliant blinding light; for one incandescent moment she saw. Damp walls green with slime; arches receding. And outlined against the walls, edged with light, the tall dark figure of a man, looking now directly towards her. Her own arms in the black velvet gleamed for a second, white, like a picture in negative. He had seen her, and she stepped forward as the light shut off.

'Julius?' she said.

She smelled the whisky on his breath, and knew, in the split second before he laughed softly, before he spoke.

'No,' he said. 'Not Julius, Luisa. Kit.'

# CHAPTER EIGHT

LUISA stood frozen, staring at him, not speaking. It was as if her tongue clove to the roof of her mouth. Fear trickled over her skin, like sweat. Kit came quite close to her, not touching her, and stood looking down at her, his mouth smiling, his eyes in shadow. With some sixth sense, she knew he sensed her fear, as if he could smell it.

'Well, aren't you going to say something? Aren't you surprised? A little word of welcome, perhaps?'

Involuntarily she stepped back. The walls pressed against her.

'What are you doing here?' Her voice came out more strongly than she would have expected, but still it sounded weak, shaky. He laughed again, and fumbled in his pockets. He must have taken out a cigarette for he lit it, and for a second as the lighter flared she saw his face clearly, lit from below, so the planes of his face appeared distorted, twisted.

'I came to see you. Isn't that obvious? I mean, I was loath to interrupt the honeymoon, especially since I'd made sure that you and Julius should have a proper chance to get together ...' He paused. '*Such* peculiar arrangements my brother had made. Separate rooms—not like a honeymoon at all. Not like a marriage, even. We can't have this, now can we? I thought. So I decided I would play Pandar—see what happened. And then curiosity got the better of me. Terrible, isn't it, Luisa? But then I was always curious, if you remember. And so I just had to come out and see how you both were. You—and my dear brother.'

He stepped a little closer, and the reek of whisky on his breath almost suffocated her.

'You're drunk!'

He laughed again. 'Very probably. Just a little. Just enough. I often am. No need to be alarmed, Luisa. I'm extremely solicitous for your welfare—that's why I'm here.' He paused, looking down into her pale upturned face. 'I had thought I might pay you a nice formal little visit at your hotel. I did call a couple of times, but whenever I enquired there seemed to be *strict* instructions you shouldn't be disturbed. I wonder why, Luisa? And so, I thought, I know, I'll pay the happy couple a little social visit, tonight, at the Principessa's. Marvellous, isn't it, how easy it is to find out my dear brother's movements? But then he's a famous man, of course. All Venice seems to know his whereabouts. Do tell me, did you enjoy Torcello?'

Luisa stared at him in silence. He laughed again, and inhaled deeply on the cigarette, the glow lighting his face again for a second. In the distance, further away, thunder growled.

'What do you want?' She forced her voice out, trying to make it sound firm, unafraid. As she did so, she turned her head a little to one side, wondering if she could just push past him, between the wall and the water. Instantly he moved, lurching sightly, so he blocked her path.

'What do I want?' He smiled mockingly, his features shadowy, gleaming with a silvery sweat in the darkness. 'I wanted you to know the truth, Luisa, what else? I think you should do, don't you?'

'The truth?' She stared at him, frozen by the menace in his voice, and felt fear prickle along her spine.

'About why Julius married you—among other matters. I always think the wife has a right to know these things don't you?'

'No, I don't.' Suddenly she felt strength return to her. She tried to push him aside, but he was immovable, rocklike. 'I don't want to listen to anything you have to say, Kit.'

'But you're going to.' He leaned forward, with a sudden movement, lifting his arms so his hands, palms resting against the walls on either side of her, were trapping her.

'Didn't it all strike you as a little peculiar, Luisa? Well, of course it did. I'm surprised a woman of your intelligence should go along with such a thing. Unless, of course, it was what you really wanted all along—to marry Julius. There is that possibility.'

'Get out of my way!' Fiercely, surprised by her own strength, Luisa pushed at him. Instantly he caught her wrist; he twisted her arm up and back behind her, so she cried out in sharp pain; then he pushed her roughly back against the wall.

'Don't do that.' He jerked her arm again, so pain shot through her like a knife. Kit smiled, his face lowered close to her own. 'I might hurt you if you make me angry, Luisa, and we don't want that, do we, not you and I? Now,' he straightened, still holding her tightly, 'a few explanations. They involve your precious sister, so I'd listen if I were you.' He saw her tense instantly, knew he had her attention now, and his hold on her slightly slackened.

'I don't know, but I'd take any wager that dear little Claudia didn't quite tell her gullible sister the truth. Did she tell you that we'd had an affair, she and I? Not a long one nor a particularly successful one. But then it was never Claudia I really wanted. She was very much second best.' He leaned forward, so his breath, sweet with whisky, enveloped her. 'Though I admit it gave me a kick sometimes, in bed with Claudia, pretending it was her sister . . .'

'You're foul! Let go of me . . .' Luisa struggled desperately to free her arm, her eyes blazing at him. Then, realising suddenly that he liked her to struggle, she stopped. In the dim light she could see his eyes now, and she saw in them something she recognised in the far recesses of her mind; something that filled her with a slow sick dread, a fear that welled up inside her out of the past. It flared in his eyes, that rapaciousness. Then, as quickly as it had come, it went. He looked at her coldly.

'Little Claudia and I came to a few arrangements then. Business arrangements shall we say? You see, Luisa, until my dear brother came on the scene, I had an interesting little sideline going—a profitable one. So easy, you see, in these inefficient old-fashioned family firms, especially when one's father is half in his dotage, and one happens to be the trusted son and heir . . .' He smiled. 'I like money, you see, Luisa. More than one is likely to receive from a solicitor's salary. And your little sister likes it too. So we had that in common. When I suggested to dear Claudia that she could be helpful to me, that she might like a little piece of the action, as our American friends would say, she was *very* quick to agree. And as it turned out, quite able. Until Julius arrived, and she panicked, of course.'

He paused, looking down at her, his eyes glittering like water in the darkness. Beyond, somewhere, the storm circled. Luisa heard thunder roll; for a second, but more weakly than before, lightning flashed.

'All might have gone well, even so, if you hadn't interfered.' He laughed softly. 'And predictably, of course, you went to Julius, didn't you?'

'I . . .' She hesitated, and he interrupted her.

'Well, then I was really in trouble. Because mixed though my feelings about Julius are, I have to admit he is rather intelligent. I don't know what Claudia said to you, or what you said to Julius, but before you could draw breath my dear brother had been through the accounts, and there it all was, as clear as daylight. *Rather* a lot of money. And most of it residing in wicked Kit's bank account. Now wasn't that a terrible thing? The family honour was suddenly involved, and Julius is rather keen on honour, have you noticed?'

Luisa drew in her breath sharply. An odd familiar fear crawled against her skin. 'I don't believe you,' she said fiercely, her voice low. 'You're lying. And anyway, this has nothing to do with me . . .'

'Oh, but it has everything to do with you. Why do you think Julius married you? Oh, come, Luisa, don't tell me you still cherish all those foolish notions of yours about a childhood romance? Did you think, at the back of your sweet innocent little mind, that perhaps Julius loved you? Was that it? I'm sure he didn't say so, did he? Julius is terribly righteous about these things. He might quite like to go to bed with you, of course, given the opportunity. It might make a nice change from women like Vittoria . . . but love? Oh no, Luisa. It's quite simple. Julius married you to shut you up.'

'*What?*' She stared at him, mesmerised by the soft insidious threat in his voice, its secret whisperings, and in spite of herself, she could not close her mind to it.

Kit laughed again, and moved a little closer, so his chest pressed lightly against her, his face a few inches from her own.

'But of course. What did you do, Luisa? Threaten to expose the whole thing, go to the police? That's just the sort of thing you would do, wouldn't you? And you see, that was the last thing Julius wanted. Because Julius, you see, had decided to hush the whole thing up. He told me so, Luisa. He was very angry. Julius is rather frightening when he's angry, don't you think? But he had some strange idea that he had to protect us. Not me, of course, he hates me—I can't think why—but our father. He got terribly melodramatic about that, said it would kill him if he found out. Well, I didn't argue, needless to say. Julius was to pay back most of the money, because I'd been rather extravagant. And I was getting off scot-free. Rather a good arrangement, I thought, in the circumstances. *Much* better than a cell in Wormwood Scrubs. There was only one problem, Luisa. You.'

'That's not true!'

'I'm afraid it is. Julius knows you, you see. He knew once you'd married him that even if you found out, you'd keep quiet, out of loyalty to him. You'd do anything he said once the ring was on your finger. He knew that. You're pliant, aren't you, Luisa? You always were. Pliant.'

As he spoke he suddenly twisted her arm again, sharply, so she cried out. With a little almost teasing jerk, Kit pulled her tighter against him, so she could feel the hardness of his thighs pressing against her own. He lowered his face, so their mouths were close, and with a sick disgust she realised it was arousing him, the pain he caused her, the fact that she could not free herself.

'Luisa.' He nuzzled his mouth wetly against her neck, bent her body back so her breats were lifted, pressed against him. She struggled, a sudden blinding fear of him pounding through her body, and he pulled her tighter, so he could hold her arms pinioned behind her back. With his other hand he reached up, pawing at the thin material of her dress.

'Come on, come on.' He rubbed his body up against her, pushing his thigh between her legs. 'Come on!' His voice was coarsened suddenly, his breath coming fast. 'I know what you want. I've always known what you want. You're like your mother, aren't you, Luisa? She was nothing but a whore, and you're not much better. Come on. Don't you remember, Luisa? All those years ago, in Scotland—even then. And you were only fifteen . . .'

'Get away from me!' Desperately she tried to kick out at him, and with a quick movement he smashed his palm flat across her face.

'I told you, don't do that!'

Her head reeled back against the stone; pain seared through her skin. Kit reached his hand to her hair, jerking her head back, pulling it so the pain brought tears starting to her eyes. She stared at him, unable to speak, as her mind began to race, as old images, jumbled and imprecise, seemed to accelerate through the recesses of her mind.

'What are you going to do, scream? No one will hear you. But just in case . . .'

He slid his hand round the base of her throat, half choking her, and then up, so the damp palm covered her mouth. She couldn't breathe. Air choked in her throat.

In that instant she remembered. Something must have shown in her eyes, because she saw him smile.

'So, you do remember. I thought so. You put up a pretence then, of course. Fought me off, didn't you? But I wasn't deceived. That's the way you like it, isn't it, Luisa? Isn't it?'

With a sharp pull he half lifted her off her feet, and then he was pushing her, pushing her back and down. Her leg twisted under her, and she fell, hard against the wet stones, so her head was against the pile of black cushions from the gondola. Kit laughed.

'Please . . .' she heard herself say. 'Please, Kit, don't, don't . . .'

'Shut up!' He smacked her hard across the face again, so the pain was like red light behind her eyes. She screamed. The sound echoed, beat back off the walls, terrifyingly loud. For a second both of them froze.

Then his mouth came down on hers, silencing her. His hand wrenched her head so she could not turn away. Her skin was wet, blood mixed with saliva, and she felt as if she were suffocating. Instinctively, with the force of fear, she reached her arms up around him, reaching for his hair, trying to pull it, to wrench him off her, trying to scratch at his skin, his eyes. Her mind seemed to be working very slowly, in a dream state of slowed consciousness; each second was like an hour. He was winning, she could feel it; he was sapping her strength; pain numbed her muscles. With some odd part of her mind she saw it all as if from the outside, with a hideous clarity; this awful parody of an embrace. Summoning her last reserves of strength, she clawed at his skin.

His breath was so loud in her ears that she heard nothing. Then, quite suddenly, without sound or warning, as if by a miracle, Luisa felt his weight pulled off her. He was off balance, still on his knees; she saw him raise one arm as if to ward off a blow. The lightning flashed, and she saw Julius.

He had Kit by the neck, wrenching him back and up to his feet. In that second of clarity she saw Kit stand, the two dark bodies sway together. Neither spoke, but suddenly as the dark came again the stones were loud with the sound of their breathing. They struggled; she could not move; her breath came in long shuddering gasps; she felt blood, or perhaps water trickle over her face; pain was clouding her eyes.

The thunder rolled, overhead again, immensely loud, and almost at once came the lightning. It lit them up for a second, the two black figures, their shadows huge and distorted against the walls, their arms locked together as they fought. Then, in the second before the dark came again, Luisa saw Julius break free. His arm came back. The light went, and she heard the crack of the blow. Dimly she saw Kit's body reel back, lifted off its feet by the force with which he had been struck, then he fell, very slowly it seemed, crumpled, awkward. He slumped back against the wall, slid down against the wet stones, and Julius stood above him, towering, motionless, watching him fall. Luisa gave a cry of fear, and as the lightning flashed again, Julius turned slowly towards her. Kit did not move.

'Julius!' she cried out, jerking herself upright.

He stood looking down at her, not moving, looking at the dress pulled up over her pale thighs, the black velvet ripped across her breast.

'Do you think he's dead? Is that what you're afraid of?'

The hatred in his voice cut off the words she had been about to speak.

'You needn't be concerned. He's not dead. I wish you were.'

Pain more acute than anything Kit had inflicted twisted in her heart. Tears burned and blinded her eyes.

'Get up. I can't bear to look at you.'

'Julius, please . . .' With pain she manged to stand, and reached out to him. 'It's not as you think . . . let me explain . . .'

'I don't want to listen to your filthy lies.' He cut her off, his face pale with anger, the dark eyes blazing coldly at her. 'You and Kit began something once, and obviously you both decided to finish it off.'

'That's not true!' She swayed, and she saw him make a tiny half-movement towards her, then draw back.

'Here.' With a quick movement he took off his jacket and tossed it to her. 'You'd better cover yourself with this. At the moment you look like what you are.'

She stared at him for a moment, and then slowly bent and

picked up the coat. Carefully, slowly, trying to keep her hands from trembling, she wrapped it around herself.

'Right, now listen to me. I shall take you out the back way. I'll take you back to the hotel. Then I never want to lay eyes on you again. Never. Do you understand?'

'Julius . . .'

'Don't touch me!'

He turned, without looking back, and disappeared through the archway. For a moment Luisa stood still, paralysed, trying to understand. Memories mixed and jumbled in her mind; she felt an aching numbness, a void. Flashes of words came to her; from the past, from now. From what Kit had said. An image of a perfect couple spinning to a perfect waltz and a white dress belling out on the air passed before her eyes. Kit stirred, and gave a low groan. She followed Julius.

No one saw them leave; the Principessa's gondolier ferried them back across the lagoon as impassively as he had brought them. Julius never spoke. In the hotel he hurried her to the stairs, pushing her ahead of him, as if he could not bear that anyone should see her. Only when they were in the room and he switched on the lights did he seem, for a second, to hesitate.

The tears were coursing down her cheeks unstoppably; she clenched her hands, but she could not stop them shaking. She saw him look at her face, and thought, surely he will understand now—there must be bruises, blood on the skin. She turned her eyes to him pleadingly, and instantly she saw something shutter in his face.

'I told you once before, don't look at me like that.'

He turned brusquely away, pulling open drawers, throwing back the doors of the tall wardrobe. In silence she watched him pull out a case, and begin to thrust clothes into it. She watched numbly, her mind seeming to work very slowly, as if the pain she felt concussed her. Then, on the upper shelf inside the wardrobe, pushed to the back, she noticed something. She stood up.

'That's my suitcase,' she said. 'Mine. The one that was lost . . .'

Julius paused for a second, following the direction of her gaze. Then he smiled grimly.

'Yes. I lied, I'm afraid. I put it there.'

'You did?' Somehow, although she knew it was trivial,

unimportant at such a moment, she could not divert her attention from it.

'Yes. I wanted an excuse to buy you something. Stupid, wasn't it? But then I didn't realise you came so cheap.'

His words were like a blow on the face. But they had the effect of freeing her mind from its numbness. Suddenly she felt a wild rush of anger, at his callousness, his injustice.

'Look at me, Julius!' She cried the words, and moved quickly to him, pulling him round so he had to face her where she stood reflected in the long mirrored doors. 'Look at my face, for God's sake! You can't think I went through that willingly!'

He looked coldly at her reflection.

'Oh, come on, Luisa,' he said quietly. 'We know you bruise easily, don't we?'

He turned away, slammed the case shut, lifted it, turned to the door.

'Julius, please . . .' She reached for his arm, and he shook her off. 'Where are you going?'

'That's none of your business.'

'I'm your *wife*!'

'Not any more.'

He strode across the room without a backward glance, and impulsively she went after him.

'Please, Julius. You can't go—not now, not like this . . .'

'Can you think of some reason I should stay?'

Luisa stopped, suddenly ashamed of her own pleading. She drew in her breath.

'No,' she said fiercely, forcing her voice not to break, 'I can't. Why should you stay? But at least don't pretend. Don't lie. I know where you're going anyway. You think me such a fool. You're going to Vittoria, aren't you?'

Julius stayed absolutely still for a moment, his face darkening.

'Just like your mother,' he said finally, his voice very deliberate. 'Slut. With a slut's imagination.'

He turned back to the door.

'Here's your key,' he said. He tossed it contemptuously across the bed. 'Keep this reservation. I'll pay the bills here. After that, make your own arrangements.'

Then he went out, and slammed the door.

# CHAPTER NINE

ALONE, the room rang with silence; memories clamoured in Luisa's head. In the bathroom she was violently sick; she could not stop herself shaking, could not control the jumbled flow of her thoughts. She made herself bathe her face with cold water, but she could not bear to look at herself in the glass. Then, trembling with exhaustion, she took off the dress, left it lying on the floor, and lay down between the cool sheets. The room spun, dipped before her eyes; she closed them and sleep came at once, heavily, like a faint, with no dreams she could remember to disturb it.

But in the morning when she woke, then she remembered. The past came back to her, clearly ordered, unravelling itself behind her eyes. She watched it as she might a film, coldly, dispassionately. Each frame in the playback was familiar; it had been there, she knew now, locked away in her mind, but before she had seen only fragments, glimpsed the edges of the images.

She and Julius had come back from the moors; it was the same evening. It had grown humid, the air heavy with electricity, the promise of storm. That evening, before supper, she had been alone in the house. Julius had driven down to the station to collect the week's mail; Aunt Con had taken Claudia to visit the ghillie whose croft was a few miles away; Kit had gone out, no one had seen him since morning. The house was still; happily Luisa had walked from room to room, thinking of the afternoon, of the evening ahead, watching the sun sink towards the horizon at the head of the loch. She had been thinking, I love Julius and when I grow up I shall marry him, and everything will be different, no unhappiness, no wavering, no lies. She had gone upstairs to her room, where the window-glass was gold from the setting sun, and had lain on her bed, her chin resting on her hands, watching the swifts dart and circle over the surface of the loch. The water had looked like gun metal; it gleamed, it was without ripples.

She had not heard Kit come in; perhaps he had stood in the doorway some time, just watching her. She never knew, until some sixth sense had told her, suddenly, that she was no longer alone. She had not liked him, even then. He repelled her; she hated the way he looked at her, the stupid pointless little lies he told, the way his eyes shifted away from you, looked always askance, slyly. So then, though there was no reason to be afraid, she had started, moving quickly, rumpling the white bedcover, pulling her skirt down over her long bare legs. And Kit had laughed. After that it was all in slow motion—Kit coming across to the bed, putting an arm round her, holding her so she couldn't move, and talking, talking, in that insidious teasing way he had. Telling her things, horrible things, about her mother, about her, about how he had watched her with Julius that afternoon.

Then he had put his hand on her leg, had slid it up, under her skirt, stroking her thigh. She remembered the outrage she had felt, the shame and the anger, and his sensing it, his pleasure in it; the mean predatory dart of light in his eyes. She had tried to push at him, realising in that moment how weak she was compared to him. It was then, quite deliberately, slowly, he had put his hand flat over her mouth, pushing her down and back on the white cover, laying his weight on her, reaching up with his other hand, under her thin shirt to her bare skin, the swell of her breasts. All the time he had talked, his mouth against her ear, the same words over and over again, like an insane litany thick with hatred. Hatred of his parents, of her mother, of Julius, of her. The hatred excited him, even in her innocence she could sense it. She writhed under him, trying to free herself; it was then that Julius had found them.

He had just stood there, in the doorway, his face white, holding the letters he had brought, not moving.

And Kit had lied—so well, so fluently. In a second he was off her, looking flushed, embarrassed, repentant. It was her fault. She had led him on, she had brought him up here, when the house was empty. It wasn't the first time, she was always begging for it. He was sorry. He had lost control. Surely Julius would understand? Like mother, like daughter. He had pointed at Luisa, as she lay there, unable to speak, and Julius had hit him.

Later that night, Aunt Con had taken her aside. One of the letters Julius had brought was from Italy. Their mother was ill; Luisa must be brave, for Claudia's sake. The doctors were doing their best, but there could be no cure, only the briefest of postponements.

'What's wrong with her?' she had asked.

'Leukaemia,' Aunt Con had answered directly in her gruff way.

'Leukaemia?'

'Yes. It's a disease of the blood.'

'And how long?'

'Six months at most. Probably less.'

She had not cried. A disease of the blood. The headache had started then. Aunt Con had sent her out to the kitchen for aspirin, and she had stood there a long time, grateful for the cold air against the heat of her skin, trying to cry. She ought to cry, she knew that. It was what people did. But the tears would not come. She had just stood there, watching the peaty water swirl and drain away in the stone sink, unable to move, unable to think. From the drawing-room down the hall she could hear the low murmur of voices, and she knew Aunt Con must be telling Julius what had happened. Pain blazed behind her eyes; every movement of her head hurt her. She swallowed the aspirin, then, crossing the room, switched out the light.

In the hall, as she was halfway up the stairs the door of the drawing-room opened, and Julius came out. Both of them stopped simultaneously, and Luisa just stood, her hand on the banister, looking down at his pale face, upturned to her in the shadows.

They seemed to stand like that for ever; then Julius spoke.

'I'm so sorry, Luisa . . .'

Maybe he was referring to the news of her mother; maybe to what had happened that evening in her room; maybe both. She had no way of knowing; she did not want to know. She had turned away coldly.

'I'm going to bed,' she had said stiffly. He made no move to stop her. Upstairs, Claudia was half asleep, but she opened her eyes drowsily when Luisa came in.

'What's happened?' she asked sleepily. 'Something has. Everyone looks cross and horrid, and Kit's cut his face, and when Aunt Con opened her letters she went white. I saw her . . .'

'Mummy's ill.' Luisa knelt down quietly by her bed.

'Very ill, or just a bit?'

'Quite ill.' She chose her words carefully. 'We shall have to go and see her.'

'What is it?' Claudia struggled to sit up. Luisa hesitated.

'It has a long name,' she said gently. 'I can't explain. It's a kind of disorder of the blood . . .'

Claudia's eyes widened.

'Like the Russian princes had? We did that at school. Hem . . . him something—when they couldn't stop them bleeding to death?'

'No, not like that at all.'

Claudia lay back.

'Can we get it?'

'No, of course not. Why should we?' Luisa pressed her hands across her eyes.

'Well, you said it was in the blood. We're her daughters. We might get it too. Like the Russian princes did . . .' Claudia's eyes widened in anxiety.

'I promise you not. No, we can't. Now, try and sleep. You mustn't worry.'

'Shall we go and see her?'

'Yes. The doctors are sending her back to London for treatment.'

'I shall like that.' Claudia settled back on the pillows. 'I like seeing Mummy. She's beautiful, I think, and she smells lovely and she wears such pretty clothes.' She smiled, a sudden sly look coming to her face. 'Kit says she's wicked, though.'

'Kit does?' Luisa stared at Claudia as the pain beat behind her eyes.

'Out on the boat the other day. He told me. He says she's wicked because she doesn't live with Daddy. Because so many people fall in love with her.' Claudia grinned, her wide mouth parting in a kittenish smile. 'I told him it was silly. It's nice to have people in love with you. When I grow up I shall have lots and lots, just like Mummy. I told him so . . .'

Luisa stood up abruptly.

'You must go to sleep now,' she said. 'We shall have to leave in the morning.'

In her room the heat felt stifling. Even when she opened the window there seemed to be no air. Her skin felt sticky with sweat, and although she washed in the ice-cold water she could not feel cool or clean. She looked at herself at last in the glass, as all the events of the day jangled together in her mind, tangling with one another. *Like mother, like daughter. A disease of the blood.*

'It's not true,' she said to the reflection fiercely. 'I'm not like her. I'm not!'

But Julius thought she was. Even then she could see the expression on his face as Kit poured out his lies could see the doubt, the revulsion come into his eyes. Guilt and shame washed over her; guilt for what she might be, shame that—even now—she could not weep for her mother, she could only fear to be like her.

In the morning she had a fever. The doctor had come; the curtains had been pulled to cool the room, she remembered that, but little after. She couldn't be moved, Aunt Con had said later. And she mustn't grieve too much that she hadn't, after all, seen her mother. The journey from Italy had been too much, it seemed to have accelerated her illness. Even if Luisa had been well enough to go, it was doubtful if her mother would have recognised her. She had been very confused at the end. Claudia had been there, that was something, and their father, and Teddy Morrell ... Luisa must get strong again. There was the funeral to be considered, although personally Aunt Con thought it would be much better if Luisa stayed here and rested ...

'Anyway,' Aunt Con had said, 'that's the last hurdle. Then you must just try and put all this out of your mind.'

'I will,' Luisa had said.

And she had done so. Until now. Until last night.

Somewhere, in that lost week of fever, of cold compresses against her forehead, of sips of water that scalded her parched throat, she must have willed herself to forget, willed it so strongly that it had all gone away, all that mixture of guilt, fear, and unhappiness. You could do that—she remembered reading about similar cases somewhere. If an event, a series of events, was so painful, so traumatic, then the mind could suppress them.... And it was true, sometimes when Julius had pressed her with his questions; when Kit had touched her arm at the wedding party ... then something had come back. But not a memory, just shadows.

Julius had been right: she had been afraid of the past, she thought. Afraid to remember what Kit had done; afraid to remember that certainty she had had then that she was tainted, that in some way she did not understand she had brought it all on herself, that it was *her* fault, Kit, even her mother's dying. She had remembered Scotland clearly only in her dreams, she thought bitterly. They took her back to the only times there she ever wanted to remember, when she had loved Julius so much and so unfearfully. But her conscious mind had remembered that, admitted that, only rarely. Mostly it had stopped at her mother's funeral, at the hatred in a pair of cold grey eyes. Hatred because of her mother, she had told Claudia, told herself.

She sighed now, looking across the darkened room, at the glint of mirrored doors, at the shutters barring the light. It had been more than that, of course. After last night she could recognise it at last. It had been hatred of herself too that she had seen, that was why that glance had been seared on her memory.

She moved her hands slowly, under the sheets, across the cold wide expanse of the bed, their bed; remembering. Could you desire someone and hate them at the same time? Yes, she thought dully, you could. Julius could.

*An expense of spirit in a waste of shame, is lust in action . . .*
From some schoolroom lesson the lines came back to her, and her heart burned as, one by one, all the memories of the past days and nights shifted, changed, became soured in recollection. She had been warned; she should have realised; she had glimpsed it sometimes in his eyes, and turned away from it. She had felt they made love; but Julius . . . What had Julius felt? She thought of the strange dark desperation in his face sometimes, and knew only that she would never understand it. Perhaps he was punishing her, or her mother, or himself, or trying to destroy the boy he had been. She would never know now, anyway. All she knew was that she, naïvely, stupidly, had imagined they were close, in that way at least, and in fact there had been a gulf between them as wide as the ocean. Turning her face to the pillow, she cried.

Later, feverishly, pacing back and forth in the room, she tried to make plans. She would stay here; then that she would return to London. That she would try and speak to him one last time, to explain, at least, about Kit, about last night. Then anger and pride dismissed that thought. Twice now he had misjudged her; if he hated her so, had such contempt, what was the point? Then, out of nowhere, came the sudden realisation. It was so obvious and yet she had forgotten it. She had no money. It had gone, all of it, to her father. She didn't have the money for a plane ticket.

No sooner had she realised that she had no means to leave than she became convinced she must. Somehow she must get money, just enough for an air ticket. She could telephone Claudia, of course, or Luke. Luke would be better. In agitation, her hands trembling, she picked up the telephone. The reception answered instantly. London? They were very sorry. They had just tried such a call. All lines to England were engaged. Would the *signora* like to try later?

'No, no, thank you. I'll decide later.'

Her hands shaking, she replaced the receiver.

Suddenly the room felt unbearable to her, its darkness oppressive, stifling. Swiftly she crossed to the windows, and threw back the shutters, letting clear light flood into the room, dazzling her eyes. As she stood there, looking out across the water, there was a knock at the door. She swung round, stiffening, but before she could speak it opened. Framed in the doorway, leaning upon a stick, was the Principessa.

'*Mia cara!*' She came into the room, and shut the door firmly behind her. Then she paused, and Luisa saw her eyes swiftly take in the tumbled bed, the damp pillows, the torn black dress still lying on the floor.

The old woman crossed to her, and took her hands.

'You must get dressed now. Pack your things—just what you need. Leave the rest, we can send for them.'

Luisa stared at her confusedly.

'Come, don't stand there dreaming.' She smiled, a wicked glint of amusement showing for a second in her dark eyes. '*Questa commedia!*'

Luisa pushed her hair back from her face and met the old woman's eyes.

'I'm sorry,' she said simply. 'I can't seem to think properly. When you knocked, I thought perhaps . . .'

'You thought I was Giulio, eh?' Her voice was dry but kind. 'Alas, no. Giulio, he has left for London, this morning. Now, you pack, I'll help you . . .'

Luisa stared at her silently, still unable to move, and the Principessa laughed.

'You have other plans, my dear? Forget them. It is all arranged. You are coming to stay with me.'

'With you?'

'But certainly.'

Luisa felt a rush of gratitude, but still something held her back.

'Does Julius . . .'

'Know about this? Of course not. It is between you and me, *mia cara*. These foolish men with their prides and their *passione*! Everything *here*,' she touched her heart, 'and nothing *here*,' she touched her head. 'What is it to do with them? When a man like Giulio is angry, he is like a tiger, yes? He prowls up and down, *so* . . .' She pulled a face. 'At such times, with such a man, one can make love, maybe. But talk, never. Leave Giulio be. Forget him for a little while. Believe me, *mia cara*—I know him. It is for the best.'

'You don't understand . . .'

The Principessa cut her off with a quick laugh.

'But of course I understand. I am an old woman. I have seen all these things before, I promise you. Oh, to you it seems very new, very painful perhaps.' She took Luisa's hand, pressing her skin against her heavy rings, her dry wrinkled palm.

'But we will not talk now. Come, pack your things.'

She took her arm, and Luisa let her lead her. Slowly, her hands curiously numb and awkward, she began to pack. She found the necklace Julius had given her, and the little card, and a small tight cry rose up in her throat like a sob. Carefully she packed them away, and left them behind in the wardrobe, with the clothes he had given her.

The Principessa turned away, looking out of the window, leaning on her stick.

'It will be a good day,' she said eventually, meditatively, her eyes scanning the horizon. 'Yesterday the storm. Today I feel the spring is coming. It was beautiful, this morning, in my garden on the Giudecca. You like gardens? Hurry, *mia cara*.'

'Then his father is ill again?'

They were sitting outside the Principessa's house, on the terrace overlooking the garden. It was evening and the smell of damp earth, warmed by the day's sun, rose up richly. In the stillness, the silence, Luisa felt for the first time that day something close to calmness; resignation perhaps.

'So Giulio said.'

Luisa looked away, avoiding her eyes, wondering if it were true. The Principessa said nothing. She was smoking, a long black Russian cigarette, inhaling deeply, her eyes on her garden.

'It is beautiful here, *no*?' She turned to Luisa with a smile. 'My husband's father, he made this garden. When I come here first it is very formal, you know? Very classical.' She wrinkled her nose with distaste. 'I do not like that too much—too much order. I like your English gardens, where there is form but also nature. Kiftsgate. You know Kiftsgate, or Sissinghurst? So lovely. I have the Kiftsgate rose, you know. There—by the wall. It is nothing now, but in the summer, so beautiful, like a bridal veil.' She laughed. 'It grows too big, of course, so I attack it. It springs up again, twice as strong. It comes from the Himalayas, yet it thrives, here in Venice . . .' She paused. 'So, will you stay here, *mia cara*? Until . . .' She broke off, and seeing Luisa turn to her, corrected herself. 'For as long as you wish.'

'If I might. Just for a while.' Luisa bowed her head. 'Thank you.'

'Giulio has told me nothing, of course.' The Principessa stood up. 'You need tell me nothing. He came here last night; you stay behind. You have quarrelled, that much is obvious.' She shrugged. 'These things happen between a man and a woman. It is not my affair. Just stay here a while, until your heart eases.'

'You think it will ease?' Luisa said quickly, before she could bite back the words.

The Principessa stood, leaning on her stick, looking down into Luisa's face, her expression suddenly more serious.

'Perhaps—who can tell? You are young. I would expect it. Here.' She drew Luisa from her chair, and took her arm companionably. 'We shall go in to dinner now, shall we? And on the way, *mia cara*, I will show you something . . .'

She led the way indoors, down a series of long arched corridors, her progress firm but slow. At the end, as they turned back into the main body of the house, she paused, lifting her stick, indicating a picture on the walls.

'You know this painting?'

Luisa shook her head, staring at it silently.

'Your mother, of course. It is a great painting, is it not? But then he was a great painter—and a very foolish young man. He was in love with her, like most of them. But he caught something most of them missed, don't you think? In the eyes, perhaps . . .'

'When was this painted?'

'Not long before she died. A year, perhaps. He died too, soon after.'

The Principessa stood still, and the two of them looked at it in silence. Luisa shivered, involuntarily.

'You don't like it? I can see why. It is very harsh, a little cruel even.'

'She looks so sad.'

'But she was sad. So much destruction, and so little to show for it. She could not give, your mother, I think. Her body, yes. But nothing from the heart.'

Luisa turned to her impulsively.

'I love Julius,' she said.

The Principessa smiled.

'But of course, I know this. That is why I show you the picture. You have not told Giulio, though, have you, *mia cara*?'

Luisa lowered her head. 'No,' she said.

The Principessa took her arm.

'Then you should,' she said briskly. 'Dare a little. Is it so hard? No one else can do it for you—and after all, what can happen? At worst, you get hurt. You get bruised.' She shrugged, and gestured back to the painting. 'It is worth it, don't you think?' She smiled. 'And now, no more sermons. *An end to preaching.* Shall we go in to dinner?'

It seemed to Luisa that time passed very strangely; hours had a will of their own. Sometimes a day would speed past, it was gone almost before she was aware of it. The next would drag interminably, and she would be possessed with agitation. There was no word from Julius, and gradually she began to force herself to accept that there would be none. Yet every time the letters were brought in, or the telephone rang, her heart would seem to stop.

There was a letter, one day, from Claudia. It was sent over from the Danieli. Luisa seized it, and hurried away with it to her room, tearing the envelope open, scanning the pages for the one name she wanted to read. But it came only at the end, when Claudia sent them both her love, and hoped they were both dancing the night away at beautiful Venetian parties. Her hands shaking, she forced herself to read the letter; but if Julius had been in England, Claudia seemed not to know it. Her letter was full of wedding preparations, of the dress she would wear, and the reception that would be held, and the tickets Harry had bought for a cruise of the Greek Islands. 'Then it's back to boring old Norfolk,' she wrote. 'I'm to have the baby there, it's decided, with the London gynaecologist in attendance, so the son and heir can give his first cries under the ancestral roof . . . Sweet, isn't it? Except I'm sure Norfolk is as dull as can be, and full of frightfully county people who can talk of nothing but horses . . .'

Luisa let the letter fall. Claudia was happy enough now, that was clear. But later? If either of them resembled their mother, it was Claudia, she thought dully. Claudia, with her restless quest for new stimulation and excitement, her sweetly obstinate refusal to consider the wishes of others. Would she continue to love Harry, three years from now? Ten years? Twenty?

But the question did not disturb her as once it would have done. She could not protect Claudia from herself for ever—in any case, perhaps there would be no need. Perhaps it was arrogance on her part to think she could help her sister anyway. She knew, in that moment, as the letter fell from her hand to the table and she stared sightlessly out of the window, that her own feelings for Julius would never change. She thought: I shall love him, three years from now. Ten, twenty—always. Just as I promised. Steadfast, she thought mockingly. And much good it had done her.

Then, suddenly, the compulsion to write to him, to reach him somehow, if only through words on a piece of paper, was so strong that she almost wrote the sentences that had been forming in her mind all these days. But just as she was about to write she caught sight of Claudia's letter, with its hope that she and Julius were enjoying themselves at Venetian parties and dances. In the instant it came back to her; Julius and Vittoria, and the slow pulse of a waltz across the warm air of a courtyard. Then she put down the pen and pushed the paper away. She could not write. Perhaps the Principessa was right, and she did not dare enough; even now.

After that, time seemed to pass even more slowly. Some days the Principessa would feel strong. On those days she would make Luisa go out. As if she were simply on holiday, the old woman took her around Venice. To the Rialto; to the market; to the Ca' d'Oro; to the Casa dei Mocenigo, where Byron had lived with Teresa Guiccioli, his last attachment. The journeys were torture to her. Each time they passed somewhere she had walked with Julius, a sense of loss so strong rose up in her that she felt the world before her fracture and disintegrate. It was less real to her than the memory in her heart.

On other days the Principessa felt weak; her arthritis would confine her to bed. Then, sometimes, Luisa would read to her, or spend most of the day alone.

'I should go back to England,' she said one day, when a week had passed.

'Not yet, *mia cara*.' The Principessa gripped her hands firmly between her own. 'You see what has happened? I come to depend on you now.'

So she let time pass. A curious inertia possessed her. She could not bring herself to write, not even to Luke, to Claudia. At least here she could shut herself away from the world; everything could be locked out, except Julius.

In the second week the weather grew warmer again; in the Principessa's garden the first bulbs, cyclamen and jonquil and wild narcissus, began to bloom. One morning Luisa picked just a few of them and took them in to the old woman. It was one of her weak days; she was lying propped up against the pillows, the great fourposter bed piled deep with books, and she smiled with pleasure at the flowers.

'*Grazie, grazie, mia cara* ...' She gestured to the windows. 'It will be a beautiful day today. You must not stay here, locked up with an old woman. I want you to promise me you will go out, Luisa. Today is a day for walking, is it not? Or just breathing the air. Say you will go now, for me.'

And so Luisa had promised, a little unwillingly. But when she had crossed the canal and stepped out on the *piazzetta*, she felt her heart lift. The air was tinged with a salt freshness; the city glittered in the light as it had done the first day she saw it. This time she did not turn her eyes away from the places she had been with Julius, she looked at them, and instead of pain they brought comfort. Almost, it was as if he were with her.

On an impulse, she walked along the quay, past the Danieli to the ferryboats, and took the one that was just leaving for Torcello. It was crowded with a party of Italian schoolchildren; they ran up and down the decks, crying out with excitement, the reds and blues of their uniforms vivid against the decks and the sea. But they got off at Lugano; she watched their teachers earnestly shepherding them into a crocodile, leading them off towards the glassworks. As the boat chugged on towards Torcello, she found herself alone.

There she clambered down, and set off across the fields, feeling the warmth of the sun upon her back, watching her shadow move before her on the straight white road. Her sense of Julius was now so strong, so powerful, that she felt that even across a thousand miles, wherever he was, it must reach him. She stopped, listening to the silence. Could the mind do that? she wondered. And standing there, in the dry flat fields, she offered up an incoherent prayer that it might. *I love him; let Julius know this*, she thought, not caring now to which deity, old or new, she addressed herself.

In the cathedral it was just as it had been formerly. Stepping into its coolness, she mocked herself for supposing it might have been different. This building had stood there for a thousand years—more, she told herself. How many women, how many men, in those centuries, had come there feeling as she did now? They were past, and forgotten and gone, but the building stood, liquiescent yet immutable, as eternal as the sea. For a moment a curious fatalism came to her. What did it matter after all? The end would be the same, no matter how fierce the grief, how sharp the lamentation in the heart.

But then, turning towards the apse, looking at the mosaic, she read again the inscription. *I am God . . . not slow to punish a fault, but at hand to aid those who waver . . .*

And suddenly all the lethargy, the fatalism, left her. She swung round sharply, staring at the empty doorway, where—before—Julius had stood. The silence was heavy. Against the opalescent glass flies buzzed. 'Julius!' she cried, her voice echoing in the stillness.

She stared at the watered marble of the great pillars, at the floor, uneven with the tread of centuries, and she felt change stir in her, perspectives shift, as if her body responded to a new tide. And she knew, in that moment, what she must do.

She must tell him, whatever happened, whatever the consequences. Nothing else mattered.

For a moment she paused, hating herself, despising herself for her own timidity, her cowardice, her poverty of spirit. Then quickly, without hesitating, she ran out of the church and across the fields.

Back at the Giudecca, she raced to the house. It was noon when she returned. The *palazzo* was shuttered against the sun, slumbrous, silent. Taking the stairs two at a time, she ran to her room, and, her hands trembling with impatience, pulled out paper, envelopes, stamps. *Julius*, she wrote. She paused, trying to order the sentences that sprang into her mind, feeling a momentary fear that now, when it most mattered, she would not be able to find the words that fitted the feelings burning in her heart. Then, fearing hesitation, she just wrote, formulating nothing. *Dear Julius, you must know. I tried to tell the air, today, in Torcello, but I must tell you. I love you so much. I have always, always loved you. And I have been so cowardly, so afraid . . .*

When it was finished she did not read it, but put it at once into an envelope, sealed it, and addressed it to his house in London. It would not bring him back, she thought, not now. But still, she had to tell him.

She took it down to the post, slipping out the side doors stealing out through the reception hall half guiltily, for she could hear voices coming from the Principessa's sitting room, but just then, she wanted to meet no one.

When she returned, feeling suddenly emptied and exhausted, as if that one impetuous action had used up the last of her vitality, there was no such escape. The Principessa must have heard her.

'Luisa? *Mia cara*, come in here!'

She called imperiously, and reluctantly Luisa stopped, opened the door. She stood there, in the doorway, staring into the room.

The Principessa was obviously much better. The look of pain that sometimes pinched her face was gone; she was gay, sitting in the sunshine that flooded through the tall windows. Beside her, on the rug, two small dark children were playing. Opposite her, leaning back, head turned enquiringly in Luisa's direction, was a beautiful woman. Again, she was dressed in white, brilliant against her tanned skin. But her thick hair was loose now, falling over her shoulders. As Luisa looked at her she pushed it back impatiently from her face, and smiled.

'Luisa . . .' the Principessa motioned her into the room, 'I have visitors, you see. I am so happy you should meet. My granddaughter Vittoria. And this is Francesca . . .' She indicated the little girl, who immediately hid her face in her mother's skirts. 'And Carlo. He is a little like me, eh? He will be a fighter, this one.' She put her arm around the little boy, who stared at Luisa curiously. Vittoria stood up.

'Luisa.' She held out her hand, and, as if she were sleepwalking, Luisa crossed to her and took it. She stared into Vittoria's face, and the other woman smiled. She was older than Luisa had realised, but very beautiful; the smile lit her eyes.

'I am so glad.' She pressed Luisa's hand warmly. 'I had hoped, the other night at the party, to meet you. I too have heard so much about you.' She paused, glancing at the Principessa. 'From Giulio.'

'How do you do?' Luisa heard her own voice come out dully, but neither woman seemed to notice. Vittoria laughed.

'We have known each other so long, Giulio and I. He is a great man, your husband. We owe him so much, my husband and I.' She turned to the Principessa with a look of enquiry. 'I may talk about it now, I think?'

The Principessa nodded. Vittoria turned back, impulsively, still pressing Luisa's hand.

'You must forgive me, but I am so happy. To be able to talk about it all openly now, after so many months. Such misery. Giulio will have told you something of that, perhaps?'

She broke off, seeing the expression on Luisa's face, and turned back to the Principessa. There was a quick exchange in Italian, which Luisa could not understand, then Vittoria laughed.

'I see. Then he has said nothing? But this is so like him. He does these things, these amazing things, but he never talks about them. He is a hero, Giulio, but an English hero perhaps, very discreet. Not like our Italians. He has not learned to boast.'

Gently she drew Luisa down so they were sitting side by side on the sofa. Then she turned to her, her dark eyes wide with happiness the light clear now on the lines of tiredness and strain around them.

'You have read in the newspapers in England of some of our troubles here in Italy, perhaps? The terrorism, the kidnappings?' She paused, her lovely face clouding for a moment. 'My husband, he is the—how do you say?—the mayor, the chief man for the province, for this area, for Veneto. We knew always that he was at risk, of course, so we took all the precautions. But they were not enough. He was taken, two months ago now, on his way to the office. They stopped his car, and the driver was shot. We had only just said goodbye. It was my birthday, and we were going out to dinner that evening...' She broke off, tears coming to her eyes, looking across the room to where her son and daughter played contentedly. The Principessa murmured something, and Vittoria nodded. 'It is true—I must not upset myself. It is over now. But you see, Luisa, still I cannot quite believe it.'

She paused, collecting herself, then went on, keeping her voice even. 'The kidnappers made terms. It was political, of course. Certain prisoners were to be released, in exchange for my husband. If not ... They made him record messages write letters. They wanted money too, naturally. That was no problem. But the Government could not agree terms. All the time, negotiations, negotiations And the *carabinieri* ... first they think he is here, in Venezia. Then no, he has been taken south. To Naples. I was in despair ...' She broke off again, glancing to the Principessa. 'And so we sent for Giulio, and he came at once. He knows Italy very well. He worked on such a case once before—an English official, from the Consulate. But now—I did not have much hope. I do not hate these people. They believe what they believe, some of them are so young, just children really.' She paused, and turned back to Luisa, who sat silently, her eyes transfixed by Vittoria's face.

'So. Giulio volunteered to be the intermediary. He took over the negotiations. It was dangerous for him, of course. If something had gone wrong, who knows what might have happened? He met with them, you know—quite alone, a month ago now. The *carabinieri* did not know, of course, they never would have allowed it. But Giulio went. He gave the terrorists the money they wanted, in person. He negotiated the terms. He persuaded them to drop some of their demands. But still, even so, we did not know, not for certain. And then, just before you came here, I think. We had a telephone call. My husband was free. They picked him up, unharmed, near Verona. It is for that the Principessa had her party, you see? For his freedom, for our re-union. And for Giulio . . .' She hesitated, her eyes looking kindly, but searchingly into Luisa's.

'You really did not know this? Giulio said *nothing*. All the newspapers . . .'

Luisa swallowed with difficulty, feeling the blood rush to her cheeks. Suddenly so many little events made sense.

'I . . . I didn't know. Nothing. I had no idea . . .' Impulsively, she pressed Vittoria's hand, guilt and self-hatred so acute she could hardly speak. 'I am so glad, so happy for you . . .' She broke off, as the tears came to her eyes and spilled down her cheeks.

A look of consternation immediately came to Vittoria's face, and she put her arm around Luisa's shoulders. The Principessa stood up, and crossed to them.

'Luisa, don't upset yourself. It is over. *Mia cara* . . .'

Luisa raised her tear-stained face.

'Why didn't you tell me? You must have realised I didn't know. And I thought . . .'

The Principessa smiled.

'But of course. But it is not for me to explain all these things. I had thought Giulio himself would return before now . . .' She paused. 'And then I thought, no, if he was not here, Vittoria should tell you. I was right, perhaps, don't you think?'

Luisa stared at her in silence for a moment, looking at her old, infinitely wrinkled face, at the sharp clever eyes, and then she nodded.

'Yes,' she said softly, 'you were right.'

'So. Now,' the Principessa straightened, briskly, 'you are friends now, you and Vittoria. It is good to have women friends. It is important when the men are difficult, when they make trouble, that there is another woman to whom one can talk. And so . . .' She paused, then said a few rapid Italian phrases to Vittoria, whose face immediately became sympathetic. She turned to Luisa with a wide smile.

'Ah, I understand now. The Principessa says you have quarrelled a little bit, you and Giulio. It is for this you cry, as well as the other. No—please, I understand. But you must not cry for this. It happens with all men. Giulio has a little of the Italian in him, perhaps. He is very jealous, very quick-tempered. It will be nothing, I promise you. Such things are of no account when two people love each other.'

There was a little silence, as if both women expected Luisa to say something, and when she did not speak, Vittoria took her hand again, pressing it.

'Luisa.' Slowly Luisa raised her head and met her eyes, which were alight with concern and gentleness. 'It hurts me you should be sad when I am so happy. When I owe Giulio so much . . .' She paused. 'You must believe me—I *know*. For instance, when all this happened, when we were still unsure how things would turn out, I went to London to see your Julius. I saw him at his house. It was the same day you were to go there to have dinner with him. He told me that he planned to ask you to marry him . . .'

Luisa flinched, and Vittoria leaned towards her.

'No, you must listen. Even then, in the midst of all these problems of mine, he was so happy, he could not hide it. He apologised to me, Luisa, that he could still feel such things, at such a time, when his friends were in trouble. But he could not hide it, you see? It shone—you can say that?—in his face, in his eyes. Then—well, I was so distraught myself, I could not take it in. I could think of nothing but my husband. But later, when I had time to think, I told the Principessa. It was extraordinary. I have known Giulio so long, and never have I seen him like this. He can appear so cold, you know? So distant. And always about him there was this sadness. But that day . . .' She broke off and smiled. 'So you see, I am sure. This quarrel, it is nothing. *Coragio*, Luisa . . .'

Shakily Luisa returned her embrace. Then she stood up. She knew only that she must be alone, must have time to think, that she could not stay in the room a minute longer, even in the face of such kindness. The Principessa seemed to sense her feelings, for she made a little sign to Vittoria, who at once stood up.

'You would like a little rest now, *mia cara*? Or a walk, perhaps?' The Principessa smiled at her. 'Vittoria wants to see my garden, and we have promised the children that they may play outside for a while.'

Luisa nodded gratefully. 'Yes,' she said quickly, 'perhaps a walk . . .' Impulsively she crossed to Vittoria, and kissed her. 'I am so happy, so glad. For you and the children.'

Vittoria laughed.

'We shall meet again soon, Luisa. With Giulio. When he returns . . .' she hesitated only fractionally, 'you shall come to dinner with us. We shall celebrate—do you promise?'

The children, sensing that the moment of release from the drawing-room had come, were crowding round her, pulling at her skirts, and it was easy enough for Luisa to avoid a direct answer, to escape.

As she left the room she saw the Principessa's dark eyes follow her watchfully, but she said nothing, and made no attempt to stay her. When the door closed behind her, muffling the cries and chatter of the children, Luisa leaned against it, in the silence of the cool shadowed hall, fighting back the tears which burned behind her eyes. All that time, and Julius had never once mentioned anything. When he had been under such stress, and she had thought only of herself; when she had seen him with Vittoria, and had imagined . . . Her cheeks burned with shame at the memory. He had been right, she thought miserably. However violently he had misjudged her, he had had some cause. What had she had? Nothing but jealousy, and a cheap imagination.

Slowly she walked out of the house, and into the soft warm light of late afternoon. Absently, not caring where she walked, she took the footpath that ran under the tall walls of the Principessa's garden, and came out at the little landing stage. There, on the edge of the canal, she could look back across the Giudecca, past the Salute church to the cathedral of St Mark, and, further along to the Riva della Schiavoni, to the Danieli. She stood there for a moment, staring silently across the water, oblivious to her surroundings, to the children playing hopscotch at the end of the quay, to the sound of the breeze rustling the trees, newly green, above her.

'Signora Morrell?'

She started and turned. It was the Principessa's gondolier, the man who had ferried Julius and herself to the Principessa's party. She knew him quite well now; he was often to be found in the kitchens, gossiping with the cook. Out of his uniform, in his work clothes, he was much less intimidating than he had appeared that first night. Now he had just finished repairing the seats on one of the gondolas. He was looking up at her with that creasing around the eyes which was the nearest he ever came to a smile.

'You would like to take a little trip, *signora*?' He gestured across the canal. 'It's a beautiful evening. To the Danieli, perhaps?'

For a moment Luisa hesitated. Then, on an impulse, she nodded.

'*Si*, to the Danieli. *Grazie*.'

He helped her down into the gondola, apparently pleased, and cast off. Then slowly he eased out of the side canal into the wide open stretch of water. They skimmed its surface, bathed golden by the low sun, crossing in silence.

At the *piazzetta* he handed her out.

'Do you want me to wait?'

Luisa looked up at the tall shuttered windows of the hotel, then shook her head. She would come back the long way, on the *vaporetto*, there was no need to wait. He shrugged, and set off back across the lagoon as silently as he had come.

For a moment Luisa stood, just looking up at the blank shuttered façade. Which of them was telling the truth about her marriage, she thought, Kit or Vittoria? And when should she have believed Julius himself; when he spoke with such apparent hatred, or when he touched her, so tenderly, in the long hours of the night?

Suddenly she was possessed by an aching desire to see again the room in the Danieli, as if it might answer her questions. She stepped forward. That was the only truth of which she felt certain, she realised. What had happened in that room, what she had felt . . . The desire to see it again, to touch like talismans the things Julius had given her, sharpened, became imperative. Quickly she crossed the *piazzetta* and slipped into the foyer.

It was empty; quiet. Motes of dust danced in the slanting light through the windows. From the manager's office came the sound of voices, a typewriter; the reception desk was deserted.

Quickly, not wanting to be seen, Luisa crossed to the staircase and mounted quickly to the first floor. The room would be locked, of course, unless perhaps one of the maids . . . She put her hand on the door handle, paused, and then turned it. The door opened. She went in, and then stopped, in confusion.

Someone was there. One of the windows was closed, the other open, on to the small balcony. A light breeze fluttered the curtains, and the cries from the *piazzetta* below drifted up into the room. The wardrobe doors were open, the bed made. On it lay a man's black leather attaché case; a black jacket was tossed carelessly over a chair. She froze; staring round the empty room. Could it have been let, was someone else staying here now? Suddenly embarrassed, she turned, fumblingly, quickly, to the door, and as she did so a gust of air from the open window slammed it shut. Instantly there was a sound from the balcony; the curtains billowed and beyond them she saw the tall dark figure of a man, turning back into the room.

'Who is it?'

Even as he spoke, he saw her, and stopped. Luisa let her hands fall to her sides. She could not answer; she felt her breath tighten, constrict her chest; she could not move.

The man moved first. Bending his head slightly, pushing the curtain to one side, he stepped into the room. Then he paused, outlined against the light, his face in shadow. They stared at each other, in silence, across the width of the room. Somewhere in the distance, across the water, near yet a million miles away, a bell began to ring for vespers.

Luisa's heart lifted. Confusedly, she thought: *He knew— what I felt today, on Torcello, it reached him*. She stepped forward, quickly, holding out her hand.

'Julius . . .' she said.

Still he did not move, and her steps faltered. She stopped, about three yards before him, and their eyes met. One glance at that cold level gaze chilled her. All the happiness and joy she felt welling up suddenly shut off, cold and tight in her heart. She saw him register her reaction; knew she had gone chalk white. He gave her a cold smile.

'Yes,' he said. 'I'm sorry if that disappoints you, Luisa.'

# CHAPTER TEN

AT that, something broke inside her. She rounded on him, feeling tears of anger start to her eyes.

'Stop it!' she cried. 'Stop it Julius! I won't let you say those things, I won't let you think them—not any more!'

Her vehemence startled him, she could see that. She saw his mouth tighten, and she knew he was about to interrupt her, so she rushed on, willing her voice not to break.

'No, you won't say anything. You'll listen to me! I swear I ... I won't let you leave this room. Not this time. Not until ...'

His mouth lifted slightly in a wry smile. 'How do you propose to stop me!'

'Don't mock me!' She cried the words passionately, stepping forward as she did so, so they were very close. Her eyes blazed at him. It's not fair, Julius! Whatever I've done, whatever I am, at least I should have a chance to speak in my own defence. I won't have you play judge and jury like this, as well as prosecuting counsel. You're not even judging me fairly. You're judging me by the past, by things that happened years ago. And I won't let you do it. You're not even judging me, in any case, you're judging my mother!'

That charge reached him, she could see it. He stepped back a little, his eyes shadowed, and his face grim.

'Is that what you think?'

'It's more than I think. It's the truth!'

He shrugged and turned away.

'Well your mother is a factor, one can't deny that.'

'Why is she a factor?' Luisa cried hotly. 'Why? It's so unfair! I hardly knew her. She's been dead ten years. Who knows why she behaved as she did?'

'You are her daughter,' he said coldly.

'And you're Kit's brother. That hateful man is your blood brother! But I don't judge you by him.'

He swung around angrily at her words, his eyes blazing

dark in his pale face. He looked at her with such an expression of fury that it was all she could do not to flinch from him.

'You mention him to me? *Now*?' For a moment she thought he was going to hit her, and instinctively, before she could stop herself, she raised an arm before her face. Instantly he stopped, an expression of disgust on his face.

'Is that what you think? You think I'd hit a woman? Oh no, Luisa . . .' He stepped back a little, his voice cold and scathing. 'You're confusing me with my brother again. That's Kit's scene, not mine—as you obviously know by now. Oh, for God's sake,' with a violent gesture he turned away, 'get out of my sight. I can't bear to look at you!'

'I will not!'

Luisa cried the words defiantly, and they rang across the space of the room between them. They stopped him, but still he did not turn. She stood there, clenching her fists tight against her side to stop her trembling, the breath coming sharp and painfully in her chest.

'Julius, please . . .'

The fatal note of pleading had come into her voice, and it had an instant effect. He turned and crossed to her, his eyes black with hatred, gripping her arm painfully, and tilting her face up to him.

'Well, go on,' he said, his voice tight. 'What are you going to say, Luisa? What excuses have you worked out these past days? That it wasn't your fault, that you couldn't help yourself? That no sooner had you lain with me in that bed then you were itching to get back to my goddamned brother? That you didn't care how and when it happened? That you'd go with him, anywhere—on the floor like some animal—at the first opportunity? You bitch! I could kill you, do you know that? Is that what you were thinking, all the time we were together, Luisa? When you lay in my arms, when you closed your eyes, when you spoke my name? Were you imagining I was Kit—was that it, Luisa?'

He shook her violently, then wrenched her round in his arms so that she faced the mirrored doors of the wardrobe, so that she had to confront her own reflection, held tight in his arms.

'Look at yourself. Go on, take a really good look! It doesn't show, does it, not on your face, not yet. You nearly took me in, with that face . . .' His voice broke, and he pulled her round to him once more. 'That sweet face,' he said softly, looking into her eyes, and his mouth twisted with pain. 'I shall see that face in my dreams until the day I die. So sweet, so apparently good, so pure, so true . . .'

'Julius . . .'

For a second he held her against him, so she heard the thudding of his heart. With a low groan he buried his face in her hair. When he spoke, it was softly, almost tenderly, his lips against her throat.

'A virgin's face, Luisa. And the instincts of a whore.'

The word, so gently spoken, cut her like a blow. With a cry she pushed him violently away from her.

'That's not true!' she cried. 'Stop punishing yourself, Julius, stop punishing me. It's not true!'

He made an odd, swift reaching gesture towards her, and she hit his hands sharply aside.

'No,' she cried, 'don't touch me! I can't bear you to touch me when you think those things, when you believe those lies. How could you have done as you did, lain in my arms in that bed . . .' she gestured wildly across the room, her voice shaking, 'and believed all those things about me? It was wrong, Julius! Never once, not once did you ask me what happened. You never gave me even a chance to speak, not even the night when we came back here when you left, when any man who wasn't blind would have known what had happened. Even then. No! You preferred to believe your brother. You just accepted everything he said, all his filth, all his lies. I hate him! I've always hated him. But you—you, Julius, you believed him because you wanted to believe him. Because it tied up the whole equation so neatly, didn't it? Because then you could believe what you really wanted to believe all the time that I was just like my mother!' She stared at him, shaking, her eyes bright with tears. 'Why did you want to believe that, Julius? So you'd feel justified in hating me—was that it?'

'That's not true . . .' He moved quickly towards her. 'And I did ask you. In Scotland—when you just ran out the room and never said a word. I asked you in London. I tried to make you talk about it—here, in Torcello. God damn it, you knew perfectly well what I thought. When we were in that bed—when I realised it was the first time, that Kit hadn't . . .' He broke off. 'Damn you, Luisa. How many times did I have to ask you and get fobbed off with one of your evasions?'

'I couldn't *remember*!'

'How convenient!'

'It's *true*.' She cried the word into the silence of the room, and he made no answer. With a gesture of despair she spread her hands. 'Julius, I can only tell you, I have no proof. I can't bring witnesses in my own defence. There's nothing. And if you don't believe me ...' She broke off, and the silence beat in on her; for a second the future yawned before her, a great vacancy. 'Then there's nothing—no truth, between us.'

Still he was silent, not moving, just looking at her, and she drew in her breath painfully, trying to steady herself.

'Julius, what happened in Scotland—with Kit—it was him. He forced me. He came up to my room. He ... he wouldn't go away. He *talked*. He said such horrible things— about my mother, about your parents, about you. He *hates* you, Julius, really hates you. It's like a sickness with him. He'd been spying on us, when we were together that afternoon ... he told me.' She paused, forcing herself to confront the memory. 'It wasn't really me he wanted—at least I don't think so. I was just a means for him, the best way he had of hurting you, of ... of breaking something he thought you wanted ... like a toy. He touched me, and I tried to push him away. It was like a dream, so slow, I couldn't believe it was happening. And then he put his hand over my mouth ...' She broke off, and an involuntary shudder shook her body. 'Julius—if you hadn't come in then ...'

With a low muttered exclamation he moved to her side, and stood close to her, his eyes dark and angry.

'Luisa. Luisa.' He put his arms out to her. 'But you said nothing. You just ...'

'I couldn't!' She lifted her face to him passionately. 'I couldn't, don't you see? He lied so well, so quickly. I could see the doubt in your eyes. You were starting to believe him, even then, when we ... when I loved you so much!'

'Luisa ...'

'And then, that night. You brought the letters, don't you remember? And there was the news about my mother. When Aunt Con told me that ... Oh, Julius, I felt so *guilty*.'

'Guilty?' He stared at her. 'Why should you feel guilty?'

'I don't know, it was all so mixed up. I couldn't think clearly.' She felt the tears start to her eyes even now, at the memory. 'It was as if that horrible illness were a punishment, for what she had been. And I was afraid I was like her—Kit said I was, he kept saying it, over and over again. I cared more about that than her dying. I couldn't weep for her, you see. I tried, and all I could think was, please, God, don't let me be like her . . .'

Her voice broke, and with a quick gesture Julius caught her to him, holding her tight against his heart. She heard herself give a low tight sob, and she lifted her face to his.

'I never saw her again, I never saw you again, except at the funeral. And I was ill. When I got better, it was all wiped out. I *made* myself forget—Julius, can you believe that? It was as if it had never happened. Sometimes, just sometimes, glimpses would come back. When I came to your office, and I thought you were Kit, and you . . . And then after our wedding, when I saw him again for the first time. He put his hand on my arm. I felt ill, I couldn't breathe . . .' She paused, fighting to keep her voice calm. 'But I didn't remember, Julius. You must believe me. Not until I was in that boathouse, that horrible place, and he wouldn't let me go. He . . . he kept twisting my arm, laughing at me. And then he put his hand over my mouth, so I couldn't scream. And I remembered. I *saw* . . .'

'Oh God!' His arms tightened around her, and she felt his fists clench. 'I'll kill him. So help me God, I'll kill him for this!'

'Julius, no!' She reached for his hands, and held them tight. 'You mustn't think that, you mustn't feel it. Don't you see, that's all he wants—to hurt us, to hurt you?' She turned her face up to him. 'But he can't, Julius, not if you believe me. Not even if you don't. Because nothing Kit does will ever change how I feel.' Gently she reached up, and touched the harsh lines of his face, trying to erase the pain and the anger that etched it. 'I love you, Julius, with all my heart. I always have. No one else, ever—there can't be.'

He drew in his breath sharply, and his lips parted to speak, but she gently placed her fingers on his mouth, stopping his words. All fear had left her now, and she knew the conviction that flooded through her body shone in her eyes.

'Julius, I wanted to tell you before. I tried to tell you, in other ways. Without words. I would have told you, that night at the Principessa's, if I hadn't seen you, hadn't thought . . . well, you know what I thought. That was why I ran away, why I went to that horrible place . . .' She broke off. 'No, listen, I want to tell you. Today, I went to Torcello. And when I was there, it was so strong, the love I felt for you. I felt as if you were close to me, by my side. And so I came back, and I wrote to you.' She smiled. 'I sent the letter. And then I met Vittoria, and she told me everything, what you'd done. And I was so proud of you, and so ashamed of myself. I hated myself. That was why I came here. I didn't know you were here—I just wanted to be in this room. To see the things you gave me. To be close to you. To remember. Oh, Julius, I love you so much. It hurts me. Here, and here . . .'

She touched herself, showing him, and with a muffled cry, his face against her hair, he held her tight to him.

'My darling,' he said brokenly, 'my darling . . .'

'Oh, God!' She pressed her face against his chest. 'Please say you believe me, Julius. Nothing else matters.'

'You know I believe you.' He held her fiercely, tilting her face up to his. 'I've always believed you, believed *that*, in my heart. How could I do anything else? It was my only truth, the one last hope I held on to in the mess I'd made of my life, the one light in the darkness all around me. But I couldn't believe it *here*,' he struck his forehead. 'Oh, Luisa, it's been like living in hell these last years, being torn in two. There wasn't a day I didn't think of you, a night I didn't dream of you. You haunted me, Luisa, your face. And then, always, I would remember the other you. It was as if I was damned to walk into that room again for eternity, and see you, and my brother. The woman I loved so much that I would willingly have died for her sake. The woman I still loved, who was in my thoughts, in my heart, night and day for ten *years* . . .'

He broke off, seeing the expression on her face change.

'You didn't know that? You didn't realise?'

Silently she shook her head.

'But you must have done. You can't not have known. It was so strong. I tried to tell you . . .'

'I thought then. In Scotland.' She hesitated.

'But not now? Here, in Venice . . . Luisa. When we were here together, when we made love . . .'

'I knew I loved you. But I thought . . . you said . . .' Her control went quite suddenly, and she could say nothing more. Silent tears spilled over on to her cheeks. He clasped her tight in his arms.

'My darling Luisa! There's never been anyone else for me. There never can be. I had to come back, you see, and . . . Oh, God, this is all my fault. If I hadn't been so stupid, so blind—and so jealous. Come here.'

Very gently, his arms around her, he led her across to the small sofa near the windows. There he sat down beside her and wiped the tears away from her eyes. When she was calmer, he took her hands in his and looked into her face.

'Will you let me try to explain? Please, Luisa. It won't excuse what I did, how I did it. But it may help you understand . . .'

'It doesn't matter now.'

'My darling, it *does*. I want there to be no more lies, no more misunderstandings between us, ever.'

He paused, glancing away from her, out of the windows to the sea.

'In the beginning . . .' he paused, turning to her with a wry bitter smile. 'In the beginning, it was like a kind of madness. You were the one thing in my life that held any certainty, and I thought that certainty had gone. So I tried to destroy all memory of you. I did the things I suppose people do in that situation—I drank a little too much, I worked a little too long, I went with other women—too many women—and tried to pretend to myself that I could forget you in their arms. It didn't work, of course. It couldn't. It just made the pain, the loss, worse, more unbearable. So I cut myself off. I didn't see my family, not even my father. I couldn't bear to be anywhere I might hear your name spoken . . .'

'But, Julius,' gently she pressed his hand, trying to comfort him, to ease the bitterness from his voice, 'there was no need for you to have felt that, whatever had happened. We were both so young. I was just a stupid girl. It was my fault . . .'

'There was every need, and you know that's not true.' He turned to her fiercely. 'Did you imagine I didn't try and explain it all away with those kind of platitudes? They didn't apply! You weren't a girl. You might have been fifteen, but you'd gone through more by that age than some women do in a lifetime. You remember what you said to me, in London, about Claudia? 'She wanted for love,' you said. Did it never occur to you, Luisa, that you might have done too? And I loved you. I'd wanted you to know that. I still did. I wanted to be with you, to protect you, to give you back a little of the things you gave so generously to everybody else—to Claudia, to your pathetic father . . .' He broke off. 'I'm sorry, I shouldn't say that, but it was what I felt, damn it. And besides, I was so sure you had loved me. I'd seen it in your eyes, in your face, every day we were in that house together. I believed in that as I never believed in anything else in my life. It was my creed, if you like, my religion. If that was not true . . .' He broke off, pain blazing in his eyes. 'Then there was no truth. Nothing. Just a void.'

'If you'd seen me then. If you'd told me . . .' she spoke gently, and he gave a groan.

'I know. But I couldn't, don't you see? Every time I thought of you, every time I remembered how it had been between us—when it was so clear that we didn't even need words, we just *knew*—then this other image would come back to me. Of you and Kit, in that bedroom. So . . .' he drew in his breath as if to steady himself, 'in the end I came to terms with what I felt. I couldn't bear to see you, and yet I had to know where you were, what was happening to you. And I did, through my father. I knew you hadn't married. I knew where you lived, where you worked. I bought that house to be near you. I even went to the gallery once, just to see the place where you spent your days. I bought a picture from Luke.' He smiled. 'And then I put it away. I couldn't bring myself to look at it. If I had one thought, it was that I hoped you were as unhappy as I was, that you were as miserable, as haunted . . .'

'Oh, Julius!'

He gave her a wry look. 'Not very noble, I agree. But how I felt.' He paused. 'Then, quite suddenly, my father was taken ill. It became obvious that the firm was very run-down, it was inefficient. I'd known that for years. But I thought it was no more than that. The worry was making my father ill—perhaps he suspected something, I don't know. But anyway, I agreed to help. I went in, the first time, about two months ago. I started looking at the books, at the transactions the firm made on behalf of clients.' He gave a harsh laugh. 'It's ironic, really. It might have taken me far longer to see what was wrong, but as it was, the first file I took out was yours. Because it was a link, a connection, because even to see your name on a piece of paper was something. And it was all wrong, Luisa.' He turned to her, his eyes dark with anger. 'Your aunt hadn't left you that much money, but what you had was disappearing too quickly. It was being siphoned off somehow. I checked and double-checked. I went through other clients' holdings and saw the same thing.' He paused and sighed. 'I suppose I knew then, really. It could only have been Kit. He was always like that with money, even when he was a child.'

Luisa stared at him, her eyes wide. 'My money too? It's not possible!'

'I'm afraid it is.'

She lowered her eyes. 'He told me he'd been doing something like that—in the boathouse, that night. And that you knew. But he said . . .' She hesitated. 'He said Claudia had helped him all along. That she'd had an affair with him . . .'

His mouth tightened grimly. 'I don't think that's true,' he said. 'Another of Kit's lies. If Claudia had an affair with him, she's a bigger fool than I think she is. And she wasn't involved in much—more or less what she told you. It was easy to see which transactions she'd diverted. She was considerably less expert than Kit. Here . . .' he put his arms around her, as he saw her tremble, 'you mustn't worry about Claudia. She admitted what she did, and it's over now. She can make a new life . . .'

Luisa nodded. 'But . . .' she hesitated, looking into his eyes, 'that means you *knew*. Before I even came to the office, before I saw you?'

He smiled grimly. 'Oh yes, I knew. But I couldn't decide what to do. I was glad, you see, that's the worst part. Glad because it gave me a reason to see you—one I couldn't argue away. And glad because it meant I could break Kit. And then . . .' he paused, 'I knew I couldn't do that. My own motives—well, they were hardly pure, were they? I'd have been punishing Kit for what had happened with you—it would have been revenge, not justice.' He shrugged. 'And it would have killed my father, destroyed the last happiness he had. He was so proud of Kit, you see. That's the irony in all this. He was always the favourite. But he could never believe it.'

'So what did you do?'

'Nothing.' He paused. 'I couldn't decide what was right. And then—well, you know what happened. The door opened one morning, and you were standing there. I couldn't believe it.' He laughed bitterly. 'I couldn't decide who had conjured you up—some god or some devil. Until you mistook me for my brother. Then I knew.'

'So you decided to pretend to be Kit—to let me go on thinking you were?' Luisa stared at him in bewilderment.

'I didn't decide! There wasn't time. I didn't think—it just happened. I was so angry, so confused . . . The one woman I loved, a woman I would have recognised in a million, and you—you mistook me, for him. Don't you see, Luisa, it just confirmed everything, all my worst fears, all my nightmares . . .'

'So you tested me?' She looked at him evenly. 'To see if I would . . . respond. To Kit?'

'Yes, damn it, I did! But you make it sound so coldblooded, as if I planned it. It wasn't like that. I kept thinking any moment you were going to realise. That if I touched you, and I wanted to touch you so much . . . Then I thought, no, it's true. She has forgotten me. And I had to find out. Then. There might never have been another chance.'

She looked at him, and tried to make her face stern.

'I passed the test, presumably?' she said drily.

A smile began to lift the corners of his lips. 'Yes. But you failed the next one.'

'When I came to your house?'

'Certainly.'

'You mean I should have acquiesed to your extremely immoral demands?'

'You wanted to, I think.'

'I did not!' she cried in mock indignation.

'Are you sure?' Very deliberately Julius leaned across and kissed her on the lips, so she trembled. Then he drew back, his eyes dark, burning into hers.

'Quite sure?'

'Perhaps a little. No . . .' she pushed him away, 'you shan't win the argument like that. If you remember, your proposals were strictly dishonourable.'

'I was waiting for some sign, some hint. Before I expressed them more directly, more honourably.'

He paused, the pain coming back into his face. 'I couldn't understand, you see. I kept thinking that if only we could talk, about Scotland, about the past, there would suddenly be a way through. A miracle.' He lowered his eyes. 'And there wasn't.'

'So you decided to change your terms?' She forced herself to keep her voice steady, her eyes never leaving him.

'Yes, I did.' He pressed her hands. 'I wanted you so much, you see. After so long. To have you in the same room with me, to touch you, to see you. To be so close to the only thing in life I wanted, and yet so far—it was torture, Luisa. I had decided, the night you came to my house, the night you were going to . . .' He paused. 'I was going to tell you,' he said abruptly, 'the truth—that I loved you, that I wanted to marry you. And then it all went wrong, it went out of control.' He gave her a half smile, a glint of amusement in his eyes. 'You moved a little too fast for me. And then, when you started to take your dress off . . .'

Luisa caught her breath at the memory, and their eyes met, sharp with the knowledge of the desire she felt suddenly quicken in her veins. She lowered her eyes.

'You mean you did perhaps want me a little then—in spite of what you said?'

'Damn you, you know I did.' Julius reached his hand up, under her hair, caressing the soft skin at the base of her throat, and Luisa felt the old sharp pull of want for him arc through her.

'Julius . . .'

'No, wait, damn it. I don't want to either, but you shall listen.' He smiled. 'If you knew, my darling, just how much control it required then, not to touch you, here——' he moved his hands to her breasts, and she trembled against him. 'Not to kiss you.' He paused, and she saw his eyes darken at the memory. 'But your face—you looked so . . . so frightened, so scornful. I'd never felt so ashamed in my life. So guilty. I nearly gave up then. I nearly let you go. Except I couldn't. I still believed, you see, even then. Put it down to obstinacy if you like.'

'And marriage?' Luisa said softly.

'Ah, marriage!'

Very gently he took her hand, its fourth finger circled with his ring, lifting it between them, so the gold glanced against the light.

'Why did you think, Luisa?'

She hesitated. 'I thought . . . to punish me perhaps. Or yourself.'

'Oh no,' he said softly, 'not that, Luisa. There could only be one punishment for us—parting, not marriage.'

'Why, then?'

'Because I hoped still. Frailly, but I hoped.'

'Just that?'

'No,' Julius said quietly, looking away. 'Not just that.' He hesitated, and then met her eyes. 'I was also involved in all this business here, with Vittoria and her husband.' He shrugged. 'When something like that happens, death seems suddenly very close, very possible. I knew I had to come back here. Something might have gone wrong—for him, maybe even for me. It was possible. If that had happened, I wanted you to be my wife first. Then—well, whatever you felt, at least I knew you would have a safe future. You would be provided for . . .' He said it roughly, quickly, as if the thought embarrassed him, and Luisa felt her heart stir with love for him, for his goodness, his kindness, that his pride would seek always to disguise.

'Hence the haste,' he said shortly.

She raised his hand to her lips and kissed it, and saw his face relax, grow gentle.

'I'm afraid it wasn't the most romantic of proposals, my darling.'

'Not exactly, no.' Their eyes met, and Julius laughed softly.

'I played the devil's advocate. You see, I did think that if I were more straightforward, if I told you the truth, you would say no . . .'

'So you thought a little coercion?'

'I thought the ends would justify the means. Just for once. I . . .' he corrected himself, 'I hoped they might. Though as I recall you chose that moment to make it quite clear you didn't love me. That you never had . . .'

'That wasn't true,' she said quickly.

'Are you sure, Luisa?' His eyes met hers once again, and for a moment she saw doubt and pain cloud them once more.

'Oh yes,' she said steadily. 'I knew, you see, Julius. I always knew, it was just that then, after what you'd said, it was too painful to admit it. But when we were in the church . . .'

'Yes?'

'I knew then. At first . . .' she hesitated, 'at first I was so afraid. It seemed such a sin, to say those things, to make those promises. To lie—because what we had agreed would have made it a lie, wouldn't it, Julius? And I wanted to stop him, the priest, to say it couldn't go on, and then . . .'

'I took your hand.'

'Yes! You took my hand, and suddenly all the fear went away. I felt such joy, I was so at peace. I knew. That it wasn't a lie, do you understand? Oh, Julius, I meant everything I promised, everything I said, with all my heart.'

'But I did too,' he said drily, and she saw his eyes suddenly lose all their coldness and their doubt, meeting hers joyfully. 'I suppose that didn't occur to you?'

'Not then,' she said quietly.

'But now?'

'Now? Oh yes, Julius.'

'My darling!' With a low groan like pain he caught her to him, and held her close against his heart. They stayed like that, neither speaking, for a long while, quite silent, locked in each other's arms.

Then, very gently, he released her, looking at her with mock sternness.

'So,' he said, 'you'd better tell me. Where have you been this past week? When I was in England, nearly insane with worrying about you. What have you been doing, Luisa— who have you been seeing? I warn you, if you so much as glanced at any other man in that time . . .'

She laughed. 'I've been thinking about you. At the Principessa's. And don't pretend. I'm sure you told her to come here and look after me.'

'I might have done.' He smiled. 'And did she give you, perhaps, the least little hint that in spite of my behaviour it might just be possible that I was wildly in love with my own wife, that I couldn't live without her? She had strict instructions not to, of course!'

'She did hint . . . but very discreetly. And she made sure I met Vittoria.'

'And you have no more stupid doubts on that score? No jealousies? You mustn't have, Luisa. There was no cause. And now, my darling, there never will be.'

'I know that.' She looked away. 'But I feel ashamed.'

'No, my sweet love, you mustn't.' Julius drew her to him.

'Jealousy is the other side of love, it's dark face. You can't pretend it isn't there. And you know I'm equally guilty.'

She looked at him, her eyes suddenly troubled, the one last question rising up, unbidden in her heart.

'And Kit?' He took her hand. 'Is that what you want to say?'

She nodded silently, and Julius sighed.

'It's arranged. My father still doesn't know—now he never needs to. He's better, but it can't be much longer. Kit will leave the firm. He'll live abroad—I shall make him an allowance, on condition he never tries the same thing again. And never comes near you—or our family. That's all.'

'A kind of banishment?'

'If you like. But Kit exiled himself years ago. No one can reach him.' His mouth tightened. 'I imagine he'll end up very like your father. The endless expatriate; he'll drink too much and . . .' He spread his hands. 'He won't bother us again. He can't touch us now. And he knows that—I told him.'

'You told him?'

'Oh yes. In London, when he eventually turned up.'

'But then . . . then you didn't know, you thought . . .'

'Not entirely.' Luisa saw a glint of amusement come into his eyes. 'The Principessa gave me the odd hint too, you know. I couldn't be certain, but I didn't care any more. I'd decided to fight, you see. I decided the past wouldn't win, no matter what. We would.' He paused, and met her eyes. 'So I came back, to tell you.' He reached for her. 'And to take care of a few other things.'

'Julius . . .'

'No more words.'

'But . . .'

'Come here, woman.' He pulled her into his arms, and bent his head swiftly to her lips. 'Wife.' As their mouths met, and her lips parted at last under his, she heard him catch his breath sharply. 'Dear God, Luisa,' he said against her mouth, 'nearly ten days, ten nights, since I touched you . . . oh, my darling!'

His arms tightened around her, and their bodies moved together with such sweet ease. The touch of his skin, the familiar scent of his hair, the strength of his body was like a shock to her, bringing at once release from longing, and the renewal of desire. She drew in her breath shudderingly, arching her neck back so his mouth could kiss the long line of her throat, her breasts lifting to the touch of his hands. Want for him soared through her body, and with a sudden feverish need, she reached to put her hands under his shirt, to feel the warmth of his skin beneath her fingers. Gently Julius drew her to her feet, so they could stand, wrapped in each other's arms, the hardness of his body pressing against her as he kissed her. With a fierce sigh he caressed her, owning her body again with the frankness of his touch, down from her breasts to her waist, to her thighs, to the small of her back so he could clasp her there, tight against him.

'My darling, my sweet love.'

He cradled her head in his arms, lifting her face up to him, and kissing her with such a sweet tenderness that she felt her heart would break.

He drew back, just a little, so he could look down into her eyes, and Luisa saw his face, alight with a happiness she would once not have believed possible.

'My darling,' his voice was roughened, 'I want so much for us. I want you to be happy, no more sadness. I want you to have my child, to feel it move, there, inside you . . .' He rested his hand gently across the soft swell of her stomach.

'I want that too, Julius.'

'Well then, come here.'

He drew her gently to the bed, and then, his hand shaking a little, reached to undo the fastening of her dress. But she stayed his hand.

'No,' she said softly. 'This time I will.'

Slowly, deliberately, she took off her clothes, until she stood in the dying light, quite naked before him. With a low groan he bent, kissing her offered breasts; knelt, and pressed his lips against the softness of her thighs. Then quickly, urgently, he took off his clothes and lay down beside her.

They lay quite still for a moment, not touching, and then, very slowly, he reached out and touched her, running his hand up over the long curves of her body, so she cried out with desire, moving to him.

'Luisa.' He kissed her, then they lay side by side, just touching, looking into each other's eyes.

'No more quarrels,' he said. 'No more lies. No more misunderstandings. Not between us, my darling.'

Luisa shook her head, then laughed, softly, her lips against his throat. Instantly he caught her, forcing her to look at him, his eyes fiercely suspicious.

'Why do you laugh? What are you thinking?'

'Nothing.' She looked at him teasingly. 'I just wondered if you were suggesting you'd never be angry . . .'

'Oh, why?'

His grip on her tightened.

'Because the Principessa told me what we should do if you were, that's all.'

'And what was that?'

'She said we should make love.'

'Only then?'

Julius shifted suddenly, so his weight was on her, his eyes mocking her, imprisoning her in his arms.

'Well, perhaps not *only* then . . .'

'I'm not angry now.'

'No. Still . . .' She parted her lips to his mouth, her thighs, languorously, sweetly, to his touch.

'Still,' he said, kissing her. '*Still*, Luisa.'

But she trembled, even so, as her body filled with the peace of his possession.

'Still,' she said, her lips against his throat. 'Always. Oh, my darling!'

An epic novel of exotic rituals
and the lure of the Upper Amazon

# THE TAKERS
# RIVER OF GOLD

## JERRY AND S.A. AHERN

---

THE TAKERS are the intrepid Josh Culhane and the seductive Mary Mulrooney. These two adventurers launch an incredible journey into the Brazilian rain forest. Far upriver, the jungle yields its deepest secret—the lost city of the Amazon warrior women!

THE TAKERS series is making publishing history. Awarded *The Romantic Times* first prize for High Adventure in 1984, the opening book in the series was hailed by *The Romantic Times* as "the next trend in romance writing and reading. Highly recommended!"

---

*Jerry and S.A. Ahern have never been better!*

---

TAK – 3

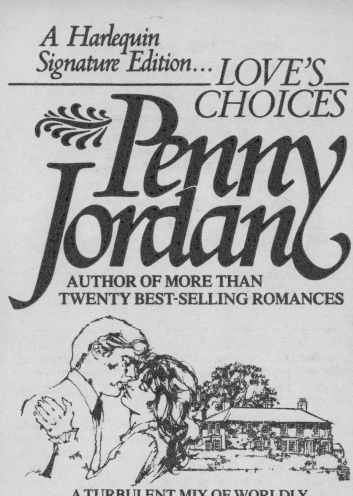